Praise for Ju

Flight to th

"Tizard's years of dedicated service in the Air Force and as a professional pilot bring authenticity and a stark level of realism to the story and all of the flying related aspects. You can truly see her experience shine from her extensive knowledge… The action is fast paced and exciting. From the plane being damaged to the survival at sea I was on the edge of my seat. Tizard is a powerful storyteller."—*Kris's Reviews*

"[T]he plane and the flying scenes were really good parts of this book. Tizard knows her stuff. Even when I didn't understand what every button meant or every switch did, I was completely engrossed in the flying scenes. They were extremely exciting and good entertainment."—*Lez Review Books*

The Road to Wings

"I have been unable to put down [this] book. Knowing nothing about the flying, I learned a lot and have much more appreciation of [Air Force pilot] training. Certainly the underlining of Don't Ask, Don't Tell permeated throughout the book. Fortunately, that law is of the past, though remnants of bias linger. Thank you for a delightful read. Well done."— Col. Margarethe Cammermeyer, US Army (Ret.), author of *Serving in Silence*

"I felt like I was in the cockpit with these ladies time and time again in this book. I loved the romance, of course, but this one has a little more than just that. If you're into military romance, learning new things, and/or planes, definitely check this one out."—*Kissing Backwards*

By the Author

The Road to Wings

Flight to the Horizon

Free Fall at Angel Creek

FREE FALL
AT
ANGEL CREEK

by
Julie Tizard

2021

FREE FALL AT ANGEL CREEK

ISBN 13: 978-1-63555-884-5

THIS TRADE PAPERBACK ORIGINAL IS PUBLISHED BY
BOLD STROKES BOOKS, INC.
P.O. BOX 249
VALLEY FALLS, NY 12185

FIRST EDITION: OCTOBER 2021

CREDITS
EDITOR: SHELLEY THRASHER
PRODUCTION DESIGN: STACIA SEAMAN
COVER DESIGN BY SUSAN RENEE AND CHRIS RICH

Acknowledgments

This book was written during a very difficult time for all of us. I'm so fortunate I had assistance from a wonderful team. My deepest appreciation goes to my editor, Shelley Thrasher. Your guidance and wisdom made my story better. And to my friend and very talented author, Justine Saracen, thank you for your keen insight and encyclopedic knowledge of grammar.

Thanks to my dear friend, Deputy Sheriff Brian van Kleef, Washington County, Oregon, Public Information Officer, your expertise in law enforcement and interagency procedures was vital to the authenticity of this book.

I would especially like to thank my special friend, exceptional writer, and overall badass, Chief VK Powell. Your generosity in sharing your vast knowledge of police procedures, your ability to spot a plot hole in a nanosecond, and your blunt advice is a great gift.

I'm grateful to the University of Southern California and US Air Force for the outstanding training I received as an aircraft accident investigator. Every aircraft accident referenced in this book was a real crash, with real fatalities, and with real lessons learned. The job of figuring out the reason a tragic accident happens, so you can prevent it from happening again, is a noble cause.

To my readers, I so appreciate your continued support and encouragement. Once again, I'm asking you to climb aboard with me and take off into another adventure. Strap in tight because it's going to be a bumpy ride!

For Sue,
Your creativity, your courage, and your love inspires me.
You are my Happily Ever After.

Chapter One

Day 1

"Get the hell out of my way. Come on, missy. Move over!"

Portland Police Detective Dee Rawlings wove in and out of traffic like a demon was chasing her. Though Dee was normally calm in emergency situations, her hands were sweating and her heart pounded. She glanced at the dashboard clock.

Crap. I'm not going to make it.

Dee flipped the switch turning on her hidden red and blue flashing lights. The other drivers moved to the right.

"That's right, people. I'm coming through."

Dee stomped the pedal to the floor, her police Camaro easily accelerating to one hundred miles an hour. She grinned broadly flying down the freeway, until guilt pricked the back of her neck. It was against police policy to use her lights for personal business, so she turned them off and slowed to normal speed. Her cheeks were hurting from smiling so much. *I can't believe I'm actually going to see her.*

It was a beautiful summer evening in Portland, Oregon, with soft breezes and the scent of pine sap in the air. The sun was setting, casting golden light on the tall evergreens and making the puffy clouds look pink and orange. It would be a gorgeous, balmy night, and Dee couldn't wait to show it to her.

She tried hard to remember every detail of her face: the flaming-red hair, the dusting of freckles across her nose, the killer dimples when she smiled. *Will she look different? Will she recognize me? Will she be glad to see me?* Dee cast her doubt aside, like she did with any other troubling thought. *Of course she'll be happy to see me. Otherwise she wouldn't have bought a plane ticket to fly here.* Dee glanced at her watch. "Crap. She's supposed to land in twenty minutes."

Fortunately, the other cars thinned out, and she flew past them. She let out a sigh of relief when she saw the giant yellow IKEA sign by the freeway exit to the airport. She was now only ten minutes away. Her heart was pounding, and her mouth was dry. What would they talk about? It had been so long since they'd seen each other. Dee didn't care if they didn't say a word. She just wanted to wrap her arms around her and hold her forever.

"No time to park. I'll have to pull up to the curb," Dee said to herself.

Stopping next to the main terminal building, she shut the engine off and jumped out of her police car. A parking-enforcement officer immediately strode over to the car.

"You can't park here. Drop-off and pickup only," the parking officer yelled in a very stern voice.

She stopped, reached into her back pocket, and showed the parking cop her police credentials. As soon as she recognized the badge, the officer let her go. "Sorry, officer."

"I'll be right back," Dee replied.

She ran into the huge terminal building and looked around for a sign showing the arrival gates. She'd checked the gate number previously, and it was E5. She didn't want to waste time reading the giant status board, so she ran to the security checkpoint and went to the far-left side to the exit lane, since she was carrying her weapon. The TSA agent standing behind a podium was about to stop her when Dee produced her police creds. The TSA agent picked up his hand radio and called for a LEO, a law enforcement officer. An airport cop came to the exit checkpoint, examined her police credentials, had her sign the LEO log, then let her pass into the secure passenger area.

Dee looked at her watch again. It was nine p.m., five minutes to landing. She turned to the right and ran down the concourse to gate E5. As she passed a news shop, she saw a glass case filled with flower arrangements. She stopped, grabbed a bouquet of yellow roses, threw down a fifty-dollar bill, and said, "Thanks. Keep the change."

As she approached the gate area, people were sitting and reading. She could see through the big glass walls that the Jetway was not hooked up to a plane yet. She plopped down into a seat near the edge of the passenger seating area and let out a big sigh. She'd just made it before the plane landed, and now she could sit and wait for the door to the Jetway to open. She tried to contain her excitement, but it was almost impossible. The Jetway door would open, and then her new life would begin, a life she had only dreamed of. She could hardly believe it was almost here.

Dee took a moment to enjoy the view of her adopted state. She could see a runway with planes taking off and landing, and the wide Columbia River just beyond it. Deep-green forests grew on the far side of the river, with the remains of Mount St. Helens visible. The sky was filled with soft, muted colors in the last light of day. Dee walked over to the windows and looked to the east. She took out her phone and selected the camera app, wanting to video the moment the plane touched down. Looking toward the east end of the runway, she could see the magnificent Mount Hood, its snow-capped peak reflecting the deep-pink color of the setting sun. A wave of happiness slowly washed over her. She'd waited so long for this moment, and now it was almost here.

Dee glanced at her watch again—9:05 p.m. The plane should be landing any second. She walked over to the podium to make sure she was at the right gate. The wall screen behind the counter showed she was at the correct place, but, under the arrival time, the display read, "See Agent."

Dee approached an older woman standing behind the podium. "Excuse me, but what does 'see agent' mean? I'm here to meet someone on flight 402 from Chicago."

The gate agent took a long look at her. "Please come with me."

She led Dee down to the end of the corridor, to a door with a cipher lock. She punched in a code and opened the door to a large conference room filled with people.

"Please go on in. They will help you with any questions." The gate agent retreated quickly.

A man in a business suit stood at the front of the crowded room. "Could I have your attention, please?"

The room grew quiet, and everyone turned to listen to him. "I'm Bob Harris, the station manager for Relax Air here in Portland. I have some important information for you all."

The hair on the back of Dee's neck stood up.

"Ladies and gentlemen, while we only have limited information so far, I need to tell you that we have lost contact with flight 402."

A gasp rose from the crowd.

"I can assure you we are doing everything possible to reestablish communication with our aircraft, and I am asking all of you to remain here in the conference room until we can provide you with more details. As a result of losing contact with flight 402, we are required to report to the FAA that our airplane is missing."

Dee fell to her knees.

CHAPTER TWO

Day 2

A jarring telephone ring woke her from a deep sleep.

"Hello. This is Dr. River Dawson speaking." Her voice was gravelly.

"Hi, River. It's Maggie. Sorry to call you so early, but I have a case for you."

River rubbed her eyes, sat up, turned on the light, reached for her pen and pad, then said, "Ready to copy."

"A plane is missing. It's Relax Air flight 402, Chicago to Portland, scheduled to land last night at 9:05 p.m. Last communication to Air Traffic Control was at 8:20 p.m., when Salt Lake Center handed them off to Seattle Center. That's all we have so far. I made a reservation for you on the 6:00 a.m. flight to Portland. Oh, and, River, it's a DC-10."

A shiver ran down her spine. "Thank you, Maggie. I got it. Talk to you soon."

River made herself a strong cup of coffee, took a quick shower, then gathered her things. Her aircraft accident investigator's go bag was always fully stocked and loaded in the back of her SUV. River did her house close-up checklist since she'd be gone for up to a month. She'd never forgotten the one time she failed to throw out some leftover shrimp in the fridge. When she came home two weeks later, the house reeked of dead bodies.

River took a moment to look out her big front window. A blue

.

line emerged from the end of a dark night on the eastern horizon, beckoning the start of a new day. It would be beautiful in Denver today. This view of the sky was her favorite—the early dawn. The air was soft, it was quiet outside, and peacefulness flowed over her. She inhaled deeply and steeled herself for the coming task, her mission. She never knew what to expect, but whatever it was would be difficult.

With her backpack, coffee, and strawberry Pop-Tarts in hand, River loaded the SUV and drove to the Denver International Airport. She didn't mind the extra twenty minutes it took to get to the new airport instead of the old Denver Stapleton. Every flight in and out of Denver was always bumpy, but Stapleton had a reputation as the windshear capital of the world, and River was glad it was closed.

She usually enjoyed her drive to the airport, but this morning her thoughts kept returning to the last words of her secretary, Maggie: "It's a DC-10."

River's shoulders and neck were tight. She rolled her head around to loosen them. She had to keep her emotions in check and not let anything distract her from the job, especially these first few days. Old thoughts about that airplane could not influence her. River would not allow it. She shoved any preconceived ideas to the back of her mind and locked it shut.

As the sun began to rise, the sight of golden sunbeams reaching from the earth into the sky calmed her. The main terminal of the airport, DIA, was a beautiful giant white tent designed to resemble the Rocky Mountains. The early light made the peaks of the terminal look pink and welcoming. She would be okay. She had done this before and knew she could get through it. Her training and experience gave her the confidence to deal with any situation.

After parking and clearing security, River boarded the underground train to the B concourse. She made sure she was in the front of the train so she could see out the big windows when the train moved. Two little kids stood next to her to also look out the train window. All the other passengers behind them appeared bored or annoyed. She loved seeing the public art in the dark tunnel as she rode the train through it. Colored light bars changed shape, and sculpture rows of small pickaxes appeared to pound the rock walls. A five-year-old next to her pointed to the axes. River bent down and said to him, "The tiny little miners who made this tunnel used those." The boy smiled at her as his mother pulled him closer.

River got off the train and ran to her gate.

"Good morning, Dr. Dawson. Here's your boarding pass. Is seat 2A all right?"

"Morning, Carlos. Yes. That seat's great. Thank you." The gate agent held the Jetway door open for her.

"Have a good trip," Carlos said.

River opened the overhead bin above her first-class seat.

"Can I help you with your bag, Dr. Dawson?"

River turned to see a young woman with a warm smile speaking to her. "That's very kind of you, but it's really heavy. I've got it. Thanks." She was clearly a junior flight attendant having to work an oh-dark-thirty departure, but she was sweet to offer.

River settled into her seat, put on her headphones, and closed her eyes for a few precious hours of sleep before she walked into a buzz saw in Portland.

❖

Dee felt the walls closing in on her. She'd been waiting all night in the conference room with the other family members. They were all desperate for any information, but so far, they'd heard nothing. Her sense of dread grew over the long night, and now, ten hours later, she was like a caged tiger.

She walked over to the conference-room door and spoke to the security officer guarding it. "I'll be right back."

"Sorry, but you can't leave this room," he answered.

Dee lowered her voice. "Are you telling me we're prisoners here?" Her level of annoyance was rising.

"Well, not exactly, but you're supposed to stay in this room." He sounded apologetic.

Dee flashed him her badge. "Look. I'm going to find a restroom, and I'll be right back."

He stepped aside and let her pass.

It was seven a.m., and her empty stomach growled. Looking for a place to eat, she noticed that all the screens in the airport were tuned to news about the missing plane. A mass of journalists with cameras crowded outside of security waiting to pounce on anyone for an interview. Dee changed direction to avoid them, then located a coffee place. After she grabbed a breakfast sandwich, she found a relatively quiet place in the airport to sit down with a view of the river, but hardly tasted her food as she ate and watched planes take off into the morning sky. Passengers were hurrying to catch their flights, as the airport, and the rest of the world, woke up to a bright, sunny day. But it wasn't a bright, sunny day for her.

She fought back the fear that churned in her stomach. As every minute passed without news, the dread inside her grew. She had to work off some nervous energy or she would explode. She walked to the end of the D concourse, turned around, then headed back to the E concourse, where she saw a Jetway door open and arriving passengers stream into a gate area.

She looked at their faces as they disembarked, searching for the one she needed to see more than any other, Naomi's. *Maybe she missed her flight. She might be on another airplane.* She held on to that thought to keep herself together, or she was sure she'd fly into a thousand pieces.

Everyone appeared perfectly normal leaving the plane except for one woman. She stood out as soon as Dee laid eyes on her. This woman walked off the plane with purpose, like she had somewhere important to go. Something was different about her, and she decided to observe her. She watched her go into the ladies' restroom, followed her, and saw her step into a stall.

The woman left her large bag outside the stall door, and Dee had her chance to get some intel. She looked around to make sure no one was watching her, then went over to the woman's bag. It was well worn, with a rainbow luggage tag and a US Air Force sticker on it. She flipped the luggage tag over to see the name: Dr. River Dawson, Aviation Accident Solutions Inc., Denver, Colorado.

Then the stall door opened, and Dee stood face-to-face with the woman she was stalking.

"Oh, sorry. My bag is in the way."

"No problem," Dee answered, then ducked into the next stall, where she continued to observe her, looking through a gap in the stall doorway. She wore hiking boots, heavy-duty blue jeans, a flannel shirt, and a green military flight jacket. At first glance, she could be a lesbian, or just another outdoorsy Oregon straight girl who loved to hike. Dee couldn't put her finger on it, but something about this woman was compelling. She certainly wasn't a typical traveler. Dee needed more information and continued to observe her.

She followed the woman down another concourse, then watched her enter a conference room filled with people. The room had a glass wall on one side with vertical blinds drawn, but Dee could see people moving around. She couldn't see clearly, but maps hung on the walls.

She observed her subject enter the room like she owned it, then shake hands with several of the men present. She needed a better look at what they were doing. Dee found a discarded newspaper, picked it up, then strolled toward the room. Then she leaned against a nearby column where she could peek into the room and pretend to read her newspaper.

As people entered and left, she caught bits of a briefing— "requested an altitude change to flight level three-two-zero," "reported turbulence," and "vector heading." She didn't know what these terms meant, but they sounded important. The woman she'd been observing raised her hand to say something, and all the men in the room turned to listen to her. She was someone important, maybe a leader or an expert of some sort. This woman knew something, and Dee had to find out what it was.

❖

River found a seat in the crowded conference room and looked around at everyone present. She recognized several faces from other aircraft accident investigations, guys from the Federal Aviation Administration, the National Transportation Safety Board, and representatives from the airplane builder, McDonnell Douglas. The rest of the room was filled with local airport managers, state Department of Emergency Management officials, airline reps, Oregon State Police, and the Portland Airport Fire Department.

A few other Feds that River didn't know were present, but she recognized their ID badges: FBI, Homeland Security, and ATF, Alcohol, Tobacco, Firearms, and Explosives. A chill ran down her spine. *Why are these guys here? What, or who, was on that jet to require these people show up?* This case had just become very interesting or very bad.

River took out her leather notebook and wrote down the flight details as the air traffic control briefer spoke.

"At 8:15 p.m. local time, they reported moderate turbulence at flight level three-six-zero to Salt Lake Center. They requested ride reports, then asked for a descent to three-two-zero. Salt Lake Center cleared Relax Air flight 402 to descend to flight level three-two-zero, then directed them to contact Seattle Center on one-two-six-point-eight. Flight 402 acknowledged the altitude assignment and the frequency change. They never checked in with Seattle Center. We called them back on the last assigned frequency, the new frequency, and on Guard, with no response to any calls. ATC officially notified Relax Air management that they had lost contact with flight 402 at 8:45 p.m. The company then reported the aircraft missing at 9:15 p.m. Are there any questions?"

River had several, but she waited for someone else to speak first. When the men in the room just sat there, she raised her hand and asked, "Did ATC try to contact other aircraft in the area to relay an air-to-air message due to the high terrain in the vicinity?"

"Yes. We did. Two other aircraft were nearby, and we asked them to relay a message to flight 402, with no success."

River went on. "Did you have any pilot reports about convective weather activity on their route of flight? Were they on any vector headings for weather, or were they on their flight's planned route?"

"Yes. Other aircraft reported scattered thunderstorms in a line from Boise to Yakima. Prior to their descent, they'd requested vectors around a storm cell. Their last assigned heading was two-seven-zero degrees, with instructions to proceed direct to the JOTBA fix when clear of the weather, then the Hood4 arrival into Portland. So, no, flight 402 was not on its filed route when we lost contact with it."

A collective groan rose from the group. Because the plane had been flying on a heading for weather avoidance instead of its planned route, it could be anywhere. River's job had just become much more difficult. She opened her terrain map to the area east of Portland—a vast area of mountains and national forests. If the aircraft had gone down in those deep woods, it could be very difficult to find.

River recognized another man who came up to the podium to speak, Ronald Moore, the chief investigator for the National Transportation Safety Board. River knew him, had worked with him on other cases, and didn't like him. He was a self-serving publicity hound who cared more about being in front of the cameras than finding answers.

"Gentlemen, and lady," he added as he looked at River, "we will depart for the Redmond, Oregon, airport in fifteen minutes. We calculated this is the most likely airport they may have diverted to, so it will be our base of operations. Bring all your gear with you, and we'll leave out of gate E1. Remember, no talking to the press. We don't officially know anything yet."

River gathered her maps and notes. She was ready to go but needed to grab some food to take with her for the very long day ahead. They would be searching for a needle in a haystack to find this jet.

As she left the briefing room, a woman came over to intercept her and grabbed her arm.

"You know about the missing plane, don't you?"

River turned to her and saw the worry etched into her young face. "I'm sorry, but I can't talk to you about flight 402. I have to go. I have a plane to catch."

"So you *are* working on this."

Obviously she was the family member of a passenger and desperately wanted answers. A wave of pity rolled over River.

"Please excuse me, but I do have to go. You can talk to the customer service supervisor over there. He may have more information for you." She tried to walk away, but the woman blocked her path.

"Hey. You don't understand. My sister's on that plane. I've been waiting for information all night." She took out her badge and shoved it in River's face. "You just got out of a meeting about flight 402, and I want answers."

Ordinarily, River would have bristled at her demands, but the compassion she felt made her pause. "Detective, has the Portland Police Bureau assigned you to this case?"

"Well, um, no, not exactly. But I have to know what's going on. Tell me." River heard a slight catch in her voice. "Please."

"I'm sorry. I can't help you." River stepped around her.

"They're all dead, aren't they?" the woman shouted after her.

Frozen in place by her words, River turned to face her. "We don't know anything yet. It does no good to speculate at this point." She took a few steps toward the stranger and looked into her pleading eyes. "I know what you're going through."

"How can you possibly know what I'm going through? I've said those same bullshit words to crime victims. We've had no word for over ten hours. The plane crashed somewhere, and you're trying to find it, aren't you?"

River could speak in front of a thousand people to deliver a report, but now, looking into the woman's face, she couldn't think of anything to say.

After a long pause, she spoke. "Detective, you're right. It's not good. And, yes, I am trying to find that airplane. But I promise you, I will do my very best to get you answers. I need to go now."

"Please call me if you find out anything." The woman handed River her card.

River took it and hurried toward her gate.

Chapter Three

The young female detective's face stayed in River's mind. As an aircraft accident investigator, she'd seen that look before. It was the look of a bewildered, surviving family member. Disbelief, confusion, then anger were the usual reactions to a crash. She'd seen family members wander around in a daze, unable to comprehend what had happened. River knew these feelings intimately.

She forced those emotions from her mind. She didn't have time to think about any victims right now. There was an investigation to focus on, one with lots of questions and no answers. The detective's anguished expression conjured up so many old ghosts. Unwelcome spirits, they distracted her with unwanted memories. She refused to succumb to them.

As the plane accelerated down the runway for takeoff, River took a moment to look out her window. She loved the takeoff, the familiar tingle of excitement in her belly. Being lifted into the air always made her happy. Flying above the wide Columbia River, with forest-covered banks and green mountains, centered her. She felt comfortable in the sky, even if she wasn't flying the plane. It was a beautiful morning in Portland, and she allowed herself a moment to enjoy the view. Soon enough, she and the rest of the team would be searching to find that plane, and the chaos would begin.

The aircraft turned to the southeast toward Redmond. It was only a thirty-minute flight, so River pulled out her notes to study the weather charts from last night. Light from the morning sun reflected on the snow-covered peak of Mount Hood. She looked up from her notes to admire it.

It was a magnificent volcano rising to over eleven thousand feet. Standing out on its own, a lone sentinel guarding the Columbia River Valley, Mount Hood was breathtaking but also dangerous. The sharply rising terrain was only thirty miles from the Portland airport and in a direct line with the runways. She remembered flying out of Portland one dark, stormy night.

The memory from ten years ago was still as sharp as if it had happened yesterday. She'd been a US Air Force pilot flying as a new copilot on the KC-10 air refueling tanker and had been at the Portland airport for a weekend air show. The whole crew was exhausted from talking to visitors all weekend and ready to get home. The aircraft commander, Bob Marks, was flying the jet back to their home base at March Air Force Base in Riverside, California, and he'd been in a big hurry to get back before the weather moved over the airport.

River had been flying the KC-10 for only two months and remembered feeling very annoyed at Bob because he rushed her through the flight planning process for the two-hour flight home. Bob took off heading east into the dark night, and they entered the clouds almost immediately. River received no answer when she called departure control after they were airborne. As the plane climbed, when she was looking up the alternate radio frequency, something told her to check their distance from the Portland airport. The display read twenty-seven miles. River shouted at Bob, "Turn right. Turn right now!" When he hesitated, she took control of the jet from him, abruptly turned the yoke full right, and yelled, "My jet."

She pulled the nose of the giant plane through the turn with the mechanical warning voice of the ground-proximity warning system yelling, "Whoop, whoop, pull up. Whoop, whoop, pull up. Caution, terrain. Caution, terrain." It was the most terrifying sound she'd ever heard because it activated only when the airplane was close to the ground. She still remembered the sickening, helpless feeling of waiting for impact.

She had looked out the front window, hoping it wouldn't be her last sight on earth, and saw a break in the clouds. A moonbeam illuminated the very close, snow-covered peak of Mount Hood, directly in front of her. She pulled back hard on the yoke as far as it would go, the automatic stall warning system shaking the yoke within her tight grip, and prayed she wouldn't hit the mountain. No one on the flight deck said a word. The only sound was the rush of air noise and the mechanical warning voices yelling at her. River remembered holding her breath, waiting for the crash.

When she was safely away from Mount Hood headed south, she vowed she would never again let anyone rush her flight planning, and she would never blindly trust her life to another person. Almost joining the carcasses of several aircraft littering the deep forests around Mount Hood had a profound impact on her. She shivered at the memory of this near-death experience. Like many things in aviation, Mount Hood was beautiful but also deadly.

After Dee watched the woman investigator board the aircraft and push back from the gate, she fell into a gate-area seat and put her head in her hands. How could this possibly be happening? Everything had been perfect until they announced the plane was missing. How had the most amazing day of her life changed to a catastrophe in an instant? She was overwhelmed, but she couldn't let herself be immobilized by fear. She had to do something.

She walked over to the gate agent. "Where is that plane going? The one that just left."

"It's a private charter flight to Redmond. Were you supposed to be on it?" the gate agent asked.

"No."

"Another flight to Redmond leaves from gate E2. Would you like me to see if any seats are available?"

Dee had a choice to make. She could continue to wait here at the airport for any word from the airline, or she could follow the woman investigator, her only lead so far. She was going crazy waiting, and this was a chance to at least do something. "Yes. I'd like to buy a ticket for that flight to Redmond."

"You're in luck. Two seats are left, and it departs in three hours."

"Three hours? I can't wait that long. Never mind. I'll drive."

Dee had no idea what she would do once she reached the Redmond airport. She knew that she had to follow her only lead, Dr. River Dawson. She rushed out of the airport carrying only the wilted flowers for her sister Naomi.

❖

Instead of studying her notes on the flight to Redmond, River kept thinking about why the pilot hadn't called "Mayday" or declared an emergency.

After they replied with their assigned heading, they didn't say another word to air traffic control, either Salt Lake or Seattle Center. When ATC tried to call them repeatedly, they gave no reply, and then they disappeared from radar. Only one possibility could account for this type of scenario, and she dreaded the thought of it.

She reached for a tissue in her pocket and felt the business card the detective gave her. She pulled it out and read, "Detective Deborah Rawlings, Major Crimes Division, Portland Police Bureau." She was impressed such a young officer had already risen to the rank of detective in a major police department. She must be very good at her job, and good at guessing, because she was correct about the fate of the passengers. Most likely, they were all dead, or some survivor would have found a way to call home by now. This would not be a rescue mission. Instead, it would be a recovery operation.

She ran her finger along the edge of the detective's business card. The image of her troubled face returned to River's mind. In another time, in a different place, maybe they would have met under better circumstances. Maybe a friend would have introduced them at a cocktail party, or maybe they would have sat next to each other on a plane and struck up a conversation. She had a beautiful face, with a strong jaw, full lips, fair skin, and very intense dark-green eyes. They were the same height when they looked at each other, but the detective was leaner, wiry, with a body built for action. With her unruly, shoulder-length brown hair, she was just the type of woman River was attracted to. But they hadn't met at a fun cocktail party or been introduced by a caring friend. They'd met on the worst day of Detective Deborah Rawlings's entire life. She just didn't know it yet.

The Fasten Seat Belt sign came on with a "ding," interrupting her thoughts. They started their descent into the Redmond airport. River looked out the window one more time, hoping to see something, anything, resembling an airplane. All she saw were dense woods, steep mountains, and a giant puzzle before her. She never allowed herself to speculate on the cause of an accident until all the evidence came in. She'd seen other investigators jump on a theory, go on a wild-goose chase, then end up disgraced when the evidence proved them wrong. That would not happen to her.

They all assembled in a large, empty hangar with terrain maps on the walls and tables set up labeled Airframe, Engines, Avionics, Weather, Cargo, Air Traffic Control, Reports/Test Results, Press, and Pax/HR. No one went near the Pax/HR table. A pilot in a green military flight suit with a Civil Air Patrol patch on his sleeve came up to her.

"What's at the Pax/HR table?" he asked River.

"It stands for 'passengers and human remains,' although it's primarily for human remains. That's why no one wants to be near it."

"Oh. I see. Thanks for explaining that. I'm Mike Bowers." He extended his hand.

She shook it. "I'm River Dawson. Have you worked a crash site before?"

"No. I'm a fairly new volunteer pilot with the Civil Air Patrol. This is my first accident."

"Are you flying the search-and-rescue missions?"

"Not so far. We have two crews flying the grid search pattern right now. I'm the backup pilot."

This was important information. River might need this man's skills down the road.

"Here's my card, Mike. I've worked on several aircraft accidents, so if you have any questions, please call me."

"Thanks. This is all very overwhelming. I'm not really sure what I'm supposed to be doing right now."

"Just listen to the briefing and be ready to help out. You'll do fine."

The different team members stowed their gear, then sat down for a status briefing from the incident commander. He was a senior Oregon State Police commander wearing a bright-red jacket, so everyone knew who he was.

"Folks, we have a big job before us, so here's what we know so far."

River sat next to her new buddy Mike for the briefing, handing him an extra spiral notebook from her pack.

"Thanks," he whispered.

"Based on the last reported position, the heading assigned by ATC, and their projected fuel remaining, our best guess on their location is this here." He pointed to a large area outlined in red on a US Geological Survey map. Rumblings emerged from the team. "I know it's a big zone, but we'll be refining the search area as we receive more information."

"Wow. That's going to take forever. It's huge. We'll be here for days, won't we?" Mike asked.

"Yes. We will," River said.

The incident commander went on. "We just received a report from a local farmer that he found an object on his land. We have a team en route to the farm now to retrieve it. We'll know more after they inspect it in the field. It may be an engine."

"Do you have the location, Boss?" A man in the back of the room shouted his question.

He pointed to a spot about forty miles southeast of the Redmond airport. "This is where we'll start our search today. The Civil Air Patrol is currently flying a low-altitude grid search over that area. We have two F-15s from the Portland Air National Guard to fly the high-altitude search. Load up your gear in the trucks outside. We depart for the search area in fifteen minutes."

Everyone scrambled to grab their gear and hurry to the trucks. Instead, River went to the front of the hangar to study the map where the farmer had reported the object. She took a ruler out of her pack, laid it horizontally, then vertically, on the map, and wrote down the latitude and longitude of the possible engine's position. She studied the terrain around the engine's location, which was mostly flat.

"That's good," she said to herself.

"What's good?" Mike asked. He'd followed behind her, probably to see what she was looking at on the map.

"The land around the engine is reasonably flat, since it's farmland, so that makes it easier to find the small metal pieces if it broke up on impact."

"What if it didn't? What if it disintegrated in flight? Or what if it caught on fire?"

"We won't know that until after we can see it and inspect it in person."

"Hey, aren't you going with everyone else to the crash site? They're leaving soon."

"That's not the crash site. It's just where one of the three engines may have landed. The main crash site is still out there somewhere."

This information from the incident commander confirmed River's first instincts about this accident. If the airplane had diverted to an emergency airport, they would have reported in by now. The fact that the crew never declared an emergency, never even said another word after their last ATC transmission, made River conclude that the airplane had blown up in midair.

This DC-10 aircraft, with two hundred and seventy people on board, had exploded into a million pieces. The fiery debris rained down on a vast area of the ground. The engines were often the first pieces found because they were big, heavy, and tended to stay intact. The real question was, why did this DC-10 blow up?

CHAPTER FOUR

After dropping off her police vehicle and picking up her personal car, Dee drove along the winding mountain road to Redmond. She worried about making the phone call she was dreading. She had to try to get in touch with Naomi's husband and family. Her husband and children needed to know the truth that her plane was missing and she was most likely dead.

Dee's eyes burned with tears. She was numb and exhausted. No sleep, no food, and constant stress made her feel like she was a hundred years old.

When she'd gotten the text message from Naomi after so many years of silence, she allowed herself to hope, which was something she rarely did. She'd learned over the years to assume the worst, so she was never disappointed. This philosophy had served her well since she was on her own at age seventeen, but it failed her now. She and Naomi needed to talk about so much after not speaking to each other for so long.

Sixteen years, almost half her life, Dee was denied any contact with her little sister because of her father. The old resentment toward him bubbled up inside her like foul garbage covered with dirt. She tried her best never to think of him, but on rare occasions, he still snuck into her consciousness to torment her again. It was as if somehow beyond the grave he was still trying to keep them apart.

Dee's father had died one month ago. The end of his life was why Naomi reached out to her after so long. When she'd received a text message from an unknown phone number one week ago, it changed her life. That message opened a door for her that had been locked closed for years.

She was initially suspicious when she received the strange text out of the blue. She and her partner, Marcus, had just finished their report on a big case involving illegal weapons and were on their way to the local cop bar to celebrate when her phone buzzed. She remembered every detail of that moment: feeling annoyed at the buzzing phone, the weight of it in her hand, being frozen in place when she read the words.

The image of that text was burned into her brain.

Hi Sissy. It's Squirt. I hope this is your number. Daddy passed away two weeks ago, and I need to come see you. This is too involved for a phone call, so I need to talk to you in person. Please let me know if this is really you, Sissy. Love, Squirt.

Dee had to turn off the road because she couldn't see. After she stopped, she put her head in her hands and sobbed. Waves of pain washed over her. It was difficult to catch her breath between racking sobs. After what felt like an eternity, she was able to stop crying. She shook her head, straightened her back, and said, "Come on, Dee. Get it together. We have a job to do."

She started the car, revved the engine, and took off again down the mountain road to her objective. She focused her mind and body on one thing: she would track down Dr. River Dawson and get the answers she needed.

River had a theory and needed transportation to check it out. Everyone else was on their way to inspect the engine in the field, but it wasn't the main crash site. If the airplane had broken up in flight from a midair collision, an explosion, or from flying into a thunderstorm, the major parts of the jet would be scattered along their route of flight.

She spread out her aeronautical section chart and used her plotter to carefully mark the last known position of the aircraft before air traffic control lost radar contact. Then she marked the position of the found engine and drew a line to connect the points. This was the track of the plane on the ground. She had to adjust for the effect of wind at altitude, plus correct their ground speed to determine their predicted position. She took out her beat-up old pilot's "whiz wheel" flight computer from her backpack.

"What are you doing?" Mike Bowers had been watching her make calculations.

"I'm figuring out their real ground track and speed so I can better estimate their flight path."

"So you don't think the team is going to the right place?"

"They're going to the beginning of the debris field, not the main part. I'm interested in the flight deck and the major parts of the fuselage. Those pieces will be found along the corrected flight path but still in a large area."

River spun the circular dials of her whiz wheel, flipped it over, and used the wind-correction dial, then wrote down her figures. "Look at this, Mike. From their flight plan, they were supposed to have a fifty-knot headwind at flight level three-six-zero, but another aircraft in the area reported winds from the southeast at ninety-five knots, so they actually had a tailwind."

She took out an orange highlighter, laid her plotter on the chart, and drew a line. "This is the real track, and based on their corrected speed, I think this is the location of the main debris."

"That is way different from where everyone else is looking. How do you know this is right?"

"Just a few years of doing this."

River extended her orange line forward, then drew a box around it and examined the terrain in the box. Parts of it were fairly flat, and then it rose sharply into the foothills of the mountain range. She needed to get there and look around. A small municipal airport was located in her search area that she could stage out of.

"Do you have any Civil Air Patrol planes available now, Mike?"

"Yeah. Our two search planes just landed a few minutes ago.

They're getting refueled. We have to wait until the Air Guard F-15s complete their high-altitude search before we can fly again."

"Can you fly me to this airport and drop me off?"

"Madras Municipal? Sure, but it's in the opposite direction of where everyone else is heading."

"That's why we're going there."

It was a short flight to Madras, and the weather was clear. They climbed into the red, white, and blue CAP Cessna 172, and River watched Mike program their route of flight. It was a four-seat, single-engine propeller plane, well equipped for search-and-rescue operations with GPS navigation and multiple radios. They took off from Redmond, and Mike turned the Cessna to the north.

"Please fly a heading of three-two-five and climb to four thousand five hundred feet."

River took out her aeronautical chart, folded it so she could see her area outlined in orange, and started scanning outside the window. She wasn't looking for anything in particular. Instead, she was trying to find something that appeared out of place, like an odd shape or something glinting in the sun. Nothing stood out.

"Can you fly us past Madras first? I'd like to see the area around the airport."

"Sure thing," Mike said.

From forty-five hundred feet in the air, River was high enough to clearly see the terrain features depicted on her chart and also close enough to make out the details. The land was lush and green, with no burning fires nearby, no big chunks of airplane, just open space. A flash of light caught River's attention. She took out the binoculars for a better look. The sun reflected on a slender, meandering ribbon of gold, a small river right in the middle of her search area.

"That's where I'm going. You can land and drop me off at Madras now."

❖

Dee made good time driving through the mountains to the Redmond airport. There, she noticed two county deputy sheriffs controlling an airport ramp access point near a big hangar. She pulled out her badge, hoping they wouldn't ask her any questions. They glanced at her credentials, then waved her through.

She had to size up this situation before she made her next move. She was way out of her jurisdiction as a police officer here, but she needed to look like she fit in. Fortunately, when she'd picked up her own car at the station, she had her gym bag in the back. She drove around the corner out of view, then changed in her car out of her detective's business suit into jeans, tennis shoes, an Oregon State Beavers tee shirt, and her well-worn leather jacket. Finally, she placed her police lanyard around her neck to display her badge.

In a chaotic emergency situation, you had to be able to figure out who was who quickly. Everyone had to recognize the symbols and uniforms of others to know their jobs. She would simply blend in with the other various law-enforcement officers, hope no one looked too closely at her, then stalk her prey.

She gathered up some discarded papers from the back seat and tried to make them appear to be something official. She observed people going into the hangar, surprised that more weren't working, especially since this was such a big case. She saw only twenty or so walking around the hangar, so she decided to slip in undetected.

"You can drop that off here, officer," a woman called out to her from behind a big table.

It looked like a registration table, except it had a sign on it. *Reports/Test Results.*

"Is this the local eyewitness list? We've been waiting for it." The woman behind the table held out her hand, obviously expecting Dee to turn over her worthless papers.

"Uh, no, ma'am. This is for Dr. River Dawson. Do you know where I can find her?"

"She's probably out in the field with the other investigators at the engine site. I'm not sure when they're getting back, but I can take it and make sure she gets it when they return."

"She's not with everyone else." Dee turned to see a pilot in a green military flight suit speaking to her.

"Do you know where she is?" she asked.

"She asked me to fly her to Madras Municipal. I dropped her off there about an hour ago."

"What's in Madras?"

"I'm not sure. She had me fly around it to the north, and then she saw something, and we landed."

"Do you know what she saw?"

"Not really, but it looked like a small river to me. I'm picking her up at five, and we should be back here by five thirty, if you want to wait."

"No. I can't. Thanks for your help. I have to go."

Dee rushed back to her car and started down the road to Madras, enjoying the familiar tingle in her spine when she was following a good lead. So many were dead ends, but when she was chasing one, and it took her to another lead, the thrill of the hunt consumed her.

She felt great satisfaction when a perpetrator was convicted and sentenced, like she was doing her part for justice. But, above all, she loved to interview witnesses, find evidence, and build a strong case. She knew what to do and was comfortable in her role. This lead was her chance to do something productive and not be just another helpless victim.

CHAPTER FIVE

Mike dropped River off in front of the small terminal building at Madras airport. She took in the panoramic view around the airport and inhaled deeply. It smelled of fresh air and pine trees, with a hint of aviation gas mixed in. She loved small airports and the happy memories they brought back. These places were busy with small planes flying around on the weekends, but usually during the week they were fairly quiet, with only one or two aircraft in the traffic pattern. River walked around the parking ramp admiring the airplanes.

It was a nice hodgepodge of aviation, with a sleek business jet parked next to an open-cockpit Stearman biplane, next to a little two-seat trainer. River looked into the two-seater through the Plexiglas canopy. The instruments were modern glass panels on a cool-looking interior. Very plush compared to the tiny Cessna 150 she'd learned to fly on.

The sound of an engine revving up made her turn to watch a yellow single-engine Piper roll down the runway and gracefully lift into the air. It was magic. No other way to describe it other than just pure magic. She could explain aerodynamics and calculate a coefficient of lift as well as anyone, but she didn't have the words to explain her love of flying.

It was out of that love that she became an aircraft accident investigator. Once again, she found herself in the middle of nowhere searching for what was left of an airliner and the hundreds of lives ended too soon. Taking a last look at the airplanes around her, she focused on the harsh reality of her purpose here. She would tuck her happy memories in a safe place in her mind, then get down to business.

She walked into the small terminal and found the local airport fixed-base operator. It provided a flight-planning room, a lounge area, fuel, repair services, and anything else a pilot might need.

"Hi. I need to get a car, preferably four-wheel drive. Where can I rent one?"

The young woman behind the reception desk said, "We don't have any rental cars here, but we have a shop truck you can borrow, if that will work for you."

"That'd be great. How much is it?"

"Don't worry about it. You're here looking for the missing plane, aren't you?"

"Yes. I am. Do you know anything about it, or has anyone here at the airport seen anything?"

"We had a couple of training flights go out this morning, but no one's seen anything so far."

She pulled out her aeronautical chart and pointed to the orange section so the receptionist could see. "I'm trying to find this area with the stream. Can you tell me how to get there?"

After River copied the driving directions, she climbed into the beat-up shop truck and headed toward the mountains. She would be searching the foothills of the Cascade Mountain range, in the Mt. Hood National Forest. It wasn't long before she left the paved roads and bounced along on washboard-like dirt roads. Traveling deeper into the forest, she steeled herself for what she might come across. She most dreaded discovering human bodies, or worse, parts.

She was thankful she hadn't had to deal with human remains in too many of her previous accident investigations. Most airplane crashes happened near the ground, so there was generally a primary impact site where all the passengers and crew would be found. If it was a slow-speed crash, such as right after takeoff, some of the bodies could be intact. If it was a high-speed crash, not much that was recognizable as human was usually left.

The human factor. This was the most difficult part of the

investigation. Not only did she have to experience the horror of seeing mangled bodies, but she had to figure out exactly how these people had died. It wasn't difficult to analyze broken pieces of metal, but dealing with dead passengers, and especially their surviving family members, was gut-wrenching.

Driving along the road to her target, she visualized the tortured face of Detective Deborah Rawlings again. A wave of remembered grief slowly washed over her, not only for the misery all these survivors would be facing, but especially for this woman. River knew with certainty that her life would never again be what it was.

She crested a hill and saw a lush, green valley with a stream wandering through it. It was beautiful and peaceful—just the place you'd like to stop and rest. Maybe here she could find some answers to ease the suffering of Deborah Rawlings. She stopped the truck, took out her backpack with her supplies, and hiked down toward the water, hoping she would find something.

Dee drove as fast as she could on the narrow state road to Madras Municipal airport. It was a typical small airport with a few hangars and a single terminal building. She found the receptionist, who assumed Dee was with the accident investigation team, got the driving instructions, and continued tracking her target.

When the paved road turned to a dirt road, Dee followed the fresh tire tracks. Bouncing along the dirt road, she was struck at the beauty of this land. She'd never been in this part of Oregon before because she was usually working and rarely left Portland. The entire state was gorgeous and green, but this area was different.

On a few occasions, Dee had taken time off for a weekend excursion to the Oregon coast. She loved walking on the wide, sandy beaches and watching the ocean waves crash on the dramatic rock formations. She never went into the cold ocean water, but she liked driving along the coast highway, stopping at places like Cape Foul Weather and the Devil's Punchbowl. She always took her weekend trips alone, wishing she had someone special with her.

Now, thinking about those pleasant drives only brought back her despair.

Dee had made such great plans for her time with Naomi. She'd taken a week off and wanted to show her sister the best sights in her adopted state. Those dreams were all gone now, with so much left unsaid. Her heart clutched, her vision grew fuzzy, and her breathing accelerated. She was hyperventilating again at the thought of what had happened to Naomi. She had to stop the car and force herself to calm down before she passed out. Images of bloody crime scenes swirled before her, this time with Naomi as a dead victim. Dee focused all her energy and self-discipline on slowing her breathing. Gradually, the horrible images faded, and her vision returned. Once she was in control, she continued down the dirt road until she came upon a well-used pickup truck.

She approached slowly, scanning the area around the truck for any movement. With no one in sight, Dee looked inside the truck for anything important, then followed the boot prints into the woods. There'd been rain last night so the ground was soft, making the boot prints easy to see. Tracking someone was one of Dee's best skills, acquired from her time as a US Army military police specialist.

Sneaking through the woods following her subject reminded Dee of her time in Iraq. Protecting her fellow soldiers deployed to the desert had become Dee's mission in life. She'd seen some of her friends blown to bits by improvised explosive devices and made it her business to find the perpetrators. As she crept through the woods following the boot prints, she could hear the words of her old drill instructor in her mind: "Keep your head on a swivel and one hand on your weapon."

Dee always had her weapon with her, tucked under her armpit, next to her left breast. She thought of her pistol as her backup, always ready when she needed it. The weight and bulk of it felt comfortable. On the rare occasions she didn't have it with her, she felt like something was missing. A noise caught her attention and she stopped to listen. She could hear birds singing and wind blowing through the pine trees, then something else. It was the sound of water.

❖

After River hiked about an hour, she cleared the trees and saw the banks of a small creek. Working several crash sites had taught her the advantage of searching around rivers and streams. Any floating debris, such as seat cushions or foam insulation, that landed on the water would be carried downstream. Also, if she was lucky, the riverbanks had grass instead of trees, making it easier to find objects.

She took a minute to look around at her surroundings. The babbling brook, the sound of birds singing, and the lush green colors combined to give this place a sense of serenity. She removed her heavy backpack to take it all in.

Dappled sunlight filtered through the trees and danced on the surface of the water. She walked down to the edge of the creek, hoping the water would be clear enough to see into its depths. The water was slow moving and crystal clear, with a good view of the creek bed and even a few good-sized fish. Looking upstream, she spotted a small waterfall with an unusual rock formation. The shape reminded her of something familiar, and a little rainbow appeared in the mist of the waterfall. For a moment, she took a break from hunting for evidence to simply enjoy the beauty. Just then, she heard a noise behind her in the woods. She froze, listening, then heard a twig snap.

Someone, or something, is following me.

She didn't have anything to defend herself with except a can of bear repellant and her heavy backpack. Assuming she was being watched, she pretended to walk upstream, then darted into the woods again. She thought about running back to the shop truck to escape, but finding out who was following her seemed more important.

She silently looped around behind the area where she'd heard the sound and saw movement. A dark figure slipped from tree to tree, hiding in the shadows. She was definitely under surveillance. She should have continued to quietly work her way back to the truck, leave the area, then come back with a couple of security guards, but now she was pissed. Who was following her? What did they want? Her heart was pounding and she approached the dark figure from behind, bear repellant in hand.

The subject spun around and hit her right hand, knocking the bear spray away. The barrel of a big gun was pointed right at her face. River put her hands up in surrender.

"Jesus! I almost shot you."

River was face-to-face with Detective Deborah Rawlings. She lowered her hands. "What the hell are you doing here?"

The woman put her gun away. "First of all, don't *ever* sneak up behind a cop. You're lucky I didn't blow your head off. Secondly, I was looking for you."

"Why?"

"I have to do something, or I'll go crazy. Please let me help. I'll do anything."

River locked eyes with her for a moment. "Look, Deborah. I'm not trying to be difficult, but you can't be here."

"Don't ever call me that. My name is Dee. Why can't I assist? I'm a trained police detective."

Just then, River noticed something green next to Dee's white tennis shoe. "Freeze."

She reached down toward Dee's right knee. "Put one hand on the tree and slowly raise your foot."

It was a lime-green piece of sharp metal. River pulled her camera out of her pack and took pictures of the metal in the ground and the surrounding area. She took a numbered white flag out of her backpack, stuck the metal shaft into the ground, then recorded the flag number, location, and description in her logbook. After putting on a rubber glove, she took a plastic evidence bag out and carefully placed the metal in the bag.

"Can I put my foot down now?"

River examined the area around Dee's feet. "Yes, but step over here."

"See? I helped you find something already."

"Dee, this is not a police investigation. It's different, and you don't know what you're doing. This entire area is an accident scene, and you're walking right through the evidence field. What would you do if a victim's family member came walking through your crime scene?"

Dee didn't answer.

River took a step closer to her. "You'd tell her she had to leave so you could do your job, wouldn't you?"

"Maybe."

River felt a twinge of sympathy, but she had to be firm.

"Then you need to leave me alone so I can do my job. I gave you my word I would contact you if I find anything, and I will. Go now, and don't come back. I will report you if I see you again."

Dee glared at her with a look that said, "This is not over," then turned and walked away.

CHAPTER SIX

Dee got into her car and drove back to Portland. River was right to demand she leave the accident site, just as she would've done, but she still didn't like it. She was hoping she'd have something to report when she called Naomi's husband, a duty she was still avoiding. It was easier to work on the case than to face this crisis with her sister's family. She didn't even know what they looked like. Naomi had texted only that she had a husband, Bill, and two daughters, Brin and Taylor. She'd also promised to bring pictures and that they would talk about everything that had happened in the sixteen years they'd been apart.

By the time Dee reached her small apartment in downtown Portland, she was exhausted, hungry, and furious. She ordered Chinese-food delivery, then started cleaning her home. The new vase with a dozen yellow roses in the middle of her kitchen table mocked her with their cheeriness. She wanted to hurl the whole thing out her tenth-story window and curse God. But she couldn't endanger an innocent citizen walking by on the sidewalk, so she grabbed the stems, letting the thorns pierce her palm, and dumped the flowers into the trash.

She ate her food without tasting it and decided she desperately needed a shower. The hot water gave much-needed relief to the spasms in her shoulders, and then it mixed with her own tears as the grief flowed from her in endless waves of pain. She had lost the person she loved most in the world and had been completely powerless to prevent her sister's death. She slid down the tiled wall to sit on the floor of the shower and let the hot water pelt her.

After the water turned ice cold, she dried off, put on clean clothes, then sat in her darkened living room, immobile. How could she go to sleep tonight, or any night, ever again? She feared her own dreams. And how could she possibly face tomorrow feeling so numb and empty inside? She'd go mad if she sat here, did nothing, and thought about everything she'd lost. She picked up the phone and called her partner, Marcus Lasalle.

"Hey, Dee. I heard the news that your sister was on that plane. Kim and I are so sorry for you. We're here for you if you need anything."

"Thanks, Marcus." She had a hard time speaking. "I do need help with one thing."

"Name it."

"I need a phone number for Naomi's husband, Bill Williams. They," she paused, "he lives near Chicago."

"Got it. I'll get back to you as soon as I get his number. Anything else I can help with? You're always welcome to stay here if you don't want to be alone."

His kindness made her choke up. He was a great partner. "Thanks for the offer, but I'm okay. Talk to you tomorrow." She hung up before she burst into tears again. She trusted him with her life, but she still didn't want to cry in front of him.

She would call her brother-in-law for the first time tomorrow to discuss his dead wife, her dead sister. The waves of loss descended on her again. Too weak to fight them anymore, she did the only thing she could think of and went to the cabinet, grabbed a quart-sized sports cup, filled it with ice, then poured it half full of Seagram's 7. After she topped it off with a can of Coke, she chugged the entire drink. She needed oblivion tonight. Maybe tomorrow she would wake up from this hideous nightmare.

❖

River drove the shop truck back to Madras airport to meet Mike for the flight back to Redmond. She kept thinking about Dee. How in the world did this woman find her in the woods? How was she even able to function right now, much less hike through such terrain? Dee Rawlings was clearly a very capable and determined police detective. River was also impressed with how easily Dee had disarmed her and shoved a gun in her face. This was a woman who demanded to be taken seriously, much like herself.

Back at Madras, River returned the shop truck and thanked the receptionist for her help. Then she took out her terrain map and pointed to the spot where she'd been exploring. "Do you know this place?"

She looked at the chart. "Does it have a waterfall with a weird rock on it?"

"Yes. It does."

"Then that's Angel Creek. It's on the edge of the national forest."

An angel. That's what the rock formation on the creek looked like. "Thanks. I'll be back tomorrow."

River took out her plotter and drew a line from the engine site to the point where Dee had stepped on the metal. She shifted her plotter along the line, extended it north, and marked it with a dashed line. This was the flight track of the DC-10 across the ground. She corrected the track for magnetic variation to give her a heading.

Mike taxied the Civil Air Patrol airplane to the front of the terminal building and shut down the engine. "Ready to go?" he asked.

"Yes, but I need you to fly us to these coordinates so I can see it from the air." River gave him the latitude and longitude of Angel Creek, then showed him where it was located on the chart.

They took off, turned northwest, and River used the binoculars to scan the area around the creek. It was five p.m., and the summer sun wouldn't set for several hours, but the ridge line of the mountain range blocked the sun, casting long shadows across the foothills. The late rays of sun might glint off some more metal.

"Can you fly an 'S' pattern over the creek?"

"Like a lazy eight?" Mike asked.

"Exactly, but not so precise. I want a good look at both sides. Just keep flying along the creek."

After a few miles, Mike climbed the plane to clear a hill, and River saw a flash of light to her right. She pointed to it, and Mike turned the plane. As they got closer, River focused the binoculars and was able to make out a white triangle shape.

"It may be part of the upper rudder. Can you climb to a higher altitude?"

She saw a second flash, farther away, then another. The last light of day glinted off more metal, and the land before her looked like it was sprinkled with glitter. Broken metal parts littered the ground for miles in every direction.

"Oh my God. Look at that," Mike said.

"I think we found the main debris field."

❖

Day 3

The next morning, the jarring sound of a ringing phone woke Dee from a dead sleep. She sat up, fumbled around for the phone, and was greeted with a screeching headache.

"Yeah?"

"You sound like you've been run over by a Mack truck. Got a pen?" Marcus asked.

"Go ahead. Ready to copy." Dee wrote down the phone number and address for Naomi's husband, Bill.

"Have you heard anything yet?"

"Nothing so far. They think it exploded in flight."

"Aw, Dee. I'm so sorry to hear that. Anything else I can help you with?"

"Not for now, but I'll let you know. Thanks for the info, and I'll call you later."

Dee had to steady herself before she tried to stand up. She was suffering from the world's biggest self-induced hangover and would be feeling bad all day because of her poor judgment last night. But she had achieved her objective of oblivion. She was grateful she hadn't dreamed last night.

After several cups of coffee and plain toast, she was able to function, sort of. Her eyes were still swollen and red, her mouth tasted like hell, and she wanted to crawl into a hole and die. She was still numb inside. How could she possibly get through this day?

She went to her front window and watched the people and cars moving about on the street below. They were hurrying along, busy in their daily lives, oblivious to the fact that her life was crushed and her future was over. Why would any of these strangers care about her pain? The only person who ever truly cared about her was gone forever, and she had no idea what to do next.

She couldn't allow herself to fall into a pit of despair again. It didn't accomplish anything except to overwhelm her with grief. She had to take action, or she would go mad. She looked at Bill's phone number and started to enter the first few numbers on her phone, then stopped herself. What could she possibly say to him that didn't sound lame? "Hi. I'm your sister-in-law. We've never met, but let's talk about Naomi's death."

She hung up. She couldn't bear to hear his voice, or his tears, right now. She had no idea how to comfort him, or his daughters, and she didn't want to hear him try to comfort her. She didn't want sympathy from anyone. She didn't want to talk about her feelings. She wanted to do something, anything, to get some answers.

❖

The entire investigation team assembled in the big hangar in Redmond as the truck bearing the engine rolled in. The General Electric engine specialists maneuvered a special lift to move it from the truck onto a maintenance stand for a detailed examination.

Mike was standing next to River, watching the delicate operation. "That thing is huge."

"Yes, it is. Each engine puts out more than one hundred

thousand pounds of thrust. The diameter of this engine is bigger than the main cabin of a 737."

River was glad it was relatively intact, with only a few sections of the exterior cowling missing. "Let's take a look."

They worked their way through the crowd to get a close-up view.

"What are you looking for?" Mike asked.

"I have just a few important questions about this engine. Was it the direct cause of the accident? Did it malfunction first, or did something else damage it?"

They started at the front with the engine intake.

"I need to know if this engine was producing power at the time of the accident. This is a high-bypass turbofan engine, with most of the thrust coming from the big fan blades of the first stage. Look how the fan blades are bent backward at the tips. This shows the engine was spinning at high speed, then abruptly stopped, which indicates the engine was operating. If they were flat, it would mean the engine was already shut down before the accident."

"So this engine was working okay?"

"So far. Let's check the engine tail-cone area."

They walked to the back of the engine through the crowd of investigators.

"What do you see, Mike?"

"Little dots of color, like tiny rainbows, splattered across the exhaust area."

"Good catch. That's a sign of molten titanium, when the temperature inside the engine gets over three thousand degrees from disintegrating metal parts. There aren't a lot of color dots here, so this damage occurred most likely after it came off the airplane."

"It sounds like you don't think this engine caused the crash."

"No, it didn't, but we have to wait for them to disassemble the engine to know for sure. Only after they take it apart will we know if any internal fire was present, or contaminated fuel, or any other issue. Let's find seats. They're about to start the morning status update."

They sat down, and River took out her leather notepad.

The incident commander from the Oregon State Police spoke first. "Good morning, ladies and gentlemen. We have secured the site where the engine was found, and that area is now safe. A new area, where additional parts were found, is located northwest of Redmond, near Madras airport. We have confirmed the area is safe from fire danger or other hazards, and it is now open for search operations. The work of the OSP is concluded, and I'm turning control over the accident site to the NTSB representative, Mr. Ronald Moore."

"Oh, great," River mumbled.

"What's the deal with him?" Mike whispered.

"Tell you later."

River couldn't stand this guy. She'd had the misfortune to cross paths with him several times, starting when she first worked for the NTSB ten years ago. He was a pompous ass then, as her first boss at the NTSB, and now he was even worse. Every word he said, every action he took was strictly for his own advantage. He was more polished than he used to be, since he loved being in front of the cameras, but he was still the same.

"Thanks, Oregon State Police, for securing our search areas. We'll take it from here." He flashed his expensive smile, his voice an immediate irritant to River. She relaxed her death grip on her pen, hoping he would say something helpful or informative.

"We had great success yesterday locating the engine, which has been confirmed as the number-two engine from the tail section. We also identified a metal piece that we have determined is part of the aircraft structure. One of our specialist investigators, River, found it, and the Civil Air Patrol discovered what looks like the main debris field. Good job, CAP. This new area is marked on your updated charts. As expected, it's a very large area, over one hundred miles across, so be sure to use evidence SOPs. I'm holding a press briefing at one p.m. today, so notify me as soon as you find anything significant. The buses leave in twenty minutes. Let's roll."

"What are evidence SOPs?" Mike asked.

"The standard operating procedures for retrieving and

cataloging everything we find. You have to photograph it where you found it, stake it with a numbered flag, mark the location on the chart, then bag it and record it."

"Thanks for explaining. Sorry, but I can't fly you to Madras today. I'm flying search missions all day."

"That's okay. I got a rental Jeep, so I'm driving out there by myself. Keep an eye out for the big parts like the landing gear, wing sections, and the other two engines."

"Got it. Why aren't you going in the buses with everyone else?"

"Because I get a lot more done on my own."

CHAPTER SEVEN

Dee tried to call her brother-in-law, Bill, a dozen times, but she couldn't go through with it. She still had no idea what to say to him and didn't want to become a pitiful, bawling mess. Instead, she managed to shower and get dressed, but then she had to sit down, immobilized again. Everything seemed pointless. She couldn't do anything but wait for news.

She wanted a call from River, but she was also afraid to hear what she might say. She'd seen dead bodies before, both in Iraq and in Portland, but she'd never had to identify anyone she knew. Maybe if she saw Naomi's body, she could accept the reality of her death. But not knowing what happened to her was driving Dee crazy. She had to get out of the house.

One thing that always helped her was shooting, so she drove to the police gun range. When she was there, she was able to focus her mind and tune out the world. She wasn't a gun nut, but she enjoyed keeping her skills sharp, even during her off time. She loved her service pistol, an H&K forty-caliber compact police special. It was lightweight, accurate, held thirteen rounds, and had never failed her. The feel of the rough grip in her hand, the sound it made when she racked the slide, the balance of it, the smell of the gunpowder, seeing her target through the clean front sight—all these sensations made her feel at one with her weapon. It was an extension of her arm and part of her body.

After the range master gave her paper targets, she put on her hearing protection and set her box of hollow-point bullets on the bench. She started with the target at twenty-five feet away for a warm-up, then mentally went through her shooting mantra: *unsnap, draw, front sight, center mass, smooth squeeze, follow through.*

"Crap." Her first shots were high and right. *I'm anticipating the recoil. Breathe.*

She soon got into a steady rhythm of draw, shoot, holster, pleased with her tight grouping in the center. She moved her target farther away after each magazine of twelve shots. After sixty rounds, she switched to the shotgun, then the M-16 rifle.

Dee was less agitated but still tense after an hour of shooting. She went and picked up a baton for some work on the practice dummy they named Bruno, the bad guy. She liked working on her defensive tactics and hand-to-hand combat skills because she'd more likely need these than her weapon. Plus, she enjoyed beating the crap out of Bruno. She whaled on the poor dummy until her arms were weak. After she wiped the sweat from her face, she felt physical relief for the first time in three days. She was also grateful her mind was calm and she could think clearly.

As she methodically disassembled and cleaned her gun, she had a thought. *If I can find a way to help the investigation, maybe she'll let me in.*

Driving back to her apartment, she decided to get in touch with an old friend who worked for the FAA. One of the tedious parts of her job was doing background checks on suspects and witnesses, so maybe she could study the passenger list and find some useful information for River. It was her only shot.

River drove directly to the area around Angel Creek to continue her search. She had confidence the rest of the team would find all the major aircraft pieces in the main debris path, now that they knew where to look. Instead, she was interested in the first pieces of the jet to fall from the sky. She had a strong feeling this debris was where the problem had begun.

After hiking to the spot where Dee had stepped on the metal fragment, River stopped and shook her head, thinking about her. Detective Dee Rawlings was as much of a mystery as this plane crash. First, she loses a family member in a terrible accident, and then, instead of waiting with the other families, she drives to the middle of nowhere to track down an investigator she met one time. Part of River understood Dee's irrational behavior as a reaction to sudden, unexplainable death. She understood because she had experienced it herself.

River still didn't like it that Dee had stuck a gun in her face, but she could comprehend a level of desperation that would drive a person to do something that crazy. Seeing the anguish in Dee's eyes brought back memories of that terrible time in her own life.

She was only thirteen when her mother was suddenly taken from her, turning her world upside down. She survived that awful experience with help from her remaining family, a special friend, and a skilled therapist. River hoped Dee had someone kind to take care of her during the days ahead, because she would need it.

She shook off thoughts of Dee Rawlings and went to work looking for the needle in the haystack. Her discovery of the huge debris field had confirmed her theory that the airplane broke up in flight. Her preliminary examination of the number-two engine from the tail section showed it was probably not the cause, but what was? Not many things could make an airplane blow up in the sky. Failure of the aircraft structure could come from unknown internal corrosion, an uncontained fire on board, midair collision with another aircraft, or even a bomb.

Whatever the cause, River was determined to find it. The definitive answer could come from something as small as a fingernail, as in the Pan Am 747 that blew up over Lockerbie, Scotland. In that case, a tiny fragment of circuit board had plastic-explosive residue on it from a bomb hidden in a suitcase in the cargo pit. That small bit of evidence proved what caused the accident and that the Libyan military had murdered all those people.

When she'd studied that case during her doctoral program at the University of Southern California, the thing that had struck her was its timing. The Libyans were clever in how they had hidden the bomb inside a small cassette player in a checked suitcase. They'd also studied the route of flight of Pan Am 103 and its flight duration. With the bomb on a timer, they had intended for the aircraft to blow up when they were over the ocean, but they screwed up and set the timer wrong. The 747 was only minutes from crossing the Scottish coastline to fly over the North Atlantic when the bomb went off. Had they set the bomb to explode only fifteen minutes later, when the jet was over the open ocean, the pieces would be at the bottom of the sea and no one would ever know for certain how those passengers died.

She remembered a grim image of that crash. The largest piece found, the side of the flight deck, resembled a great dead bird lying on the ground, shot out of the sky by a hunter. At the time, those images had made River feel the heaviness of the enormous loss of life. And all the accidents she ever worked made her feel the same loss, yet she pushed through because of her mission. She was determined to find the cause so she could prevent future accidents and, hopefully, eliminate the devastation of so many lives from an aircraft crash. Like the devastation Dee was going through right now.

Thoughts of her drifted into River's mind several times as she methodically searched both sides of the creek. She wasn't looking for a specific component, but she hoped she would get lucky and find something, anything, so she could report it. Maybe if Dee heard that the investigation was progressing, she would have the relief of knowing some answers. River could only hope.

❖

Dee hadn't looked up Marci's phone number in a long time. Her time with Marci had occurred in her distant past, half a world away. They met on Dee's first deployment to the Middle East in the dining hall at Bagram Air Base, Afghanistan. Dee's unit of military police had been sent there to beef up base security after increasing attacks. She smiled, recalling her first encounter with Marci on that hot, dusty day fifteen years ago.

"Hey, soldier. Where'd you get the Tabasco sauce?" The voice of a woman caught Dee's attention.

Dee stopped with her tray, turned, and saw a very cute US Air Force woman speaking to her. "I brought it with me from Texas. Would you like some?"

From that brief conversation, Dee made a big move and sat at the table next to the woman, instead of with the guys in her squad. She got a few looks from them because army and air force troops generally didn't mix, but she didn't care. She and Marci clicked from the beginning and met in the dining hall as often as they could, which soon led to them very carefully coming out to each other. That was during the bad days of "Don't ask, don't tell," when your career could be over from just a rumor of being gay.

After that, Dee had her first real affair with a woman. Marci was an air traffic controller at the busy base, and she worked the swing shift in the tower. Then she had mandatory crew rest because of her critical job. The good part was that Marci had a private room, unlike the army grunts crammed into tents. This arrangement gave Marci and Dee privacy, a luxury very few people had in the service. She and Marci were hot and heavy, sneaking around for three months before Marci got sent back to Barksdale Air Force Base in Shreveport, Louisiana. They planned to see each other when Dee returned to Fort Hood in Killeen, Texas, but it never worked out, mainly because Marci already had a lover before she deployed.

Dee remembered feeling crushed when Marci told her she already had a girlfriend. That's when she realized it had been just a wartime romance. Even though they were never lovers again, Dee remained friends with Marci, and now she needed her. Marci left the air force after her enlistment was up and now worked at the FAA Headquarters in Washington, DC. Dee called her office number.

"How's my favorite grunt? It's been a while, Dee. How are you?"

"Not so good. That's why I'm calling."

"What's up?"

The concern for her in Marci's voice gave Dee the courage to continue. "I assume you heard about flight 402?"

"Of course. This place has been crazy with it the last few days. What about it?"

Dee could hardly choke out the words. "My sister, Naomi, was on that plane."

Marci was silent. "Oh my God, Dee. That's so awful."

"That's why I'm calling. I really need your help."

"I'll do whatever I can. You know I could never say no to you."

"Can you get me a copy of the passenger information? I need it to do some research."

"Research? What kind of research? Have you been assigned to the investigation?"

"Well, no, not yet. But if you help me, I think I might be able to work on it."

Marci paused before answering. "Dee, you know I'd do anything for you, but this is not possible. All that information is under tight lockdown, and I don't have access to it. I wish I could help you."

Dee was quiet. She had to find a way to convince Marci to help her.

"I don't want you to lose your job, but is there any way I can at least see just the names of the passengers and crew? I don't need anything else, but please help me, Marci. I have to do something, anything, or I won't make it through this. I'll never ask you another favor again."

"First of all, we both know that's not true about asking for favors, but it's all right. I do have one idea that might work."

"What is it? I'll try anything." Was there a glimmer of hope?

"I have seen the passenger manifest and the crew list. The Airman Certification Branch sent it to my office as part of their review of the pilot records. They're looking for any violations, failed check rides, or training problems with the three pilots."

"There were three pilots on this plane?"

"Yes. The captain, the first officer, who is the copilot, and the flight engineer. I remember the names of the pilots but not all the flight attendants."

"So how can I see this?"

"Well, I could attach the passenger list to an email on my personal account, save it as a draft, let you open it to look at it, and then I'll delete the draft. This may not work, but it's all I can do."

"That would be great. Thank you, Marci. I owe you."

"You don't owe me anything. I wouldn't have made it through Afghanistan without you, so we're even. I'm sending it now."

Dee was overwhelmed by her old girlfriend bending the rules to help her. She'd always wondered if Marci was the one that got away. Maybe she should have waited until Marci was single, which happened six months after they got back stateside when her lover was transferred to South Korea. Very few women were able to make a relationship work in the military, mainly because everyone got sent to different bases every three or four years. If a soldier was legally married to another soldier, as in a male and a female, the army would try to assign the couple to the same base. As lesbians, they had no rights and had to lie about their lives every day to avoid a dishonorable discharge. She still loved Marci and was pretty sure Marci still loved her, but they never spoke of it. Dee was grateful she had one person left who still cared about her enough to help her.

Dee copied the database as soon as she opened the draft email from Marci, then deleted it. She hoped this wouldn't cause any problems for her at work. She printed the database so she could write notes on it and scanned the sheets. So many names on page after page, each one a life cut short, leaving grieving families behind.

Dee found Naomi's name on the list and ran the tip of her finger across the printed letters of her name. She wanted to touch her sister, but this was as close as she could get. What was she hoping for? That it wasn't true? That she'd missed her flight? That Naomi was waiting at the airport to be picked up? Her tortured thoughts just brought more tears.

She wiped her face. "I don't have time for this."

Dee went to work studying the passenger list. It was organized by seat location in the airplane. Using a few different sorting methods, she rearranged the names on the list, looking for any patterns or any names that stuck out. She expected to see common last names, like Smith or Jones, but was surprised to find six passengers with the last name of McClain. These six passengers also used only first initials instead of spelling out their first names.

Returning to the original list with names arranged by seat location, she found the six people with the same last name sitting in different locations throughout the cabin. If they were related, wouldn't they want to sit together? She also sensed something familiar about the name, McClain.

It was something Marcus had said recently when they were working on an illegal weapons case. This felt like a lead she needed to follow, and she called her partner.

"Marcus, do you remember the big weapons case we did a few months ago?"

"Of course. What about it?"

"You mentioned the name McClain to me. Who is that?"

"And why do you need to find this out right now? Aren't you off duty?"

"Yes, I am. I just want to help the investigation team by doing some computer work. That's all."

"Have you made an appointment with the shrink yet?"

"No, and I'm not going to until I finish this job. So the sooner you help me, the sooner I'll make my appointment."

"No point in arguing with you anyway. I always lose. At that time I was referring to the case against E.J. McClain. He's the head of the anti-government McClain Militia, near Bend, Oregon. He's been financing his white-supremacist operations by selling guns to felons. We've never been able to get anything solid enough to arrest him."

"Does he have any family you're aware of?"

"Oh, yeah. He's got five sons, and they all go by initials, like J.R. and P.J."

Dee looked at her list. Those initials matched the McClain names on the manifest.

"I think E.J. and his sons were passengers on flight 402. This could be significant."

"Damn. That's quite a coincidence."

"Yes, it is. Thanks, Marcus. I need to report this to the investigation team ASAP."

"And after you report it, you're going to call the shrink and make an appointment, right?"

"Of course. Bye."

Dee's mind was spinning. Could these militia guys actually take down an airplane? Did they smuggle explosives on the plane and either accidentally or intentionally blow it up? Did someone try to take them all out and kill everyone else on the plane as well?

She had to find River and show her this information right now. She would volunteer to do more forensic research on the McClains. If she could see credit card records, past travel information, and emails, she'd have a much better chance of finding any connection between these men and the plane crash. She'd uncovered vital information and had to convince River to put her on the investigation team. Nothing else mattered.

Chapter Eight

Dee drove as fast as she dared across the mountains to the Madras airport. She wished she was driving her police Camaro with her lights on so people would get out of her way. She was energized and on task, a condition she was very familiar with. When she was able to dive into a case and see connections others might miss, she was in her element and using all her skill and experience. That's how she'd gotten promoted to sergeant, then detective in only three years.

For the first time since this nightmare started, she was calm, her mind focused, her body feeling normal. Concentrating on the passenger list was the only thing giving her a respite from her grief. Since she'd fully immersed herself in this case, she was too busy to think about her loss. Work was her salvation.

River would probably be somewhere near the place she'd stepped on the metal piece. After parking her car, she set out on foot to find her. She kept checking behind her in case River tried to come up and blast her with bear spray again. Following the sound of water, she emerged from the woods onto the grassy bank of Angel Creek. She stopped searching for River to watch the water flow by. It was a pretty, quiet place, with only the sounds of birds and the wind. She wanted to sit down on the bank, take her boots off, and put her feet in the cold, clear liquid. She looked upstream at the small waterfall and found River staring back at her. *Oh, shit.*

River stomped toward her with an angry expression. "Why are you here?"

"Look. I know what you said, but I can explain."

"You're not explaining anything. You're leaving right now, and I'm reporting you to the chief of the Portland Police Bureau. This is completely unacceptable, Dee."

"I found some evidence for you." She tried to sound enticing.

"What evidence?" River still sounded pissed off.

"I discovered a connection between six of the passengers."

"How do you know who the passengers are? Did you get a copy of the passenger manifest? Oh, my God, Dee. What have you done?" River started pacing in front of her.

"It doesn't matter how I got the information, but I found six family members of an anti-government militia who have an illegal-weapons business. Isn't that significant? Could these guys possibly be connected with a bomb?"

"I wonder if that's why ATF and the FBI are here? This is certainly an interesting development. But, Dee, you can't know this."

"Why? It's important to the investigation."

"You're right, but you don't have the security clearance necessary to see the passenger manifest. Every piece of information about this crash is classified until the investigation is complete. It's a federal crime for you to even have it, much less analyze it and talk about it. You could get arrested."

"I don't care. I have to know what happened to Naomi. If these crazy-assed militia nut cases had anything to do with destroying that plane and killing my sister, they'll answer to me!"

They stared at each other for a long moment.

River lowered her voice and spoke very deliberately. "I know what you're going through is horrible, and you did find valuable information that I will definitely act on, but you cannot be involved in this case. I'm sorry."

Dee couldn't say anything. She knew she'd stepped out of bounds when she got the passenger list from Marci, but her plan to become involved with this investigation was backfiring. She was getting tossed out and would probably suffer severe consequences. She might even lose her job when River reported her to the chief. She didn't bother asking for a pass on reporting her. Dr. River Dawson would offer no professional courtesy of looking the other way. She was clearly a stickler for the rules. Dee was toast, and she knew it.

"Well, I had to try. Here's what I found out about the McClain Militia in Bend. I hope it's useful. Sorry to bother you."

Dee turned and left the beautiful creek, her heart shattered.

❖

River was stunned by what Dee gave her. How the hell did she get the passenger manifest? Everything about this crash was locked down tight. *Why did she bring this to me?*

Watching Dee walk away with her head down, part of her wished she could put her arms around her and tell her she would survive this. That the rest of her life wouldn't be filled with sadness and death like it was today. But Dee wouldn't believe her, because she hadn't believed it either when her therapist had told her she would have a life after her mother's death.

For an entire year after her mother died, her life was filled with darkness. Then, very gradually, a few cracks of light appeared. They were tiny rays of hope that River clung to. She learned how to put one foot in front of the other to get through the day, and also to fake it until she made it. She couldn't bear to talk about what had happened, so she acted like her life was all right just so people would leave her alone. River wanted to share her advice with Dee, but it simply wasn't allowed. If anyone knew she was working with a victim's family member, they would assume she was compromised, and her conclusions would be suspect. The NTSB Chief, Ronald Moore, would definitely try to get her kicked off this case, and she couldn't let that happen.

She took the few items she'd found—a small piece of scorched insulation that had probably floated down the creek, and another piece of internal metal with lime-green anti-corrosion paint on it—with her. Then she drove back to Redmond to turn them in and to discuss Dee's findings with Ronald. He was an ass, but this was a significant finding he needed to know about. Plus, they had to pursue it.

After looking at Dee's report for quite a while, Ronald finally said, "How did you make the connection to this local militia group?"

"I have a contact with local law enforcement."

He picked up a hand mike for the public address system. "This is Ronald Moore speaking. ATF and FBI, please report to my table."

He could walk over there to them just as easily.

Two guys hurried over to Ronald's table, and he handed them the report. "What do you think of this?"

"We knew the McClain boys were on this flight, but we hadn't figured out they intentionally didn't sit together. The airline also told us they checked five rifle cases before they boarded. We're still looking for those."

They both turned to River. "Did you do this analysis? It's very helpful, and we'd like to run down this lead."

"Actually, I did it."

They all turned around to see Dee Rawlings standing behind them with her hands on her hips. River was shocked to see her again and scrambled to think up a cover story.

"Gentlemen, this is Detective Dee Rawlings of the Portland Police Bureau. She is my local law enforcement contact and the person I worked with to obtain information on the McClain passengers."

"Is she the liaison with Portland police?" Ronald asked.

"No, but she's a subject-matter expert on militia and illegal firearms activity in the local area." It was an exaggeration but mostly true.

Dee took the hint, walked forward, and shook hands with the team members like she belonged here. "If you're interested in an even more detailed analysis, I'd be happy to assist if I could access the full passenger data."

"We can read you in, Detective Rawlings. Come with us," the ATF agent said.

"If it's all the same to you, I'd like to continue to work with Dr. Dawson. We have an established professional working arrangement."

"Whatever you want do to. Just copy us on any further

intelligence you're able to find on the McClain family." They walked away, seeming grateful for Dee's assistance.

River pulled Dee aside. "We need to talk, now."

❖

River was clearly mad at her. Too bad, because she would do whatever she had to do to work on this investigation. She understood she now had some negotiating power because the ATF and FBI were interested in her report. What she didn't understand was why River hadn't reported her, like she'd threatened to.

"What are you doing here? I told you it wasn't possible for you to be involved in this case." River spoke through gritted teeth.

"Why didn't you report me?"

"Well, I was just about to when Ronald Moore brought in ATF and the FBI, and apparently they like your work. So you accomplished your goal. You got yourself on the team, and I'll be held responsible when they discover you're a surviving family member."

"How will they find that out if I work with you? I won't mention it if you don't."

They stared at each other, unblinking, waiting for the next move.

"Fine. I can't seem to get rid of you, so I guess I'll just have to keep you busy, but stay out of my way."

Dee smiled at her victory. Her stubbornness had served her well, once again. "So what is all this?" She waved her arm across the huge hangar.

"This is where we reassemble all the parts of the airplane we find." She led Dee on a tour of the investigation headquarters. "We place everything we discover on this DC-10 scaffolding frame to reconstruct the airplane in order to see the big picture. Look over here."

River showed her the first items found. "This is the number-two jet engine from the tail section. They're taking it apart to determine if it was running properly at the time the airplane broke apart."

"Why do you say 'broke apart' instead of blew up? Isn't it obvious it exploded?"

"It may appear obvious to you, but we have to prove it by finding the origin of the explosion on the airframe and the cause of it. You can't jump to conclusions. We have to examine every aspect of the evidence to see where it leads first, and then we determine the cause. I'm sure it's similar to what you've done as a police detective."

"Yes, of course. So was this engine the cause of the accident?"

"I don't think so, but let's talk to the engine guys."

They walked over to the engine disassembly area. Hundreds of metal parts were spread out on tables, neatly arranged and tagged. River slowly walked along the tables, looking closely at each part.

"What is all this, and what are you looking for?" It was an organized mess of a zillion sharp, twisted metal pieces.

River pointed to the various parts. "These are all the internal parts of the engine. This engine has seventeen different stages inside it, where the air is accelerated and compressed by each stage to produce jet thrust. These are rotors, the parts that turn, and these other things are the stators, the stationary parts. The engine stages rotate at high speed, three thousand RPMs, to produce power."

River went into excruciating detail explaining how all the parts of a jet engine work. She pointed to the rainbow-colored drops of molten titanium in the tail cone and explained the significance of the bent blade tips.

Then she walked over to a technician wearing General Electric coveralls. "Have you found any internal damage? How are the fluids?"

"All the discs are intact, the main fan blades are deformed backward, and all parts are accounted for. No internal fire or lines burned through. Oil, hydraulic fluid, and fuel have tested normal, and no indication of ice present. It looks like this engine was operating normally. They found number one yesterday and are bringing it here later today. Still looking for number three."

"Thanks, guys." River led Dee to a less noisy place in the hangar.

"Translate for me what he just told you."

"Essentially, this engine is normal and did not cause the plane to break up. We don't know anything yet about engines one and three, which are on the wings."

"How do you know all this stuff, River?"

"Because I flew this airplane for four years in the US Air Force."

Dee was stunned. She knew River was very smart—she had a doctorate, after all—but there was a lot more to this woman than Dee had first assumed. An air force pilot who flew this giant plane? Dee needed to learn a lot more about Dr. River Dawson.

CHAPTER NINE

After driving two and a half hours back to her apartment in Portland, Dee couldn't wait to log in to her computer and look up background information on River Dawson. She wanted to know this woman's full story. Based on what she saw back in the big hangar, River could think on her feet when she told the ATF and FBI guys that Dee was her "subject-matter expert" on local militia activity. She also wasn't nearly the rule-follower Dee had first assumed. The fact that River didn't rat her out after she threatened to showed that she could bend things a little when she needed to.

The first search inquiry revealed some basic information. River was listed as the president of Aviation Accident Solutions, Inc. out of Denver, Colorado. The business website had independent aircraft accident investigation and aviation safety consulting as primary missions. The website showed River's resume: US Air Force Academy graduate with a bachelor's degree in aeronautical engineering, master's degree from Embry-Riddle, and her doctorate from the University of Southern California. It also listed papers she'd written in professional publications and major aircraft accidents she'd worked on. Her company had stellar ratings.

River's work history verified what she'd told Dee about being an air force pilot, although she served for only five years before going to school for her doctorate. She'd worked with the NTSB, but only for two years. Then she'd started her own company. The real question Dee needed to answer was, who was River working for? It certainly wasn't the NTSB or any other government agency, although she knew most of these people, so she must be representing some other organization, or another person, with a vested interest in this accident. What was River's agenda? Dee dug deeper and was surprised River had had the same mailing address for the last ten years in Denver. River projected an air of sophistication, so Dee had assumed she'd lived all over the world. She also checked property, marriage, and birth-certificate records. Interestingly, River had bought a house with another woman in Los Angeles after she left the air force. Had River been dishonorably discharged for being a lesbian? The time period was right for that possibility.

Just then her phone rang. Dee looked at the display and saw it was the main number for the police department.

"Hello?"

"Detective Rawlings, this is Assistant Chief Diana Ward. I need you to come to my office tomorrow at nine a.m."

"Yes, ma'am. Can I ask what this is concerning?" Dee was nervous.

"I'll discuss that with you tomorrow at nine. Good-bye." Then with a *click*, she hung up.

Oh, shit. Now Dee was worried. She rarely spoke to the assistant chief. In fact, it was her goal in life to never step foot in her office, and here she was being called before her. It must have something to do with the investigation. Could River have reported her to the chief of police after all?

Had Dee misjudged River and she really was that tight-assed rule-follower? Maybe River was just placating her when she explained all that complicated stuff about jet engines. She was disappointed that River might try to get her kicked off the investigation team, behind her back, after she'd pretended to work with her.

She needed sleep, but her mind was still buzzing. She poured herself another stiff drink to try to relax. It had been a very eventful day with the intel from Marci on the passengers, then getting invited to help with the investigation against River's objections.

She noticed the slip of paper she'd left on her kitchen table with the phone number for Naomi's husband, Bill. She still needed to call him, but she'd been too busy today. She promised herself to definitely call him tomorrow and collapsed on her bed, grateful for the work today. When she was busy, she didn't have time to think about Naomi.

❖

River was exhausted when she got back to her hotel room in Redmond. She was physically tired from hiking around all day looking for aircraft parts, and she was worn out mentally with Dee Rawlings. Part of her understood Dee's desperation to help with the investigation to keep busy. Being alone in loss was a very frightening place.

She remembered clearly that abyss of nothingness after her mother's death. She would have done anything to run away from that pain. Unlike Dee, who needed to take action to avoid her own grief, River turned her despair inward. Motherless at the age of thirteen, River had lost the will to live and wished for her own death to be with the woman she loved most in the world. But she'd been luckier than most because of her father. He'd found her a good therapist and a grief support group for kids. *Did Dee have anyone looking out for her?*

What was she going to do with Dee? She had to work with her on the investigation team, but she was a loose cannon running around the state causing problems, and River didn't want to have to babysit her. She would simply keep Dee occupied with busywork, like more computer research, so she wouldn't get in the way out in the field.

Keeping her busy could be very difficult, based on what she'd seen of Dee's resourcefulness. River still couldn't figure out how Dee had accessed the passenger manifest, but her analysis of the very limited information was impressive. The detail about the McClain family members not sitting together was significant, because that's what the 9/11 hijackers had done. Intentionally sitting in different parts of the cabin enabled them to control the passengers during the attack. The 9/11 attackers wore fake bomb vests during the hijacking, and perhaps the McClain men had a real bomb on board. Not only did Dee uncover this connection with the passengers, but she did it very quickly. What could she figure out when she got access to the full passenger and crew data?

River ordered room service, having declined an invitation to go out for dinner with the guys. She preferred to be alone when she was off duty from working an accident scene. The urgency to find the remaining pieces of the plane, the difficult terrain conditions, seeing unrecognizable human remains, the pressure to provide answers all combined to cause a high level of stress. River had to take care of her own health or she would be useless. She needed quiet time in the evening to process everything that had happened in the field. She also had to have sleep, or she could get a migraine headache that would keep her down for two days. She'd spent so much time in hotels over the years that sleep was often elusive, so she meditated to calm her mind. Sometimes, in that twilight between consciousness and sleep, the answer to a question in the investigation would come to her. Tonight, the last image she saw before drifting off to sleep was Dee's face.

❖

Day 4

The next morning, Dee put on her best navy-blue pantsuit and drove to work for her meeting. Walking into the familiar building felt different. She had the sensation that everyone was watching her and whispering about her. The only thing she hated more than being gossiped about was pity. She felt uncomfortable in her workplace for the first time ever, and she didn't like it. She had to walk through a gauntlet of her fellow detectives to reach the assistant chief's office. They tried to look busy, but a few stole glances at her. She stood tall, tried to ignore them, and kept her eyes forward. Then she saw Marcus and almost lost it.

The look of sympathy on the face of her partner made Dee's

eyes well up. She couldn't speak to him right now, or she'd be a crying mess in front of the assistant chief. He understood, gave her a head nod and a small smile, then walked off. She stood outside the assistant chief's office and knocked on her door.

"Enter."

"Morning, Chief." Dee stood at attention.

"Dee, have a seat." She gestured to the leather chair in front of her big desk. "How are you?"

"I'm okay, ma'am," she lied.

"One, stop calling me ma'am. And two, don't ever lie to me. You are clearly not okay. You look like hell, as a matter of fact. Have you been to see Dr. Lopez yet?"

She hesitated. "Not yet. Sorry. No, I haven't seen her, but I'm planning to call her to make an appointment as soon as I can."

"Call her today. Next issue, can you explain to me why I'm getting calls from the Feds about you out at the airplane crash site? You need to tell me exactly what you've been doing out there. I do not care to look like an idiot when the Feds ask me questions and I have no idea what they're talking about."

Dee took a deep breath. "I had information from my work on the McClain weapons case that might be useful to the investigating team, so I took it out there to give it to them."

"And how did you know the McClain family was on that flight?" Diana Ward was staring holes into her.

"I called an old friend from the military who's at the FAA to get the passenger list. I had to do something, Chief, or I'd go crazy. I know I crossed a line, and I'm sorry."

"You sure as hell did. How would you react if the sister of a murder victim showed up at your crime scene and started doing your work?"

Dee had nothing to say for herself. She had such enormous respect for Diana Ward, and now she'd made her look bad. Assistant Chief Ward had worked her way up years ago from beat cop, through every major division, to running the day-to-day police operations. She was a six-foot-tall Black woman with command presence who'd earned her position through hard work and dedication. Everyone respected her, and most people feared her. Dee had hoped Diana would be her mentor someday, but now that would never happen.

Diana walked around her desk, sat in the chair next to Dee, and looked her in the eyes.

"I can't imagine what you're going through, and I'm so sorry about your sister. I checked and saw that you haven't taken any vacation in four years, so I've extended your leave for one month. Since the Feds have now requested your assistance, I will authorize you to be detailed to the aircraft investigation for thirty days. I understand the need to work to get through loss. I want you to help the team, but I also want you to take care of yourself. Dr. Lopez has helped many of us navigate some real hard times, and I think she can help."

"Thank you."

"Dee, I want you back. I'm here for you if you need anything."

Diana stood up, indicating the meeting was over, and opened her office door. Dee couldn't say anything because of the lump in her throat. She left the room overwhelmed by Diana's kindness.

❖

River was back at the Redmond airport early, along with rest of the team. They were just about to start the morning briefing, and Dee wasn't here. River was annoyed with her, and she hated starting the day in a foul mood.

"How do you expect me to do my job if you don't show up?"

"What was that, River?" Mike Bowers had apparently overheard her.

"Oh, hi, Mike. It's nothing, I was just talking to myself."

"I don't think this is a safe place to mention that. I'm sensing tension in the air. Do you know what's up?" He stepped closer to her so others couldn't hear them.

"This is when the long knives come out. As more evidence surfaces, all the different parties will claim they're not responsible for the accident. They also start blaming, or implying, that someone else is the cause. They almost always blame the pilots."

"Even before all the facts are in?"

"Especially before the facts are in. Every accident is the result of a mishap chain of events. Something wrong occurs first, then something else, and finally the pilots are just the last link in this chain. In fact, the pilots rarely cause aircraft accidents. Most of this posturing is for PR purposes anyway when they're attempting to sway public opinion."

Ronald Moore continued to take credit for others' work and updated them on the locations of other major parts of the airplane. River looked at the big area map with colored pins marking the new spots. She was pleased the line of major parts was on the ground track she'd discovered. She took a few more notes, then waited for Ronald to stop talking.

"Let's get a closer look at the crash map."

River and Mike maneuvered through the crowd to the wall map. River took out her plotter and measured some distances and angles to the newly found objects.

"What are you trying to do?" Mike asked.

"If this was a symmetrical blast pattern, I can give you a more accurate location to search for the third engine. The distance from the ground track line to the left-wing engine might be the same for the right-wing engine, which should put it right about here." River held her fingertip on the map, moved her plotter, then wrote down the coordinates of her point. "Why don't you start here today, then do an outward spiral search pattern, and you might get lucky. It looks like it's densely wooded, so watch for broken treetops too."

"Thanks. I'll start there. What could cause a symmetrical blast?"

"I can think of several possibilities, but we haven't found the magic bullet yet. That's the first piece of evidence from the initial blast, and the most critical, because it gives us information about the origin of the explosion."

Mike added, "Thanks for the tip about flying low near sunset. I did that yesterday, saw the sunlight reflect off something, and it was an aileron. I need to go. I'll see you back here later. Why don't you join us for dinner tonight? We're all going out for barbecue."

"Thanks. I'll try to. Have a good flight."

Mike was a nice guy, but he was barking up the wrong tree. River wanted to wait for Dee to show up, but she needed to get moving. Rain was forecast for later today, and it could wash away, or even bury, evidence. Still annoyed, she left a note with instructions for Dee at the call desk. Dee was getting off on the wrong foot with her today.

CHAPTER TEN

Dee couldn't wait to leave the police headquarters building. She was itching to get back out to the accident site, but first she had a task. She'd already missed the morning briefing and had a long drive ahead of her, so she decided to detour to Bend, Oregon. The McClain family compound was just outside Bend, and she needed more intel on them. She thought she'd stop by and have a chat with Mrs. E.J. McClain.

Dee was familiar with this area from earlier surveillance operations. She approached the main gate slowly, knowing they were watching her. They tried to camouflage their cameras, but Dee could still pick them out. She came up the driveway, got out of her car, and walked up the steps to the front door of a big lodge made of pine logs. Two bearded men carrying AR-15 assault rifles rounded the corner to intercept her.

"Hey. Who are you?" they shouted.

Dee was careful not to make any sudden moves. "My name is Dee, and I'm here to see Mrs. McClain. I'm from the aircraft investigation team."

Just then four more guys showed up with rifles. Dee could feel the tension rise and heard grumbling amongst the men. She was outnumbered six to one in what was becoming a very tense situation. *Maybe this wasn't such a good idea. I should just leave and return with backup.*

The armed men started moving closer to her, but then the massive front door opened.

"Hello?"

An older lady stood in the doorway staring at her. She wore a frumpy cotton dress and had uncombed hair. Her eyes were red and swollen.

"Mrs. McClain? Hello. My name is Dee Rawlings, and I was hoping to speak with you."

"Well, I don't know."

The woman was hesitating, so Dee had to think fast. She started to reach for her badge, then stopped. Maybe now wasn't the time to reveal she was a police officer. "I'm from the aircraft investigation team, and I'd like to ask you just a few questions, if I may?"

"Oh, my gosh. Please come in." She opened the door wide to let Dee in. "Please have a seat." She gestured to a couch. Mrs. McClain sat on the opposite facing couch, leaning forward, and a young woman carrying a baby on her hip came in and sat down next to her.

"Have you found them? My husband and my sons, where are they?" Mrs. McClain held the hand of the young mother next to her.

Mrs. McClain assumed she was with the NTSB team and was here to bring them news of her missing family. *Oh, my God. She doesn't know they're all dead.*

"Mrs. McClain, I'm sorry to report we haven't found any of the passengers so far, but we are still looking. I can assure you of that." Dee tried to make her voice as gentle as she could. "I was wondering if you could tell me the purpose of their trip?"

Mrs. McClain looked confused. "They're very late. They should be home by now. Are you from the airline? Where's my husband?" She looked around like she was expecting him to walk in from another room. Dee felt sorry for her in her bewilderment, but she needed answers. She tried again.

"Mrs. McClain, do you know who your husband was seeing on this trip? Why didn't they sit together on the plane?"

She couldn't respond to the questions. She looked frozen on the couch with a blank stare on her face, then buried her face in her hands and started to cry.

"Please, Mrs. McClain. Could you answer my questions?"

The woman was sobbing uncontrollably now.

The young mother with the baby stood up. "Why are you making her cry? Hasn't she been through enough? What are you doing to find my father and my brothers?"

"I'm very sorry, and I'm not trying to make your mother cry. I need to get answers so we can figure out why the plane crashed." Dee tried to sound sympathetic.

"We know why the plane crashed. The US government shot it down with a missile. People saw it blow up. That's who you should be talking to, not us!" This woman was growing increasingly agitated.

"Who exactly saw the plane blow up?" If this information was accurate, it could be critical for the investigation.

"How should we know? Isn't that your job?" She was shouting at Dee, the baby was screaming, and Mrs. McClain was wailing and rocking.

The men from outside came in with their guns. "What's going on here?"

The situation was quickly getting out of control, and Dee needed to get out of here while she still could. She slowly stood up and turned to Mrs. McClain. "Ma'am, I'm so sorry to disturb you, and I'll be leaving now." She knelt in front of her and gently took her hand. "Mrs. McClain, I promise you as soon as I know anything definite about your husband and sons, I will get back to you." The poor woman could only nod, her face lined with tears.

Dee carefully retreated from the compound as the group of armed men watched her leave. Once on the road to Redmond, Dee couldn't believe what the young woman had told her. Was it possible the airplane had been shot down? She remembered the compact shoulder-mounted radar-guided Stinger missiles used in the desert when she was deployed there with the army. They were very effective weapons against aircraft, with deadly accuracy.

If this was true and the plane had been shot down, then who was responsible, and why? If this plane crash wasn't an accident, then

Naomi, and every other person on that plane, had been murdered. She had to find River and tell her about this incident immediately.

❖

River was back at the hangar in Redmond watching the technicians attach the big parts found onto the DC-10 scaffolding frame with wires. Mike had discovered the number-three engine from the air in the area she'd suggested, and they were wheeling it in to analyze it. They'd also located two main landing gear trucks and some big flight control sections. What they were putting together was beginning to resemble what used to be an airplane.

Nothing so far pointed to any reason for the accident. All the parts they'd found appeared to operate normally. River hoped they'd determine the cause, but that was never guaranteed. Some accidents were still a mystery, like the Malaysia Air Boeing 777 that vanished over the South Pacific in 2014. She'd heard rumors of what'd happened, but it was never found. They were fortunate that this accident had occurred over dry land, instead of a swamp, like the ValuJet crash in Florida, or over water, like the Airbus 320 that landed on the Hudson River. It was still a great challenge to find everything, especially spread out over such a large land mass, but at least they had a chance of figuring out what happened.

Nothing from the flight deck had turned up so far. They were still looking for the cockpit voice recorder and the digital flight data recorder. These boxes were in the tail section of the aircraft and were bright orange, not black. They both had radio transmitters that emitted a *ping*, making them slightly easier to find.

River kept scanning the hangar looking for Dee. She should have been here hours ago, and now she was not only annoyed but worried about her. Even though she looked okay on the outside, Dee was barely keeping it together.

Just then, across the crowded hangar, River locked eyes with her, and they walked directly toward each other.

"Where have you been? I've been waiting for you."

Dee looked surprised. "You were waiting for me? Well, I'm here now, and I have some information on the McClain passengers. I went and talked to the wife."

"You what? You shouldn't have done that. They could've killed you."

Out of the corner of her eye, River saw one of the FBI agents marching directly toward them. He stopped in front of Dee's face.

"Hey. Who told you to go interrogate a surviving family member? I just got off the phone with the lawyer for the McClain family, and he accused you of harassing E.J. McClain's wife. What's going on?"

Dee had stiffened and looked like she was about to let loose on him, when River stepped between them.

"So sorry about that, Agent. It's my fault. I told Detective Rawlings to canvass witnesses and survivors, but I didn't explain our interview protocols to her. It won't happen again."

"Make sure it doesn't. All interviews go through us." He turned and stomped off.

"That's the second time you've covered for me. I thought you were going to report me to the chief."

"The day's not over yet, and I may still do that. That's the last off-book interview you do around here. So what did you find out?"

"Shouldn't we brief Ronald Moore?"

"Not necessarily, but go ahead."

"McClain's wife is very upset but also confused. They're on high alert at their compound, with lots of armed men. The daughter told me they have witnesses who saw the airplane hit by a missile."

"Shot down?" This was a revelation to River, but, if true, it could explain a lot. "Were you able to get names of witnesses?"

"Not so far, but I think this is a good lead."

"This is a stretch, but it could explain a motive. If a rival anti-government group got ahold of a Stinger shoulder-fired missile, or even a mobile rocket launcher, they could take out the whole McClain family with one missile."

"That's what I thought too." Dee looked excited.

"This possibility brings up new questions, such as, who wanted the McClains dead, and how did they get a weapon like a Stinger missile?"

"All good questions. Have you ever heard of something like this happening to an airplane?"

"Yes, unfortunately. A Malaysia Air 777 was blown up over Ukraine by a Russian surface-to-air missile in 2014. Three hundred people died, and worst of all, several of the passengers were AIDS researchers. Just recently, the Iranian military shot down a 737 passenger plane after takeoff and killed a hundred and seventy-six people."

"Wow. I didn't know that."

"In the first case, the Russians deliberately took down the plane. In the second one, it was a supervisor's error. Both mishaps had no survivors. Please write a report of your interview with Mrs. McClain and turn it into the Tests/Reports table."

"Is that all? Just write up an interview report? Don't we need to go back to their compound with more firepower to get some answers?" Dee was clearly frustrated.

"What is considered the least reliable type of evidence?"

"Eyewitness testimony. Why are you quizzing me?"

River went on to make her point. "And why is eyewitness testimony the least reliable?"

Dee seemed pissed off now. "Because people don't remember details correctly, they can mix up facts."

"Exactly, and it's even more true with airplane accidents. A plane falling out of the sky is not normal, so the human brain has to create a logical reason for seeing something that doesn't make sense."

"Create a reason? What do you mean?"

"In previous investigations I've worked, I've had witnesses tell me things like, 'I saw smoke coming from the engines,' or 'the plane was on fire before it hit the ground.' In both cases, the witnesses were mistaken, and no fire or smoke existed before the crash. Their brains fabricated an explanation for the plane crash. Therefore, they thought they saw fire when there was none."

"Yes, that can happen, so what's your point?"

"We can't rely on what someone thinks they saw. We have to prove it with physical evidence. We'll have to find punctures going into the aircraft skin from missile shrapnel, explosive residue on parts, or pieces of the missile mixed in with aircraft parts. If we can locate any of this evidence, you might have figured out the magic bullet that brought this plane down. Let's go see what they've found so far."

River led Dee to the big structure with parts attached to their locations on the airframe with wires. As they walked around it, River pointed to the various structural parts they had gathered so far.

"This is the outboard left aileron, this is the right main landing gear truck, and here is the upper rudder. I don't see any scorching or inward punctures on any of these parts."

Dee came up close to River and whispered, "What's that, on the outside of the engine they just found?"

"That's the number-three engine from the right wing."

The engine had been loaded onto a movable stand for examination by the General Electric technicians. Dee tilted her head back to look at it.

"This thing is huge. There, on the left side of it, is a gash. And what's all this stuff in the front of it?"

River watched the GE guys wheel the engine past her to their teardown area. Pine branches stuck out of the front intake, along with dirt, and the outer cowling had a three-foot-long tear in its side. "I need to talk to Mike Bowers about where he found this."

They went to the Civil Air Patrol operations table and saw Mike doing flight planning for his next search mission.

"Hey, Mike. Good job locating the engine. Do you have any pictures of the terrain it impacted?"

"Sure. Here they are. And thanks again for the tip on where to search. I saw it from the air only about fifty yards from the point you gave me."

Dee stuck her hand out toward Mike. "Hi. I'm Dee. I'm with the Portland Police Bureau."

"Oh. Sorry I didn't introduce you. Look at these pictures.

The tops of several evergreen trees were broken off as the engine crashed through them. On this view, I can see a definite line from the missing treetops. This is the angle of impact."

Mike jumped in. "Yeah. They told me this engine was half-buried in the forest floor when they retrieved it. It took them quite a while to dig it out."

"That explains the dirt in the intake but not the gash in the side of the engine."

"Could the trees have torn that hole in the side when it fell from the sky?" Dee asked.

"Not likely. This engine is made of all metal and is very heavy. A big tree would break before it could damage something this massive. Look at the hole on the side of it. It's a three-foot-long tear that is deformed inward, meaning something hit this engine hard from the outside."

"Like a missile or a bomb?"

"Possibly, but we won't know anything definitive until they tear it down and look at the internal damage."

"River, if something hit this engine, is that enough to bring down an entire airplane?"

She mentally reviewed the list of major aircraft accidents, each one a fascinating but tragic story. "Yes, it is. An American Airlines DC-10 crashed over forty years ago because the left engine broke off from the wing and severely damaged the plane. It happened just after takeoff, when they were close to the ground. They never had a chance."

Dee was quiet. "What do we do now? Wait for these guys to take the engine apart?"

"No. We need more evidence, and lots of it, to figure out what happened. Let's get back out in the field and find the rest of this jet."

Chapter Eleven

Dee and River returned to Angel Creek and walked around for hours with nothing to show for it. This was very different from what Dee was used to as a police detective. She didn't even know what she should be looking for. Most of the mangled parts on the scaffolding frame looked like trash, not valuable evidence. Instead of directly pursuing a bad guy, River was methodically and thoroughly searching for pieces. Dee was getting frustrated at River's slow pace.

"Why are we still in this area instead of searching where everyone else is in the main debris field?"

River stopped and turned to her. "If you don't like the way I do things, you're free to leave and join them."

"Hey, I'm not trying to pick a fight. I just want to understand the big picture of what we're doing. I don't know what I'm looking for."

River looked irritated. "Do you know what a hydraulic fuse looks like?"

"No."

"How about the difference between a pitot tube and an angle-of-attack probe?"

"Of course I don't. What's your point?"

"You don't know this environment or how it works. If I walked into a crime scene with you, I wouldn't know what to do either."

"Okay. You're right, but you could help me out a little and explain what you're up to. After all, I'm trying to help."

"Really? So far, you've been nothing but in my way."

Dee felt like River had just slapped her. After a moment, she said, "If that's how you feel, I'll go. Maybe I can be of use to the FBI or ATF." She turned and walked off.

❖

Watching Dee walk away, part of River was glad she could do her work in peace. Another part of her felt guilty for what she'd said. She didn't want to be unkind, but Dee's questions were interrupting her process. She also felt sorry for her because she understood the need to keep busy. But Dee Rawlings was a loose cannon and a distraction she didn't have time for.

As River continued to search the area, not finding anything, she wondered if Dee was right. Maybe she should join the rest of the search team, because she wasn't discovering anything new at Angel Creek. But something about this area made River think she could locate something significant. It was nothing more than a hunch, but she continued. She did prefer to work by herself, but she had to collaborate with the other team members when they presented their findings.

A clap of thunder in the distance drew her attention to the sky. It was dark and ominous to the south, with lightning flashes getting closer. She packed up for the day before she got drenched. With a twinge of melancholy, she looked back at Angel Creek on her way out. It was such a peaceful place in the midst of such destruction.

Back at the hangar in Redmond, Ronald Moore was holding a press conference. "Ladies and gentlemen, Ronald Moore here. We've made significant progress on the investigation today, starting with the discovery of parts of the main cabin. Sadly, we also discovered the first human remains. Based on the amount of damage, we must report that we have found no survivors of this tragic accident. Our deepest condolences to the families."

"Oh, no." River looked around the hangar, hoping Dee wasn't here. Then she saw her standing in the corner. Hurrying through the crowd to get to her, by the time she reached Dee, she was shaking.

"I need to see her, River. Take me to where the bodies are."

"Oh, God. I can't do that."

"Don't give me that 'you don't belong here' bullshit. She's my sister."

"You don't understand. There are no bodies to identify."

"What are you talking about? More than two hundred and fifty people were on that plane."

"When the airplane exploded, the bodies were vaporized. The impact forces at five hundred miles an hour were enormous, and she died instantly. I'm so sorry, but nothing is left."

Dee buried her face in her hands.

"Come on, Dee. Let's get out of here."

Dee fought to control her breathing as River drove them to the Holiday Inn. Even after River had explained about the impact forces, she still couldn't believe nothing was left of Naomi. Up to this point, she'd thought she might be able to survive Naomi's death by working on the case. She now understood how impossible that would be. She was immobilized.

River pulled up to the hotel entrance. "Let's get you a room."

"I don't need a hotel room. I have to drive back to Portland."

"You're not going anywhere tonight."

"Do *not* try to tell me what to do." Part of Dee realized she'd just sounded like a three-year-old.

River shut off the car and turned to her. "Dee, I would never force you to do anything. But I need you to listen to me. You are not safe to drive right now. You're in shock, and you're not thinking clearly." She took Dee's hand. "Please let me help you."

Dee nodded, and they went into the hotel lobby, where the front-desk clerk said, "I'm sorry, but we're full with the investigation team. I don't have any more rooms available."

"It's okay." Dee turned to River. "I feel better. I'm all right to drive home."

"Wait. What about the room next to mine? Why don't you give her that one?"

"If that's all right with you, Dr. Dawson. I'll make you another key," the clerk answered.

"Hey. I don't want to put you out. I'm really okay to drive."

"Humor me, please." River led them to the elevator.

"I have two hotel rooms at the end of the hall, connected by a door. I use one as an office, but you can have it." River unlocked the hotel room door and held it open for her.

Dee looked around. "This is nice, but where will you work?"

"Sometimes I need space to spread out my maps to see the big picture, but that's all. Besides, my client, the liability insurance company, is paying for both rooms. Are you hungry? I was thinking of ordering room service."

"Not really, but you go ahead. Aren't you having dinner with the team?"

"No. I prefer to be by myself in the evenings."

"Oh." Dee felt bad for imposing on River's space and quiet time.

"I'll order room service." River walked through the adjoining doorway to her room.

Dee was very uncomfortable as she looked around. She was in this woman's space, a woman who clearly didn't want her anywhere near this case, and now she was supposed to spend the night in the room next to her. *I should leave.*

She went to the door between their rooms and knocked. She wanted to thank River, but she also needed to flee.

When River turned to her, she said, "You need to sit down. You don't look good." She led her to sit on the edge of the bed, then sat next to her.

She stared into River's eyes. "How can you be sure all the bodies are gone?"

"Because I've seen it before, and it's the laws of physics. They will find some personal effects, like clothing or maybe jewelry, but it's not much. They'll have to do DNA testing to determine the identities of the remains."

"I don't even know what she looks like now. I probably wouldn't have been able to identify her body anyway."

Tears slowly ran down Dee's cheeks, and she sensed herself sliding down the pit of despair into darkness again. She struggled to breathe, then felt warmth across her shoulders. It was River's arm holding onto her, holding her from descending into nothingness.

She felt the muscles in River's strong arm flex against her back. *Hang on, hang on.*

Waves of grief crashed into her, trying to dislodge her from River's grasp. She clung to River's waist as the sobs came. She lost track of time. When she was finally able to raise her head, she was dizzy and thirsty, and saw the wet, tear-stained front of River's shirt. She was mortified.

"I'm so sorry about your shirt." She tried to get up, but River held her firmly.

"It's just a tee shirt, and it's all right. Can you breathe?" Her voice was soothing.

Dee sat up. "Yes. I'm fine. I'm sorry I'm such a mess."

River released her shoulders and held her hand. "It's not a problem, and I understand what you're going through."

"How can you possibly know what I'm going through? You've worked a lot of aircraft crashes and are used to people being vaporized, but you've never had your sister taken from you in an instant."

"You're right, I don't know what that's like, but I do understand about sudden loss, because my mother died in a plane crash thirty-one years ago."

Dee's anger turned into stunned silence.

❖

River dreaded this conversation, but she knew it was necessary for Dee. She hated telling this story because it brought back the pain as if the crash had happened yesterday. But letting Dee know she wasn't alone in her grief was more important. Dee was sinking into depression and needed a lifeline to hold on to. She grabbed some tissues, took a deep breath, and began. "My mom and I were passengers on United flight 232, the DC-10 that crash-landed in Sioux City, Iowa, in 1989. I was thirteen, and my mom and dad had just gotten a divorce. We lived in Denver with my grandparents, and I was going to Chicago to spend my first summer with my dad, but I didn't want to fly by myself, so I begged my mom to come with me."

River got up from the bed, walked around the room, drank some water, then continued.

"I'd been on airplanes before with no problems, but that day I was really nervous. It was bumpy at the beginning of the flight, like it always is out of Denver. Then it was smooth, and I was just reading my book, when I heard this loud *boom*. The plane lurched, then slowly turned, and we thought everything was fine. But then we saw the flight attendants move quickly up and down the aisles and knew something was very wrong. The plane almost went upside down, then leveled out and slowly rolled back and forth. They told us it would be a very rough landing, and I remember them yelling, 'Brace! Brace! Brace!' at us. I was holding on to my mom's hand as hard as I could."

She had to stop a moment to control her breathing, then sat down to continue. She couldn't look at Dee.

"The last words I heard ever from my mother were, 'We'll be okay.' Then we hit really hard, my mom's hand was ripped out of mine, and everything went dark. The next thing I remember was waking up in a hospital room with my dad looking down at me. He told me I'd been unconscious for two weeks and was lucky to be alive. Then he told me my mom was gone."

The memory of those words from her father were burned into her brain for all eternity. Her eyes overflowed onto her already-wet shirt. She didn't try to fight her tears because it was futile. For thirty-one years, every time she talked about that moment, the result was the same—overwhelming sadness.

After drying her face, River returned to Dee and sat next to her on the bed. "So you see, we do have something in common."

They gazed at each other, then someone knocked on the door.

"The food's here. Let's eat something and continue this later."

By a mutual unspoken agreement, they didn't talk anymore about the accident. River was happy to see Dee dive into the bacon cheeseburger she'd ordered for her. They ate in companionable silence and watched *Jeopardy* on TV.

"How do you know the answers to all the questions? Have you seen this episode before?"

"No, but my mind is filled with useless information. The only thing my freakish memory is good for is trivia contests," River said.

Someone knocked at the door, and when River answered it, Mike Bowers was standing before her. "Here are the car keys and the bag. You ladies have a good night." Then he turned and walked away.

"I asked Mike to bring your car over from the hangar." She handed Dee the keys to her car and her gym bag from the back seat.

"Thanks, but you didn't have to do this."

"I was just looking out for you, like I would for any team member. This is difficult work for all of us, and sometimes we need to take care of each other."

"I get that. We had to do the same thing when I was in The Sand Box."

"When were you in the Middle East?" River asked.

"When I was in military police in the army. I did three tours— one to Iraq and two to Afghanistan, from 2005 through 2007."

"That must have been difficult duty." River wanted to know more about Dee's past, but she had to wait until Dee was ready to talk about it.

"Yeah. It's a nasty place, next door to Bum Fuck, Egypt, but we were busy, which was good." Her voice trailed off, and a blank stare filled her face.

It was the look of nothingness. River had seen this look before on the faces of other soldiers, usually when she was flying them on a KC-10 back home to the US. It was the classic PTSD stare. She recognized the signs of exhaustion in Dee and knew she needed rest.

"Hey, I don't know about you, but I'm really tired. I think I'll get a shower, and then I need my beauty sleep." River took the food trays and set them out in the hall.

Dee got the hint and went into the other room with her gym bag.

River put her hand on Dee's arm before she closed the door between their rooms. "I want you to know, you don't have to keep working on this investigation. There will be very difficult days ahead as we uncover more evidence. There's no shame in just taking care of yourself."

Dee was quiet for a moment, then looked at River. "I have to keep working. It's the only thing I can do."

Chapter Twelve

Dee was glad to shut the door between herself and River. She appreciated her for trying to be helpful, but she wasn't in the mood to talk about her past, her sister, the plane crash, or anything else. She opened the minibar looking for something to help her sleep, but closed it in frustration. No amount of alcohol would take away her pain or give her the oblivion she craved. If she had one drink, she'd drink them all, and that would be pointless. Plus, she didn't want River to see a pile of little booze bottles by the bed.

The hot water felt good on her tight shoulders, and she stayed in the shower a long time. She thought about everything River had said, surprised at her candor. Initially, River came across as someone very intelligent and competent, but also rather cool. She didn't hang out with the guys and preferred to eat alone in her room. Maybe she wasn't comfortable working with men. Dee knew all about that after working with men for eight years in the army and another eight at the police department.

She'd developed a tough skin from living with her father for seventeen years, so she was used to getting yelled at in army training. She figured out how to work with her male coworkers, earn their respect, socialize with them just enough, and avoid dangerous situations, especially after she was almost assaulted in Iraq. She shivered as she recalled that incident.

She'd finished an all-night patrol and crashed on her cot, grateful that her tent mates were on duty and the hooch would be quiet. She remembered waking up with a start when a hot, sweaty hand covered her mouth. She couldn't move, pinned by his heavy body on top of her. Struggling, she was able to free her right hand, feel for her gun in the cubby next to her cot, and jam the hard, steel barrel into his thick neck. He froze, then removed his hand from her face only a second before she was about to blow his brains out. Remembering the vivid details made her heart race. She was one of the lucky women in the army who got away, although she'd always regretted not shooting him in the ass as he ran out her door.

Well, that was another cheery thought.

This crash and her thoughts of Naomi were triggering her PTSD. She would have to use all her coping techniques to get any sleep. She went to the door between their rooms and heard soft, steady snoring from River's room. Reaching for the lock, she stopped herself and slid her fingertips down the face of the door. Then she turned and closed the bathroom door, left the small light on, and double-checked the deadbolt lock.

Her alarm was set, her pistol lay on the nightstand, and the bed was comfortable. She concentrated on tightening, then releasing all her muscle groups from her feet to her head. Then she counted her breathing, a three-count inhale, four-count exhale, and repeat. Her normal sleepiness wouldn't come. She conjured up her well-used meditation images: the beach, small gentle waves, sunlight dancing on the ocean. *Feel it. Smell it.*

She inhaled deeply for the scent of salt air, felt warm sand between her toes and a cool breeze across her face. She saw herself walking toward the waves, letting cold seawater splash over her feet. Raising her face to the sun, she let peace enfold her in golden light until sleep mercifully took her as she tasted the salt of the ocean in her own tears.

❖

A sound awoke River from a deep sleep. She listened for more and heard a noise coming from Dee's room. She went to the door separating their rooms and heard sounds of a struggle. Throwing open the door, she saw Dee thrashing in the bed, her arms and legs flailing wildly. She ran to the bed and touched Dee's shoulder to wake her so she wouldn't hurt herself. In the dim light, River saw movement and ducked just before Dee hit her in the face.

"Dee. Wake up. You're having a nightmare."

River lay down on the bed next to her, put her arms around her, and threw her leg over Dee's lower body to stop her from thrashing. "You're safe. I'm with you. It's me, River. Stop fighting, please. I won't hurt you."

She kept repeating these words over and over, making her voice as soft as possible. Finally, Dee stopped, and her body relaxed.

"Wha…what's going on? River?" Dee's voice was hoarse.

River let out the breath she'd been holding. "You were having a nightmare. Are you okay?"

"Yeah. I think so, but I'm cold." Dee started shivering.

"You're soaking wet. I have a spare tee shirt in my room."

She started to get up, but Dee held her arm tight against her. "Please don't go."

She was still shivering.

"All right."

She nudged Dee to turn onto her side, then pressed herself against Dee's back. She reached down, pulled the covers over them, put her arm around Dee's waist, and pulled her close. Finally, she whispered into the back of Dee's neck. "Do you think you can sleep like this?"

Dee laced her fingers through River's hand. "Yes. If you'll stay with me for a minute."

Dee's breathing deepened, then slowed.

"Sure."

❖

From the depths of sleep, Dee sensed delicious warmth along the length of her back. More lusciousness pressed against the back of her legs. A soft hand rested on her belly. This was a beautiful dream she didn't want to wake up from. Steady breath on the back of her neck made her want to stay in this place forever. She moved her hips into the velvety skin against her bottom, wanting more. The hand on her belly pulled her in closer.

"Mmm."

Then, the arm around her waist tightened, and breasts pressed into her back. It was pure heaven. She put her own hand on top of the fingers caressing her stomach, gently urging them to move lower. Just then, all movement froze. The soft hand on her belly was withdrawn, and cold air assaulted her back as the warm body next to her left. She was fully awake now and realized she'd been rubbing her backside against River. *Oh, hell, what have I done?*

She didn't move from her spot, even though she wanted to grab River's hand and pull her back into bed. She pretended to be asleep because she didn't want to have some sort of awkward conversation. River got out of bed, put the covers back over her, and left the room. Dee had been warm and happy for a moment, but now she was alone and cold again.

Maybe this whole thing was an incredibly bad idea after all. Working on this investigation with River made her feel useful and gave her a temporary escape from her grief, but was the cost too high? River didn't want her here, that was very clear, and the accident was triggering her PTSD in a big way.

She remembered having a hard time getting to sleep earlier, and the nightmares coming. Various images of the horrors she'd seen in combat, at crime scenes, and now airplane crashes swirled together and tormented her all night. In her dreams, she'd tried to fight them, but she was paralyzed, until River woke her from the nightmare. When River held her in her arms, she felt like she'd been saved. Then River had showed her kindness by staying with her all night.

Dee had no idea what to do next. She just pulled the covers tighter around her, humiliated by her behavior in front of River. Not only was she an emotional mess, but now River knew she was psychologically damaged. Usually, she was able to manage her past trauma with the techniques she'd learned during her army PTSD treatment, but Naomi's death made her feel like she was at square one again. Then, on top of that, Dee had thrown herself at River in bed.

The only recourse was to use the tried-and-true "I can't remember what I did last night" excuse. If it worked for drunks to avoid consequences for bad behavior, it should also work for PTSD. If that didn't take care of it, her only other option was to crawl into a hole and die. Hopefully, River won't bring it up, and they could pretend it didn't happen.

As Dee tried to relax and go to sleep again, whenever she closed her eyes, all she could think about was the sensation of River's body next to her. It took her back to a time in her life when she was briefly happy with Marci. Even though she and Marci had to sneak around on base, were in the middle of a war zone, and didn't know if they'd be alive from one moment to the next, they'd been happy together. Even understanding it would never work out for them, she couldn't keep from falling in love with Marci all those years ago. They'd had amazing sex, but her favorite memory with Marci was when she fell asleep in her arms, safe from the chaos and war around them.

River had given her that same comfort, and she responded by making a pass at her. River was just trying to take care of her, like she would do for any other team member, and it didn't mean anything. River was only interested in being kind, as a fellow surviving family member, and nothing more. As she tried to sleep, she forced thoughts of the sensation of River's closeness from her mind: three-count inhale, four-count exhale, beach, small waves, sunlight.

❖

River closed the door between their rooms as quietly as she could when she went into her bathroom. She turned the light on and looked at her reflection with disappointment. "What the hell are you doing?"

She shook her head, not knowing what she should do next. Her heart was racing, and her skin tingled where she had been next to Dee. She had only intended to help Dee through this trauma, but then she ended up in bed with her, touching her stomach. She was no better than a lecherous man taking advantage of a helpless woman. On top of that, the symptoms of a migraine headache were beginning.

She found her medication in her travel bag and downed it with a big glass of water. The light in the bathroom hurt her eyes, and everything had a golden shimmer around the edges. She hoped it wasn't too late for her meds to work. Otherwise, if this turned into a full-blown migraine, she'd be incapacitated for two days.

River looked at her watch. It was already three a.m. If she was lucky, she'd get five hours of sleep and might be able to make the morning briefing at nine. She blocked all light in the room, put in her ear plugs, set her alarm, crawled into bed, and tried to stay as still as possible. Her head was throbbing in waves of pain, but she hated the nausea worst of all. She tried to relax and wait for her meds to kick in, slowed her breathing and cleared her mind, but thoughts of being next to Dee continued to creep into her consciousness.

She'd found Dee thrashing in bed throughout the night, fighting her invisible demons. River used all her might to keep Dee from hurting herself, but she was very strong despite her slight build. Dee would calm down for a few minutes, then start twitching, which would turn into moaning, and then her fists went flying. As the night wore on, she repeated this cycle, with less and less fighting. After Dee finally calmed down for more than a few minutes, River drifted off to sleep holding her. She'd been worried about Dee and was so relieved when she finally slept that she let her own guard down and closed her eyes. The next thing she was aware of was a warm body next to her and a lovely round bottom sliding against her hips. Soft, velvety skin under her fingertips invited exploration. When Dee put her hand on top of River's and urged her to move lower, her own arousal almost took over, before she realized what she was doing and stopped.

Even through Dee wasn't herself, her own reaction surprised her. Out of professional necessity, she'd learned how to always keep her emotions in check and was careful not to reveal her feelings unless it was important. When she'd felt Dee next to her, part of her had wanted to let go of her tight control and simply enjoy the sensations. Then she remembered she was in bed with Dee, supposedly trying to help her. River's behavior embarrassed her, and she hoped they would never speak of it. Both of them were exhausted and stressed out. It was nothing more than that. At least she hoped so.

Chapter Thirteen

Day 5

Sunlight streamed into Dee's room through a gap in the curtains, and she woke up disoriented. She looked around the room to get her bearings, checked the clock, and made herself some coffee. When she examined herself in the mirror, she hardly recognized the woman looking back at her. Her hair was a rat's nest, she had dark circles under her eyes, her skin color looked grayish, and she ached all over. Another hot shower gave her sore muscles relief, but she was still tired from her restless night.

As she dressed, she listened for any sounds from River's room and heard nothing. River was probably still asleep, and she was relieved she didn't have to talk to her right now. Maybe later today it wouldn't be so awkward to converse, and she could just gloss over last night's embarrassing incident. She would never forget it, but she hoped she wouldn't have to discuss her behavior face-to-face with River.

Her stomach growled, and she got dressed and went downstairs to the hotel's breakfast buffet. Many team members were already there, busily stuffing their faces and talking. She got more coffee and a plate of food, then saw Mike Bowers sitting with a group of guys.

"Mind if I join you?" she asked.

"Not at all. Have a seat," Mike said.

"What are you guys working on today?"

"We're continuing our search flights and are hoping to find the location of the black boxes. We have a direction finder in our airplane that can point to the radio signal from the pinger. I was thinking of asking River where she thought they might be. She's been spot-on with helping us find other stuff."

"I'm sure she'll have some suggestions."

"We're going to head over to the airport for the morning briefing in a few minutes. Do you need a ride?"

"No, but thanks. I'll see you guys there."

Dee kept watching the doorway of the dining room, expecting to see River walk through it, but she didn't. Where was she? Maybe she'd already left for the airport without telling her. Maybe she didn't want to speak to her this morning either. Whatever the reason, she'd better check on her before she left the hotel for the day.

Back in her room, she listened at the door between their rooms for any sounds from River. Hearing nothing, she gently knocked on the door. No answer. She turned the knob and poked her head into the room. It was pitch-black, the clock radio alarm was beeping, and River was moaning.

"River? Are you okay?"

No response. Dee walked into the room, opened the curtains so she could see, then went over to the bed. River was buried under the comforter in a ball.

She gently shook the lump under the covers. "River? Do you need help?"

"No, no, no. Close the curtains, close the curtains." She sounded frantic.

Dee quickly pulled the drapes shut and turned off the clock radio. "Okay. They're closed. What's wrong?"

River slowly unburied herself from the covers and carefully sat up on the side of the bed, her hands covering her eyes. Her voice sounded rough. "Migraine. No lights. Please stop shouting. Give me a minute." River rocked back and forth with her head down and her eyes covered. "Oh, crap."

She tried to stand up but looked like she would fall over, so Dee put her arm around River's waist to steady her.

"Please help me to the bathroom."

River was very wobbly as Dee maneuvered her there.

"Don't turn on the light. I can see well enough with just the night light."

As Dee got her to the sink, River abruptly turned to the toilet and emptied the contents of her stomach.

"Oh, fuck," River mumbled, then flushed the toilet and rinsed her mouth at the sink.

"Can I get you anything?"

"Please bring me a 7-Up from the fridge."

Dee found the soft drink and brought it to her, then watched River sip it and swallow a pill with it. It was awful to see her in such pain. She wished she could do more to help her, especially since River had helped her so much last night.

River drank some more 7-Up, then tried to walk back to bed, but she was still unsteady.

She put her arm around River again. "Here, let me help you."

After getting River back into bed, she spoke very softly. "What do you need?"

"I just have to sleep and hope this migraine goes away eventually. Can you go to the morning briefing and take notes for me? Also, bring me a copy of any new test results or reports they have. I'm not going to be able to do anything today, so you're on your own. Sorry."

"Got it. I'm leaving now to go to the briefing, but if you need anything, please text me. Are you sure you're okay here by yourself? You really don't look good. Do you need me to call a doctor for you?"

"No. I'll be fine. Please just let me sleep, and thanks." River buried herself under the covers again.

Dee hung the Do Not Disturb sign on the outside door handle, turned off the bathroom light, checked that the drapes were securely closed, and quietly left the room through their adjoining door. On the short drive over to the airport, she kept thinking about River. She felt sorry for her suffering from the effects of a nasty migraine. Being so helpless and in pain was such a contrast to the usually self-assured accident investigator. And then there was the other side of River, the side of a woman who was kind to her and who had taken care of her.

She sat in the back of the hangar listening to the briefing. Though she didn't understand a lot of the technical airplane stuff, she dutifully wrote it all down for River. While listening to Ronald Moore conduct the briefing, she had to agree with River that he was a self-serving, pompous ass. He talked about all the tremendous progress they were making and mentioned that they had retrieved a few parts from the flight deck. He concluded the briefing with a description of their major findings so far.

"We have the fluids tests completed, with no irregularities found, and the engine analysis and tear-down is complete. The GE engine experts report that all engines were operating within normal parameters at the time the aircraft broke apart. We did find one thing we are still working on. The number-three engine from the right wing sustained a large puncture on the inboard side of the engine nacelle. We have concluded that an unknown object penetrated the outer casing and damaged the internal engine components.

"This impact significantly damaged the engine but not enough to cause it to separate from the wing. At this time, we believe it was damaged during the explosion and did not cause the airframe failure. We're still looking for the object that impacted the engine. Additionally, we've received the Relax Air training records and FAA pilot records on all the flight crew members. All these reports will be available after the briefing. We'll continue to be relentless in finding what caused this terrible accident. I will now entertain any questions from the press. Thank you for your attention."

Dee hurried over to the Tests/Reports table to get River copies of all the reports. She really didn't know what she could do to help with anything in the search area today, so she bundled up all the reports and decided to take them back to River at the hotel. Plus, she wanted to check on her to see if she was feeling any better. As she turned to leave, one of the ATF agents intercepted her.

"Here's the rest of the information on the passengers, with

everything we know so far. Can you go over this to see what else you can find out about the McClain family? Get back to me as soon as you can." He shoved a thick file folder into her hand, turned, and walked off.

"Why, yes, Agent. I'd be happy to do your job for you, and I'll be sure to get back to you in a jiffy."

No one was around to appreciate her sarcasm, but it made her feel better to say it. Most of the Feds she'd worked with in the past thought they were hot stuff and felt entitled to order local cops around. She didn't normally put up with their crap, but they were the reason she was allowed to participate in this investigation, so she had to comply with their "requests."

After adding this file to her stack of reports, she drove back to the Holiday Inn and quietly entered her room. She listened at the adjoining door for any sounds from River. Hearing nothing, she opened the door to River's room to check on her. The room was still dark, with just a tiny amount of light coming from the bottom of the drapes. She could see through the dim light that the big lump in the bed appeared to be breathing. She was glad to see River resting comfortably, especially after the misery she'd been in earlier. She turned to leave the room and let her sleep.

"Dee? Is that you?" River's voice was weak.

"Yes. It's me. I'm sorry to disturb you. Do you need anything?"

"What'd they say at the morning briefing?"

"I picked up the reports you asked for. Do you want them now, or do you want to read them later?"

River slowly sat up in the bed. "For now, just give me the highlights. I'll read the reports later, when I can see."

"According to Ronald Moore, everything is going well, and they are making progress. He talked about the engines and said he didn't think they caused the crash. Then he said they had some reports completed."

"That means he's in trouble."

"Why do you say that? He seemed fine to me."

"Because I've had to work with him long enough to know

when he says 'Everything is going well and we're making progress,' it means the opposite, and he's getting big pressure to identify the cause of the accident."

"Getting pressure from who?"

"His boss at the NTSB and everyone else, because of the size of this accident. Three hundred passengers and crew were killed, and that's a lot of blood priority."

"What's that mean?"

"Blood priority means that the more blood spilled in an aircraft crash, the more attention the accident gets. Ronald Moore is under a lot of pressure to produce results and find the cause, fast."

"That makes sense, I guess. Hey, do you want any breakfast? I can go down to the buffet and get you something."

"No. My stomach is still a little iffy. I'm just going to sleep some more. Then I'll be better. Thanks for getting the reports."

River crawled back under her covers, signaling it was time for Dee to leave.

❖

River listened for the sound of the door latch, then buried herself in the bed and tried to go back to sleep. She stayed very still and tried to breathe slowly. She would survive this migraine, but just barely. She hadn't had one this bad in a long time because she was usually better about taking care of herself. As long as she didn't get too tired or hungry and stayed away from Parmesan cheese, she could generally prevent her migraine attacks.

She hated feeling vulnerable when she had a bad headache. She couldn't move, couldn't think, couldn't defend herself, and could barely manage to take her meds. When she'd heard noises in her room, she'd been relieved Dee was back.

Dee was sweet to check on her, but she was also the reason River was incapacitated. She couldn't be mad at Dee. It wasn't her fault she had a traumatic reaction to her sister's death. River didn't regret staying with Dee all night to keep her safe, because Dee needed her. She did regret being down the entire day, but was this another reason Dee shouldn't be working on this accident?

River didn't want anyone to know about the weakness these migraines imposed on her, but now Dee knew her secret and had leverage over her. All because of that piece of shit in Louisiana. That was another moment burned into her brain. River remembered every detail like it had happened yesterday, even though it was over sixteen years ago.

She'd been driving her silver Corvette back to Barksdale Air Force Base after being named Top Graduate of the US Air Force Flight Safety School. Life was good, River loved her flying, and her future was limitless. She'd just been selected for promotion to major, was starting KC-10 instructor pilot school, and had met a beautiful Southern belle who called her every day she was away at school.

As she was enjoying the drive and thinking about possibilities with her new lady, a drunk driving a pickup truck ran a red light and plowed into the passenger side of her car. The impact was so hard, the car spun around three times before stopping against a tree.

River found this out later when she woke up in the base hospital with a collar around her neck. She was sore all over, had lost consciousness for thirty minutes, and wanted to go home. The doctor insisted she stay, threatening her with bed restraints if she tried to get up. Compared to a plane crash, River thought she wasn't doing too bad, and she was ready to leave the next day.

Two days after that, she was stricken with the worst pain she'd ever known. Back at the hospital, the neurologist told her she had migraine headaches as a result of a concussion from the car accident. His parting words stabbed her in the heart.

"Oh, sorry to tell you, but you're now permanently grounded."

CHAPTER FOURTEEN

Dee set down her coffee and spread out the reports on the desk. The ones labeled "Engine Analysis" looked like they were written in Greek, and she set those aside for River. She skipped to the summary at the end of the Fluids Analysis report.

1. Hydraulic fluid, Jet-A fuel, engine oil—Normal parameters.
2. Presence of ice—Unknown.
3. Causal factors—None.

The reports from the airline and the FAA regarding the crew members looked more familiar, and the detailed passenger data was already in a database. Dee began with the FAA pilot records. Most of the reports were typical government paperwork with copies of the captain's, first officer's, and flight engineer's pilot's license, medical certificate, driver's license, arrest record, and any FAA violations.

Dee was surprised to see copies of every physical exam the pilots had ever taken throughout their flying careers. She scanned the documents and started a timeline for each pilot. The first thing she noticed was the age of the flight engineer. She was shocked that he was seventy-five years old and still flying. Flipping through his file, she learned that he'd been flying continuously for over fifty-five years and never had any significant medical issues.

Next, she reviewed the information regarding Captain Joe

Davis. He was fifty-seven years old and had been flying for more than thirty years, but she found some gaps in his records. She'd have to ask River to explain the codes on the documents. First Officer Michael Lee was only twenty-nine and had the least experience of the three. He had no medical issues and was probably a young hotshot at the relatively new airline. She decided to go over these reports with River when she felt better.

Dee quietly opened the door between their rooms to check on River, relieved to hear steady, deep breathing. She left the door open a crack in case River called out to her. Opening the folder of passenger information put her in an area she was familiar with. She scanned the pages of data, looking for irregularities to pop out, specifically searching for all information about the McClain family and anyone associated with it.

They had purchased their round-trip tickets from Portland to Chicago only three days before they departed and paid a high price for the last-minute fares. They stayed in the Chicago area three days, and then J.R. McClain had called Relax Air to change their reservation to return a day early. That's why they ended up sitting in different parts of the plane, because the earlier flight had only a few seats left. They all got stuck with middle seats throughout the cabin for the four-hour flight home. She still didn't know why they went to Chicago, what they did there for three days, or why they took an earlier flight home. She would need to dig deeper with this lead.

Scanning the rest of the passenger data, she stopped when she saw "16A—Naomi R. Williams." She ran her finger across the printed letters of her name and saw the rest of Naomi's data on the page: her address, cell-phone number, emergency contact (Bill Williams), and his phone number. *I can't believe I haven't called him yet.* Her eyes welled up, and she couldn't fight the wave of loss as it rolled over her. She was still upset, but not as bad as the day before. *That's because River helped me last night.*

Dee closed her eyes, leaned back in the desk chair, and turned her chair to face the sunlight streaming into the room through the windows. The sun was warm, and she inhaled deeply. She took her mind back to the moment she was aware of River holding her from behind. She'd felt cared for and knew River would keep her safe. She clung to that feeling to ride out the wave of grief. After a few minutes, warmth replaced melancholy, and she felt better. Focusing on a positive thought helped her get through the rough spots. She skipped over the part where she tried to put the moves on River. She could handle only so much humiliation in one day.

Dee checked on River again, happy to hear the shower running. She didn't realize how much she'd worried about River, who'd looked so unsteady this morning. The water stopped, and she stepped away from the door. Then River walked into her room with her blond hair slicked back and wearing only her towel. *Oh, my.*

❖

"I'm so sorry about this morning, Dee, and I'd really appreciate it if you didn't mention to anyone that I was sick."

"Certainly. I would never tell anyone your personal business."

"Thank you. Well, I guess I should get dressed. Be right back."

River finished drying off in her room and put on her flannel shirt and sweatpants. She still had to be careful and not move too quickly, or she'd get dizzy. She still felt shaky from her migraine, but much better than earlier. It was similar to a nasty hangover, but without the booze. She had to get back to work, or she might miss something important. When she walked into Dee's room again, she saw neat stacks of tabbed folders spread out on the desk. "You've been busy."

"I looked at some of these, but I need you to translate the other ones. Here are the notes from the morning briefing."

She took the notepad and noticed Dee's tidy handwriting. The notes were well organized, thorough, succinct, and exactly what she needed. Dee was clearly skilled and had covered for her well today.

"These are great." Then she smiled and laughed.

"What's funny?"

"The way you spelled a word. That's all."

"Did I write down something wrong?" Dee was staring at her.

"It's the word 'chock.' In flying, it's a wheel stop used to keep a plane from rolling. You wrote 'chalk,' like what you use to write on a board. It just looked funny on the paper."

"Oh. Sorry I'm such a dummy about all this flying stuff." Her voice had a definite edge.

"No. That's not what I meant. It's just cute."

"Well, you can look at the reports on the desk. I'm going downstairs to get more coffee."

She put her hand on Dee's forearm to stop her. "I'm sorry. Please don't be upset with me. I'm not thinking too clearly yet." She needed to sit down. "Could you please close the drapes partway? I'm still a little sensitive to light."

Dee closed the drapes halfway and turned down the lights in the room. "How's this?"

"Better. I'm going to order room service. Would you like anything to eat?"

"Yeah. I'm kind of hungry." She looked around the room for a menu.

"They have nachos, French onion soup, chili, hamburger, chicken Caesar salad, BLT, and chocolate cake."

Dee turned to look at her. "How do you know what they have?"

"This is kind of sad to admit, but I've spent half my life in hotel rooms, and they are all the same. Here, check it." River handed her the room service menu.

"You're right, again. I'll have a BLT sandwich." Dee still had an edge to her voice.

River called room service and ordered hot tea with plain toast for herself, and the BLT for Dee. Then she turned to her. "Hey. I wasn't trying to insult you. I appreciate you getting the meeting notes and for organizing all this for me. It helps a lot. Thank you."

Dee's expression softened. "I know I'm not a jet jockey like you, and I don't know airplane stuff, but I was trying to be productive."

"You're very helpful, and I'm not a jet jockey anymore."

"Why's that?"

"It's these migraines. They started when I was injured in a car accident and this disqualified me from any type of FAA medical certificate. They ended my air force flying career."

Dee looked at her for a moment. "I'm sorry to hear that. I didn't know something like that could stop you from ever flying again."

"Yeah. Now I just ride in the back of airplanes and put the broken pieces back together."

Their food arrived, and they sat down to eat. River had to admit she did enjoy having someone to eat a meal with for a change. She wasn't good at idle chitchat. Usually she was giving information, asking questions, making reports, or processing evidence. Some people thought she was abrupt or unfriendly, but she was just very focused on her job. But now, River felt like having an actual conversation with Dee instead of her usual shop talk.

"So how did you get into police work?"

Dee looked surprised. "I was a military police specialist in the army. I really liked it, got out, and was hired by the Portland Police Bureau. I've been a cop for sixteen years—eight in the army and eight with Portland PB."

"Did you always want to be a cop?"

Dee laughed. "Ah, no. I thought I wanted to go to college and be a doctor, but that didn't work out, so I joined the army when I was eighteen." She paused. "The army saved my life."

River was intrigued and wanted to know more. She didn't want to pry into Dee's personal life, even though they'd already crossed that line when she'd climbed into bed with her last night.

Dee turned the question back to her. "How did you become an aircraft accident investigator?"

She took a deep breath. "Before I was medically grounded, the air force sent me to USAF Flight Safety School, where I was trained as an accident investigator. After I recovered from the car crash, I was the chief investigating officer for a KC-10 Class A mishap. That was a major accident, and we were lucky no one lost their life in that one."

"How come?"

"It was a ground mishap that occurred during a maintenance engine run. Two mechanics were involved and didn't get hurt, but they caused over five million dollars in damage to the airplane."

"What happened?" Dee leaned closer.

"They'd fixed some mechanical issue with the right-wing engine and had to do an engine run to make sure everything worked correctly. That's where one mechanic is in the cockpit with the engine running and another one monitors the engine from outside. Then they run it through different throttle settings from idle to full power.

"But the KC-10 engines put out one hundred thousand pounds of thrust, and Barksdale didn't have a reinforced engine-run area on the airfield, so they used the edge of the ramp to test it. When the mechanic pushed the throttle up, the jet exhaust ripped up the asphalt pavement behind the engine and smashed it into the tail section. Chunks of asphalt punctured the rudder, the elevators, and the vertical and horizontal stabilizers. Worst of all, the air refueling boom was badly damaged. That's the critical part of the plane where we transfer fuel in midair to another jet. It was a mess."

"Were they able to fix it?" Dee was transfixed.

"The manufacturer, McDonnell Douglas, was able to replace the damaged parts, but it never flew right again. The airplane was written up for flight control problems after every mission, so it became a hangar queen."

"A hangar queen?"

"That's a plane that spends more time in the hangar being fixed than it does flying. After finishing that investigation, since I couldn't fly anymore, I was medically discharged from the air force. I went back to school to get my doctorate, worked for the NTSB for three years, and then started my own business."

"What do you do with your business? If you don't work for the NTSB anymore, why are you here at this accident?"

"I do independent aircraft investigation, and I produce my own accident report, for an insurance company. This company pays the liability compensation to the victims' families, and they need to know who's responsible for causing the accident. As I found out when I was with the NTSB, outside interested parties can sometimes influence investigations, so the final report may not be correct. No one influences my reports."

"Are you talking about falsified accident reports? Why?"

"Because some groups want to shift blame away from themselves. For example, an Egypt Air 767 crashed into the ocean on a flight from New York to Cairo in 1999. Nothing was mechanically wrong with the airplane, and the cockpit voice recorder proved that when the captain left the flight deck, the copilot intentionally put the plane in a steep dive, shut off both engines, and flew the jet into the ocean, killing himself and everyone on board. The government of Egypt refused to accept this conclusion, because suicide is forbidden in Islam. Therefore they claimed the plane crashed for 'an unknown flight control problem.' It was a made-up excuse."

"So the copilot killed all those people? And I thought I dealt with some bad guys. Speaking of pilots, I found some gaps in their records and need you to explain them."

River scanned the records and looked at the tabbed sections Dee had questions about.

"Why is the flight engineer seventy-five years old? I thought they had mandatory retirement," Dee asked.

"He was a captain at a major airline until he had to retire at sixty-five, then got hired by Relax Air. You can work as a flight engineer after sixty-five, and he was supporting three ex-wives. No training or medical problems here. Just poor judgment."

"The flight engineer's background doesn't list any arrests or convictions. What about the copilot?"

"He's young, low in DC-10 flying time and overall experience. Looks like he got hired by Relax Air right out of school, and no medical issues."

"Why would a low-time guy be flying this plane? I thought the pilots who flew the big jets were all very experienced."

"Because not many pilots want to fly for this company. Their pay is low compared to the major airlines, and they're a non-union company. Relax Air has been in existence only a few years, and their hotshot CEO has branded them as an ultra-low-cost airline. This company has the worst pay and work rules of any US airline, so they don't get the best and brightest. Most young pilots use a company like this only as a stepping-stone to build flying time so a better company will hire them."

"Is that why the captain had gaps in his employment? Did he have some sort of flying problem in his past?"

River studied his FAA records more carefully and noticed some discrepancies in his file.

"Look at this." She pointed to the records for Dee. "He worked for different small companies for several years, got hired by a big airline for five years, they went bankrupt, and he lost his job."

Dee added, "I found out his house went into foreclosure, and he got divorced. A job loss could explain that. After his company went bankrupt, there are few records of him for eight years, and then Relax Air hired him. What happened to him?"

River flipped through more papers. "A regional airline in Asia employed him, and he flew DC-10 cargo operations for them, but then there was some incident in Jakarta, and he got let go. We'll need to get ahold of his flying records from that company." She jotted down some notes.

"I found some possible issues with his finances," Dee added. "He declared personal bankruptcy after his divorce, has a mountain of debt, has been audited by the IRS for the last five years, and bought a two-million-dollar life-insurance policy last year. Those are red flags to me. Do you think he might have done something intentional to crash the plane?"

River paused. "In the history of aircraft accidents, death by pilot suicide is extremely rare. Pilots work their entire careers to avoid a plane crash, but we have to consider this as a possibility. We need more information on him." She rubbed her eyes.

"Are you feeling all right? You still look kind of pale." Dee had concern in her voice.

"I guess I am a little tired. I probably need to get a little more sleep. Thanks again for sorting through these records."

River went back to her room, drank a large glass of water, closed the drapes, and collapsed on the bed.

❖

Dee was still worried about River. She looked hung over, and her stomach was obviously still bothering her, as she ate only tea and toast. She waited until she heard sounds of steady breathing from River's room, then left to drive to her apartment in Portland for more clothes. Her mind was swimming from everything she'd heard. River's analysis of the pilot's records showed one was older, one was inexperienced, and the other one had personal and financial problems. The story about the pilot suicide where he took hundreds of people with him was chilling. Could any of the pilots of Naomi's flight have intentionally caused the airplane to crash? She needed to look deeper into their backgrounds.

Having had the difficult duty of dealing with suicides both as an MP and in the police department, she knew how awful the aftereffects were. Could someone really be so desperate to end their life that they'd take three hundred innocent passengers with them? And who would you hold accountable? The murderer was dead, followed immediately by the passengers, who had trusted their lives to him. She couldn't let herself go down that rabbit hole and chose to hang on to River's assurances that pilot suicide was very rare.

Dee felt sympathy that River had lost her air force flying career. It was another thing they had in common. She had such mixed feelings about her military service. She loved the army and had hated leaving her promising career because she was a lesbian, but she'd had no choice.

She'd planned on a career in the army and had completed online classes to earn her bachelor's degree. Then she got accepted to Officer Candidate School, became a second lieutenant, and went to advanced training in the Criminal Investigation Division. It was her dream job until her commander told her she had to spy on fellow soldiers accused of homosexuality so they could be dishonorably discharged. This was during the bad old days of "Don't ask, don't tell." She couldn't lie about who she was, then investigate the soldiers she'd sworn to protect, so she had to leave.

Like River, she'd made a new life for herself after the military. She was happy to be a civilian cop in a very gay-friendly city like

Portland, glad soldiers no longer had to worry about losing their careers for being gay, but she did wonder what her life might have been like had she stayed in the army. Maybe she would have been spared the agony of losing Naomi.

CHAPTER FIFTEEN

Dee stuffed clean clothes into a duffel bag, checked her mail, and disposed of her smelly trash before she got on the road back to Redmond. This was going to be a lengthy investigation, and she wanted her apartment secure. Her cell phone rang. It was the ATF agent calling her.

"Hello. Detective Dee Rawlings speaking."

"Detective Rawlings, this is ATF Agent Paul Marshall. We met at the airplane hangar yesterday."

She remembered his voice. He was the guy who'd shoved a stack of folders at her and told her to get back to him.

"Yes, of course. What can I do for you?"

"Do you have any more information from the passenger files? Particularly regarding the McClain Militia?"

"So far, I've found that they sat in different parts of the airplane because they took an earlier full flight with only middle seats left. This information does not indicate that they sat apart for strategic purposes. I'll be working on further analysis this evening."

"We'd like you to rendezvous with us at 1800 hours at the McClain compound. We'll be interviewing witnesses about possible missile sightings, and your local connections would be helpful."

He sounded polite, but this was not a request.

Dee responded. "I'll be there. I recommend that you secure your visible firearms in your vehicle and use a rental car rather than a government one."

"Roger that." Then, *click*, he hung up on her.

This was progress, and Dee was looking forward to being more involved. She didn't mind doing computer research and document analysis, but she much preferred working in the field with real people. On the drive to Bend, she mentally reviewed the eyewitness-interview checklist River had given her after the McClain family complained about her last visit. She would need to be very gentle with Mrs. McClain this time. This poor woman had lost her husband and five sons. Dee only hoped she could still function.

A silver van was parked around the corner from the compound entrance. Dee slowly approached, then saw Agent Marshall. Six men in dark suits who emerged from the van had "Fed" written all over them. This wouldn't do at all. She motioned them over.

"We won't get past the front gate with all of you. You men stay here, concealed, and monitor the situation on the private frequency. Paul, you need to take off your jacket and tie, roll up your shirt sleeves, and leave your ATF badge and service pistol here. I'm only going in with my ankle holster. Carry this notepad in your hand, wear your accident investigation team ID around your neck, and try not to look so much like a Fed. These people are heavily armed and trigger-happy. Let's go."

The ATF agents complied with her instructions, Paul looked less conspicuous, and they drove up to the main gate in Dee's car. She recognized the faces of the two guys with long rifles at the entrance. They walked up to her car, looked in at her and Paul, then asked, "Why are you here?"

"We're from the aircraft accident investigation team and received a request to talk to some folks about what they saw. Can you tell me where we need to go?" Dee used her sweetest, most non-threatening voice, with a hint of her old Texas drawl thrown in for good measure.

He gestured with his rifle. "Over there, big log house on the left. Don't go anywhere else. We'll be watching you."

As she parked, she discreetly counted the number of men with weapons walking around the compound. Then she noticed Paul feverishly writing notes on the positions of the armed men. She whispered, "Paul, be cool. You're my assistant. Don't write notes until we get inside, and walk behind me." He glared at her but did what he was told.

She walked up the steps to the big porch and raised her hand to knock, when the door opened before her. It was Mrs. McClain's daughter.

"What are you doing back here? You've already upset my mother, and you're not welcome."

Dee had to be careful with this family because they were very much on edge. "First of all, we are so sorry for your loss. We were informed that some people here saw something the night of the plane crash, and we're hoping to speak with them. Also, I was wondering if I might express my condolences to Mrs. McClain? It'll only take a minute."

"Well, I suppose so. Come in."

Dee looked around the space using her peripheral vision, while she walked toward Mrs. McClain. She was dressed entirely in black, sitting in a chair in front of the large stone fireplace, staring into space.

"Mrs. McClain? It's Dee Rawlings. I wanted to tell you how sorry I was to hear about your husband and sons."

The old woman slowly turned to look at her, clearly bitter and angry. *She's dangerous. Be careful.*

"You again. Why should I talk to you? Just leave me alone." She turned back to the fire, and her daughter started toward them. Dee had to think fast. She went over to Mrs. McClain's chair and kneeled down next to her so she could look her in the eyes. Then she gently touched the back of Mrs. McClain's hand.

"You don't have to talk to me, Mrs. McClain. I just wanted you to know that I lost someone I loved in that plane crash too."

"You did? How can you bear this? It's all too much." She put her hand on top of Dee's.

"Yes, ma'am. It is." Her eyes started to well up again, but she had to keep it together.

"Did they tell you there are no bodies? How can that be? My husband and my five boys were on that plane, and they can't find them. What are we supposed to bury? I just don't know what to do."

A tear rolled down her cheek. Dee reached into her pocket and handed her a tissue. As she took it, they locked eyes and recognized the helplessness of grief in each other's face. Dee's own tears came, and she leaned near to hug her. They held each other for a minute, and then Mrs. McClain mumbled, "Thank you."

Dee wiped her eyes and composed herself because she had a job to do.

"Ma'am, I was told you have some folks who might have seen something the night of the crash. Would it be all right with you if I spoke to them? It might help us figure out why the plane crashed."

"So what if you figure out why it crashed. It won't bring them back, will it?"

She was angry again, and Dee had to win her over.

"Mrs. McClain, if we can find the cause of this accident, we can prevent this from happening again. You don't want any other family to suffer like we are, do you? Then please help me."

"No, I don't. No family should ever have to go through this. You go talk to my nephew and find out why this plane crashed. If somebody took that plane down on purpose, I want to know about it, and we will deal with them."

Her daughter led Dee and Paul to another room and introduced her to Christian.

"Hi, Christian, I'm Dee, and I'd like you to tell me where you were and what first caught your attention on the night of the accident."

"Who's he?" Christian asked.

"This is Paul, my assistant, and he's going to help me by taking notes so I can correctly record your recollections."

"Okay. Well, I was walking around outside the night of the crash, near Lone Mountain Road, and I looked up and saw a white streak zoom across the sky. Then I heard an explosion and saw stuff on fire, falling out of the sky. It was horrible."

"Was anyone with you when you saw this?"

"Yeah. My buddy Daryl was down the road from me, but he saw the same thing."

"Do you think I could speak to him?"

"No. He's busy. But he'll tell you the same thing. We saw a missile shoot down that plane."

This was all she would get from him tonight.

"Christian, before we leave, is there anything else you'd like us to know? Is there anyone you know of who would want to take down that airplane?"

"I have nothing more to say. I need to get back to work."

She and Paul left the house and the compound. This was important information, and she needed to talk to River about it.

❖

After a couple hours of sleep, River felt better and was eager to get out in the field and back to work. She looked for Dee, disappointed she'd already gone, but also a little relieved. She wasn't ready to talk anymore about awkward personal stuff with Dee. She'd run into her later, and maybe they could just discuss the investigation. She drove over to the hangar to see the latest finds and check on any more reports.

River heard a voice behind her that made her skin crawl.

"Nice of you to finally show up. Where have you been?" It was Ronald Moore.

Gritting her teeth before she replied, "I've been working, Ron."

She knew he hated being called "Ron." Using that name was childish, but it made her feel better to get in a little dig.

"What exactly have you been working on? I haven't seen any reports from you so far."

"You will have my reports when they are complete. By the way, we are missing training records for the captain from the Asian cargo company he flew for before he went to work for Relax Air. Do you think you could track those down for us? Thanks so much." She turned and walked away from him before he could answer.

"All reports come to me first. Don't forget that," he shouted after her.

"Ass wipe."

River had more important concerns than Ronald Moore's

delicate ego. She was behind in the investigation and didn't like being at a disadvantage to anyone. She went over to look at the aircraft reconstruction. They'd made a lot of progress in finding most of the big pieces: the flight control surfaces, the three engines, parts of the fuselage, and the landing gear wheels. Most of the pieces they'd found had no burn marks or visible damage, except for the hole in the side of the right-wing engine. The shape of the opening reminded her of something familiar, but she couldn't quite put her finger on it. That puncture to the right engine was their closest proof of some kind of explosion big enough to bring down the plane. They still hadn't found the critical part yet. She needed to get back out in the field and look for it.

Driving back to Angel Creek, River decided to widen her search pattern. She'd followed the creek upstream about a mile when she saw something pointed and silver in the trees ahead. She trudged through the thick brush to it, then stopped when she recognized the corner of a cargo container. As she cautiously approached so she wouldn't step on any evidence, her heart raced, and her breathing quickened. This was the excitement of the hunt, the part of the job she loved most. Discovering the critical piece of evidence to solve an aircraft accident was like finding a big gold nugget. The chance was slim that this cargo container could be that critical piece of evidence, but it might be important.

As she got closer, she could see that it was a luggage container, and most of it was missing. The metal was in the curved shape of the belly of the plane, with clear plastic on one side. A few bags were stuck in a bent corner, but the rest of the luggage had been sucked out when the airplane blew up. She detected a faint odor of jet fuel. Not surprising since the fuel tanks had most likely ruptured during the explosion. She examined the exterior and couldn't find any indication of scorching or bulging, classic signs of a bomb inside a suitcase.

River put on her gloves and carefully maneuvered around jagged metal, working her way into the container. She spotted an odd pink suitcase, intact, and resting on top of a few other bags. She photographed the torn container and the luggage, then reached in and pulled out the small pink object. It was an old Samsonite case from the 1960s. These had been marketed as the most indestructible you could buy, with a TV commercial featuring a gorilla trying to smash one open. She was drawn to it and had to know what was inside.

After she got the suitcase free of the container, she found a boulder with a flat spot, placed the case on top of it, and examined it more closely. No luggage tag—probably ripped off by explosive forces, no markings, and it was locked. River took out her multi-tool and pried open the lock. Inside, she found a layer of bubble wrap and, under that, a photo album and a leather satchel. She flipped through the photo album of mundane birthday and graduation pictures, then put it back. Then she took out the leather satchel, opened it, and found a stack of blue envelopes and white envelopes tied up with twine.

She sat down on a piece of soft grass, leaned back against the boulder, and read them. As she untied the twine, she noticed that most of them were sealed, except for two white envelopes with red Minnie Mouse stickers on them. She slowly removed the yellowed paper from the envelope and read aloud the words in a child's handwriting:

> *Dear Sissy,*
>> *Where are you? I need you to come home! Mother and Daddy are yelling all the time. I miss you SO MUCH. Please come home.*
>> *I love you, Squirt*

River flipped over the envelope to see who it was addressed to and read:

> *PFC Deborah Rawlings*
> *Ft. Leonard Wood, Missouri*

The return address was from Naomi Rawlings, Killeen, Texas. *Oh my God. This is from Dee's sister.*

Chapter Sixteen

Dee was eager to leave the McClain compound. She much preferred working with her partner, Marcus, than the ATF agent, Paul. She also preferred to have much more firepower when going to chat with rabid white-nationalist, anti-government hate groups. Grateful to get out of there in one piece, she hoped her eyewitness interviews would help River. Actually, she was hoping River would say something positive about her work. She didn't need her approval, though she wanted her to respect her as a professional.

Then she recalled how bad River had looked this morning. After watching her get sick last night, Dee was worried about her. Hopefully, she'd gotten some more sleep and was feeling better. She was looking forward to speaking to her when she got back to the hotel, not only to update River with the investigation progress, but also to just talk to her.

Some of the things River told her over lunch intrigued her, and she wanted to know more, like how she became an air force pilot. She also wanted to know how River worked through the death of her mother in that plane crash thirty-one years ago. Dee wasn't dealing with her grief, and she knew it. She was staying busy so she wouldn't have to think about it, but she couldn't run from it forever. Dee would have to face Naomi's death, her husband and family, and the aftermath of this crash, but she had no idea how to do that.

Dee hoped she could have dinner with River. Maybe they could actually leave the hotel and go eat at a restaurant, instead of just having room service again. She didn't just want to talk about the interviews she'd completed with the McClains. She wanted to understand more about River as a person, not just a coworker.

Back at the hotel, Dee was glad River was in her room, almost like she'd been waiting for her. "Hey. Have you eaten dinner? I have some info to go over with you about the McClain interviews, and I'm kind of hungry."

"No. I haven't eaten yet. The guys like the barbecue place down the street. Want to go there?"

"Sounds good. It's nice outside, if you'd like to walk."

It was evening but still light, with a soft breeze and the scent of pine in the air. It was pleasant walking with River, away from the loud guys and the tension of the investigation.

When they entered, the smoke smell made Dee's mouth water. "I hope their barbecue's good. I'm kind of a snob about brisket."

"Why's that?" River asked.

"Because I'm from Texas, and we have the best brisket in the world."

River smiled. "Is that so? Please don't tell me you're one of those obnoxious Texans who thinks everything from their state is the biggest and the best."

"Yes. We do have the best barbecue. And, no, I'm not one of those obnoxious Texans. When I was growing up, we used to go to this giant western-clothing store in Lot, Texas, to buy school clothes, and they had the best brisket I've ever tasted."

River was smirking at her. "Why was it the best?"

Dee leaned back, closed her eyes, and tried to recall every detail of her favorite meal.

"The brisket would cook all day in a huge black smoker outside, where the amazing smell would surround you. Then they'd give you a big paper plate full of sliced brisket with just the right amount of sauce, potato salad, ranch beans—which are tangy, not sweet—and a big piece of Texas toast. The brisket was charred on the outside, tender and juicy inside, with the most amazing flavor. It would melt in your mouth. Naomi would eat so much she'd almost make herself sick." The sweet memory made her ache inside. "I guess we'll never do that again."

River looked at her but didn't say anything. Their food arrived, and they ate together without talking much.

After the server took their plates, River asked, "So is their brisket acceptable?"

"It's very good, but not as good as the barbecue in Lot."

"My food was excellent. Good suggestion to come here. It's nice to take a break from the investigation."

"Can I ask you a personal question? How did you get through your mother's death in that plane crash? I'm having a hard time with everything. Just talking about barbecue makes me tear up. Do you have any suggestions?"

River was quiet for a moment, then reached across the table to hold Dee's hand and looked into her eyes. "Surviving that accident and my mother's death was the most difficult thing I've ever done. But I was lucky, and I had help, starting with the nurse who rescued me the day of the accident."

"What happened?"

River took a deep breath. "I found this out after I woke up in the hospital when a nurse named Betty came to see me. She was in the Iowa National Guard, at the Sioux City airport, and was on duty the day of the crash. A whole lot of National Guardsmen helped with the accident because they were there for training. Betty told me she found me unconscious, hanging upside down by my seat belt, in a part of the plane that came to a stop in a cornfield. Betty and another Guardsman freed me from the seat and carried me away from the plane before it caught fire."

River took a big drink of iced tea.

"You don't have to talk about this if it's too hard, River."

"No. I want you to know. When I saw the video of the landing, I couldn't believe any of us survived. Betty saved me and came to visit me several times in the hospital while I was recovering. She also introduced me to a man who helped me tremendously.

"Six months after the accident, my body was recovering, but not my mind. My dad found me a good therapist, but I was overwhelmed with PTSD. I couldn't sleep, I was afraid and anxious, and I couldn't talk about it. Then Betty called me and said I had to come to their National Guard training assembly. They had a guest speaker who'd come to thank them—Captain Al Haynes."

"I've heard that name before."

"Captain Haynes, the pilot of the DC-10, was famous for making the impossible landing. The plane had lost all hydraulic fluid and had no flight controls, except for asymmetrical thrust from the wing engines. They tried to recreate the accident in the flight simulator, and no other pilots, including instructor pilots, were able to land the plane. He was amazingly humble and never took credit for what he did, but insisted on giving credit to his crew. Betty introduced me to him, and he became a mentor to me. He talked to me about his injuries and took me with him to an accident-survivor's group therapy. We all had PTSD from the crash, and I realized I wasn't the only one who suffered from guilt that we survived."

"Why did you feel guilty? You couldn't have done anything."

"I was consumed with guilt because I'd asked my mom to fly with me. If I hadn't been afraid to fly by myself, she wouldn't have died that day. I thought my life was over at the age of thirteen, and at times I wished I had died with her, because it was too hard to go on."

River had to stop speaking for a moment. Talking about her past was clearly difficult for her, but she continued.

"Betty and Al Haynes would call and check on me, and we'd just talk. They were lights at the end of a long, dark tunnel for me. I'm not sure I would have made it without them. Eventually, it did get better, and Al helped me find a purpose for my life—flying."

River withdrew her hand from Dee's and leaned back. "Dee, you will get through this, but it will take time. I can tell you only that you can't run away from loss. You have to face it, get a good therapist, and walk through the grief to get to the other side, or it will cripple you forever."

Dee listened to her advice and appreciated that River was trying to help her. "I'm not sure I can do this, but I do understand guilt. If it wasn't for my actions sixteen years ago, I wouldn't have lost contact with Naomi for so long, and she wouldn't have been on that plane. I'm responsible for her death."

❖

They were both silent on their walk back to the hotel. River had spilled her guts to Dee but didn't know if it had done any good. Watching Dee tear up when she talked about Naomi made her question her decision to let Dee work on this investigation. Someone personally involved should not be allowed to participate in a case concerning family, for good reasons. Their judgment was impaired by grief, and Dee had a great deal of guilt to work through. She was fragile emotionally, and one wrong word, or memory, could put her at risk for a psychological breakdown.

After seeing Dee tormented by her PTSD all night long, she couldn't take the chance that the letters she'd discovered would trigger her to have another attack. If she did, River wouldn't be able to give her the care she needed and still do her own work. Plus, if she turned in the suitcase with the letters, the investigators would confiscate them and test everything for chemical residue, and Dee might not get them back. Removing anything from an accident site was forbidden, but these would be important to Dee, and River had to safeguard them.

She also had to admit she needed Dee's help with this case. Her own health was questionable right now, and Dee could be her eyes and ears if she was stricken with more migraines. It was very clear to her that she couldn't tell Dee about the letters she'd found in the pink suitcase. River would give the letters to her later, when she was more able to handle reading them. For now, she needed to keep them to herself.

After they returned to the hotel, Dee said, "Do you want to go over my interview notes from the McClain family members?"

"I'm a little too tired to process them tonight. How about tomorrow?"

"Sure. Well, good night then. See you tomorrow."

Dee appeared disappointed as she entered her own room, then closed the door between them. River could hear Dee moving around.

She went to open the door between their rooms a little so she could hear better, in case Dee had any more nightmares and needed help. Dee had locked her side of the door. She obviously didn't want, or need, any assistance from River tonight.

CHAPTER SEVENTEEN

Day 6

Dee woke up to the sound of her alarm. She was still tired, after tossing and turning most of the night, but grateful she hadn't had her recurring PTSD nightmare of mangled bodies last night. She could hear River in the shower next door and wondered how she'd slept.

She sat on the side of the bed remembering her dinner with River last night. It was a nice evening of sharing a meal, until she'd had that memory of eating brisket with Naomi in Lot. The whole tone changed after that. Realizing she'd never have a chance to experience something so simple as eating barbecue with Naomi again made her feel so empty.

River showed her kindness when she talked about her own survival from a plane crash. She couldn't imagine being only thirteen years old, losing your mother, and having to go through this. But Naomi had been only thirteen when their father kicked Dee out of their home. She'd had no choice at the time, but she still felt guilty for abandoning Naomi all those years ago.

River was right. She did have guilt and grief mixed together in a toxic concoction and had to find a way to get through it. Not today, but very soon, she had to call Dr. Lopez to make an appointment, and she had to talk to Naomi's husband, Bill. Today, she had to get to work and find some answers. She heard a soft knock at the adjoining door between their rooms.

"Ready to go?" River asked.

"Yes."

River looked different today, certainly a lot better than she did yesterday, when she'd had the migraine, but there was something else. She wore her same uniform of hiking boots, Levi jeans, and a plaid flannel shirt, but she looked lighter. She seemed to be not so tightly wound, almost relaxed, and she even smiled. Whatever it was, Dee was glad to see the change. They ate breakfast at the hotel buffet with the other team members, then went to the hangar for the morning briefing.

As they sat at the back of the briefing area waiting for Ronald Moore to start, Dee looked around. "Why are more press people here today?"

"Because there's more pressure to come up with answers. The families, the FAA, Homeland Security—they all want to know why this airplane fell out of the sky, and they want results now."

The briefing was starting. "Good morning, ladies and gentlemen. I'm Ronald Moore, NTSB Chief Investigator, and we have significant progress to report. We recovered a baggage-cargo container, largely intact, with a few suitcases inside, which we are currently processing. We interviewed more persons of interest and have recovered more airframe pieces. We've also identified flight training problems with Captain Joe Davis, now that we have his records from his previous employer. Most important, we found the cockpit voice recorder early this morning, and it's en route here for analysis. We should have preliminary information from the CVR later today."

Some of the briefing information confused Dee. "Was he saying the captain had flying problems? I don't remember seeing anything to suggest that when we looked at his training records, do you?"

"No, but a dead captain is an easy target to blame because he's not here to defend himself. I need to see the records they got on him from that Asian cargo company."

"Can we check out the luggage they found? There might be something from Naomi."

River hesitated a moment, then said, "Sure. But it's unlikely."

They walked over to the Cargo/Hazardous Material table.

"Have you finished processing the luggage?" River asked.

"Not quite, but we will," the technician answered.

Dee jumped in. "Have you identified the owners of the suitcases?"

"No. Only three were inside, and the luggage tags were ripped off at some point."

"Any information from inside the suitcases?"

"Just the usual—clothing, toiletries, shavers, but nothing significant so far. We're still waiting for chemical analysis of the exterior and interior of the luggage."

"Thanks," River said. She turned to Dee. "Sorry."

"It was a long shot."

Dee saw movement and turned to see Ronald Moore making a beeline toward her.

"Detective Rawlings, I'd like to speak to you about your interview report of the eyewitness. ATF Agent Paul Marshall said in his report that he didn't think the eyewitnesses' report of a missile strike was credible. Yet in yours, you think it is. Why the difference of opinion? Are you new to this?" He looked at River as he said the last part.

Dee squared her shoulders so she stood directly in front of him. "No. I am not new to dealing with extremist hate groups in Oregon. I reported that the subject displayed a strong belief in what he witnessed and that it warranted further investigation. Does the ATF agent know how many rival groups want the McClain family dead? Does he know what kind of weapons they have? Well, I do. I stand by my assessment."

"Thank you for clarifying. I'll set these for follow-up investigations."

Dee heard a commotion on the other side of the hangar, where a crowd of investigators had gathered around something. It was the CVR orange box, the cockpit voice recorder.

❖

Walking across the hangar to the CVR, River was still nervous that Dee had insisted on looking at the luggage. The small pink suitcase should've been with the other found bags, but River didn't want Dee to learn of its existence just yet.

As they gathered around the CVR, it looked to be in fairly good condition, with only one damaged corner. They hooked it up to a computer to download it, and to a speaker.

"Will we really be able to hear what went on in the cockpit?" Dee asked.

"I hope so, if it's not too distorted. It's designed to withstand high G forces, fire, even water, and it records all sound, including, cockpit conversation between the pilots, radio transmissions, engine noise, and any other sounds in the area."

Everyone stopped talking to listen. A man with a deep voice spoke first.

"This is a crappy ride at three-six. Seat belt sign coming on."
Ding.
"Michael, let's request lower."
Click.
"Relax Air 402, at flight level three-six-zero, in moderate turbulence, requesting descent to flight level three-two-zero."

"That must be the first officer on the radio, so the captain is flying," she said to Dee.

Pop.
"Relax Air 402, descend and maintain flight level three-two-zero. Contact Seattle Center on one-two-seven-point-six."
"Relax Air 402, out of three-six-zero for three-two-zero, Seattle on one-two-seven-point-six."
Click, click, click, click.
"Three-two-zero, set."
"Three-two-zero, checked."
Crackle.

"I see some flashes. I'm turning the weather radar on."

Hum.

"Damn it, this radar isn't working again. I think there's a cell at twelve o'clock. I'm turning right, thirty degrees."

Click, click, click.

"Tell Center our new heading."

Crackle.

"Roger."

BOOM.

Silence.

No one moved. Hearing the last words spoken by people just before they died was sobering. Then someone behind them spoke. It was the ATC representative.

"He turned directly toward a thunderstorm cell. If he'd asked us for a vector to avoid weather, we would have told him to turn the other way. Oh, my God."

The whole crowd buzzed.

"River, what's going on? Why are the press people on their phones?"

"Just a second."

She ran away from the crowd to a quiet corner, took out her notepad, and wrote down every word she could remember from the CVR as fast as she could. Dee followed her.

"Tell me what sounds you heard in the background, Dee."

"I heard some pops and clicks. Why?"

"Did you hear a buzz or a crackle sound?"

"Yes, toward the end."

"That's what I heard too. I think there was lightning around them."

"Do you think they got hit by lightning? Is that why the plane blew up?"

"Most big planes can withstand a lightning strike. They're designed to dissipate the electrical energy across the skin of the airplane. I actually got struck by lightning when I was flying the

KC-10 once. It's quite startling, but the plane had only minor damage. It's more likely that he accidentally flew into a thunderstorm because his weather radar was out. That could definitely tear an airplane apart."

They heard an announcement coming from the briefing area.

"Ladies and gentlemen, in light of this most recent evidence from the cockpit voice recorder, we'll be looking at pilot error as the cause of this accident. For an unknown reason, Captain Joe Davis either intentionally, or inadvertently, flew the aircraft into an area of thunderstorms, causing the aircraft to break up in flight. More information will be released as we get it."

"That's bullshit." River was furious. She turned to Dee. "He's blaming this crash on the captain."

Chapter Eighteen

"We need to talk to the weather desk," River said.

Dee followed her across the hangar, still trying to process everything she'd heard on the CVR.

The weather charts tacked to the bulletin boards looked like nothing but jots and squiggles. River pointed to the aircraft ground track overlaid onto the weather chart.

"This is the SIGMET forecast I've already studied. This was given to the flight crew during their preflight planning, and only scattered thunderstorms were supposed to be in this area. It's possible the thunderstorms built up more quickly than forecast or that there was a wind bust. I need to see more charts."

River turned to the meteorologist at the desk. "Can you get me the winds aloft forecast for flight levels three-six, three-four, and three-two, any SIGMETs from Oakland Center for southern Oregon, and any pilot reports."

"How far out do you want the PIREPs?"

"From altitude blocks two-zero-zero through four-zero-zero, two hundred miles south of the crash site, and within one hour of estimated crash time."

"Sure thing, Dr. Dawson. I'll have those for you in about ten minutes."

River took her elbow. "Let's go over here where it's quiet."

They went over to the food area and sat at a plastic table. "All right. What's going on?"

Dee kept her voice down.

"The fastest way to end an aircraft accident investigation is to blame a dead pilot. Ronald Moore wants to wrap this up because none of the big boys—Relax Air, GE, ATC, McDonnell Douglas—want to be held responsible, but I think he's wrong."

"Why's he wrong?"

"Mainly because he's a jerk, but he's also wrong to say the captain caused this accident."

"Well, it did kind of sound like he was having trouble with the weather."

"Dee, no pilot would ever intentionally fly into a thunderstorm. It's madness. If he couldn't see a storm cell because the weather radar was out, it was an accident, not pilot error."

What the hell?

Dee's ears were hot, a clear sign she was getting angry. "Do you mean to tell me that if a pilot is stupid enough to fly into a storm, it's *not* a pilot error? It's just an accident?"

"You don't understand. I meant to say—"

"I certainly don't, and I don't understand why you want to defend him."

She had to remove herself from this situation before she said something she'd regret later. As she jumped up to leave the table, River put her hand on her wrist. Her hand was warm and her grip, tight.

"Dee, please sit down. I need you to understand. I'm not defending the captain of this flight. I'm trying to get to the truth."

Dee returned to her seat. She owed River the courtesy to listen. "Go on."

"If Ronald Moore can blame this accident on a dead pilot, he stops the investigation, and we may never know why the plane really crashed. If it broke up due to a collision, a bomb, a maintenance problem, or airframe metal fatigue, we won't know. Then other DC-10s will still be flying around the world, filled with people, not knowing there's a serious problem with their jet."

River released her wrist. "I can't let this happen again, Dee. I have to find out what really killed all these people. I think you deserve to know how Naomi died." She paused. "Unless this is too hard. I don't mean to push you."

"No. You're not pushing me. It is very hard, but I need to know the truth."

The meteorologist came over to their table with the new weather charts, and River flipped through them with a practiced eye, marking some numbers. "Well, it's not exactly surprising."

She turned the charts so Dee could see them, then got out of her seat and stood behind Dee's shoulder to point to the area she was speaking about.

"This was the SIGMET, that's short for significant meteorological forecast, issued the night of the crash that showed storm systems in northern California and southern Oregon. They were moving north but not expected to be in this area until after their time of flight. This other chart shows the forecast winds aloft at their flight level, which was from the west at sixty knots. Look at this. It's a PIREP, a pilot report, over Eugene, Oregon, thirty minutes before we lost contact with flight 402. A pilot reported winds from the southwest at one hundred and ten knots. That's a wind bust, when the actual wind is way off from the forecast wind. They thought they'd have a sixty-knot headwind, but they really had a tailwind, and the actual wind blew this storm system into the crash area sooner than expected."

"So he didn't expect to have thunderstorms, and his radar didn't work, so he couldn't see them. Sounds like this guy had two strikes against him."

"Exactly, so to suggest that this captain intentionally flew into bad weather is incorrect. He might have made a mistake by turning the wrong way, but he had unforeseen bad weather and inoperative equipment happen first."

"Do we need to take these charts to Ronald Moore and show him this?"

"Well, there's one other thing I can't prove."

"What?" Dee leaned in to hear better.

"I flew the KC-10 for four years, and it's a very tough plane. I've personally witnessed new pilots prang on landings when they were learning to fly it, landings at maximum weight on short runways, multiple bird strikes, and I've even had an aircraft commander fly us directly into a thunderstorm. The aircraft was not damaged, even when we got hit by hail, which sounds like you're being shot by a machine gun, by the way. I just have a feeling that even if the captain inadvertently flew into a storm, the plane would have survived. I can't shake the sense that we're still missing something, the real reason this plane blew up. Until I can prove my hunch, it's useless to take this to Ronald Moore because he will only dismiss it."

"Well, you have to trust your gut. I guess we'll just keep searching until we find the proof."

"If any metal pieces of the skin or structure have scorch marks, that could indicate a lightning strike. I'd like to see what progress they've made on the airplane reconstruction."

They went to examine the aircraft supported by the scaffolding frame. Overall, Dee could tell it had once been an airplane, even with the mangled parts. River walked to the front of the plane.

"This is where the nose cone goes, when we find it. It's made of composite fiberglass, and the weather radar antenna is inside it. If lightning strikes a plane, it often hits in this area. The nose cone has special lightning strips designed to burn off the massive electrical charge, and sometimes you can see burn marks from the lightning on the outside of the skin."

She slowly walked from the nose toward the back of the plane, scanning the skin pieces. Dee followed her, craning her neck back to see the sides of the huge airplane. She couldn't spot any burn marks.

"This is the cargo container found yesterday. It's from the forward baggage compartment."

Dee looked at the twisted silver metal. She would never have known what this was if she came across it in the woods. "Was it damaged from an explosion?"

"Maybe, but we won't know until the chemical-residue tests come back."

River turned to face the back of the plane. "What the hell is that?"

Dee couldn't see what she was referring to, but she followed River to the middle part of the airframe. "What is it?"

"This is a fourth landing gear. What the hell? How did I miss this?"

River looked irritated.

"Explain, please."

"Most commercial airliners have three landing gears: a nose wheel, and left and right main wheel trucks. They've just discovered a fourth landing gear, the center main wheels, located between the left and right main gear. Only the DC-10 freighter aircraft has center main wheels. This plane was originally a cargo plane, then modified at some point to carry passengers."

"Why does that matter?"

"Because of weight. A DC-10 freighter weighs a lot more than the passenger airliner. The original DC-10 was built for long-range passenger service, but because the plane was huge and the engines were so powerful, they also made a freighter version for international cargo. The DC-10 airline version was modified to carry extra weight because cargo is not only in the forward and aft baggage compartments, but also on the main deck, where the passenger seats were. A plane carrying cargo, even after a long flight across the ocean, usually lands near maximum weight. That's why it needs a fourth landing gear—to support the increased weight. Max-weight landings put more stress on the airplane, especially the main wing spars, where the wings are attached to the fuselage."

"River, are you saying that because this plane used to be a freighter, the wings might have broken off?"

"No, not in this case, but it has happened to other aircraft. If a wing had separated from the fuselage, the plane would have gone into a tight spiral and fallen straight down to the ground. All the debris would have been in a single hole, not spread out over miles. We need more data. Let's get out to the crash site."

❖

"Would you mind driving to Angel Creek while I read the aircraft maintenance records?"

"Sure thing. I like driving," Dee said.

River had to keep her temper in check because she didn't want to take it out on Dee. She was upset with herself for missing the fact that the plane had previously been a freighter. She hadn't had time to study the maintenance records when she was incapacitated with her migraine. In the aircraft accident investigation business, knowledge was power, and she hated being caught short.

"Why don't you tell me what you're looking for? Maybe I can help."

"Dee, you don't know the difference between an A and a C check. I don't think this would make any sense to you."

"Humor me. What's the most important thing you're looking for?"

"Well, the maintenance records have several parts—the repair history, the deferred items, compliance with airworthiness directives, aircraft modifications, maintenance inspection schedule, weight and balance, plus—"

"What's the most important thing?"

River was quiet for a moment. "Well, it would be the mechanical condition of the airplane just before the crash. Specifically, what equipment was inoperative at the time of the explosion?"

"So we know the weather radar was broken, because of what they said on the CVR. Was anything else not working?"

River flipped through the maintenance write-ups for the previous month. "Wow. This baby had some mileage on her. Lots of write-ups for small stuff, like cabin lights, but also some recurring issues. This plane had chronic problems starting the APU—the auxiliary power unit—and several flight control write-ups."

"Could that cause them to lose control of the airplane?"

"No. It's written up that the plane flies crooked, which may mean that the flight controls just needed to be adjusted. It's another chronic problem, but not bad enough to bring down an airplane."

"So it sounds like the main airplane problem before the accident was no weather radar, but that alone wouldn't cause it to blow up. What's the next most important thing to look at?"

"The aircraft's modification history. We know it was once a freighter, and then it was converted into a passenger jet. It was modified twelve years ago at a Chinese maintenance facility in Shanghai, and then the plane flew passengers for ten years out of Nairobi, Kenya. Relax Air acquired it two years ago."

"If this plane was converted from flying freight to flying passengers, wouldn't the manufacturer do that?"

"McDonnell Douglas could certainly have modified the plane, but it was done in China because it's cheaper."

"Really? Doesn't the FAA check their work?" Dee asked.

"Yes, they do, sort of. I'm familiar with this maintenance facility, and it's huge. They can overhaul an entire aircraft, or rebuild engines, or modify airframes, but only a few FAA-certified maintenance inspectors oversee the repair work of hundreds of mechanics. How closely is their work supervised? We can only guess. It's aircraft heavy-maintenance work being outsourced to foreign countries for cheap labor."

"That doesn't really inspire confidence. I kind of wish I didn't know that."

"Well, this isn't good."

"What?"

"We don't have any maintenance history before it was modified. The history starts when it left the Chinese facility in 2008. This airplane was built in 1985, but the maintenance records go back only twelve years."

River took out her phone and dialed a number. "Can you connect me to the Maintenance Records table? Thanks." After a slight pause, she said, "We're missing the first twenty-five years of this airplane's life. That's a big problem, and I need those records immediately."

❖

Dee parked, and River got out her backpack of supplies.

"So where do you want to start today?" Dee asked. "Are we looking for anything in particular?"

River put her hands on her hips and scanned the horizon around Angel Creek. "Let's start downstream and each cover one side of the creek, working our way upstream. I don't really know what I'm looking for, but there's something we haven't found yet."

"Would it be parts from that big empty space in the middle of the plane?"

River stopped and turned to face her. "What big empty space? Do you mean the forward cargo pit?"

"No, the space on the airplane in front of the fourth landing gear, where no pieces were in place."

River had a look of concentration. "I'm not picturing it."

"If you're standing at the center main landing gear, look toward the nose. On the belly of the plane is an area that appears hollowed out, with no skin sections attached."

"I must have been focusing on the fourth gear and lightning marks so much that I walked right past it and didn't notice."

"Yeah. The floor pieces above it looked like they were bowed out. I thought you saw all that. Otherwise, I would have asked you about it," Dee said.

"Well, I'll just have to examine that part of airplane when we get back. Sorry I missed it."

"I don't know how you can tell what any of that twisted metal is anyway. I know it's evidence, but it looks like a scrapyard to me. So I guess the mission today is to try to find something from that missing middle section."

They walked in silence for a while, with only the sounds of birds singing and the breeze through the pine trees to accompany them. Dee took the opportunity to ask River some non-technical questions.

"Did you say you've been struck by lightning when you were flying a plane? What's that like?"

River stopped walking and a smile came across her lips. She had a very nice smile.

"Let's sit down for a minute, and I'll tell you what happened."

They found some rocks to sit on, in a grassy shaded spot next to the flowing water.

"I was in Saudi Arabia flying a KC-10 air refueling mission one night. We'd had a flawless rendezvous with the AWACS airplane, offloaded one hundred thousand pounds of fuel to them, and were headed back to Riyadh."

"That's the plane with the giant Frisbee on top, isn't it? I saw those in Oklahoma."

"Yeah. They're based at Tinker Air Force Base, in Oklahoma City, home of the famous Tinker Burger, which is a fabulous cheeseburger they serve at the snack bar in Base Ops."

"Did you fly a US Air Force airplane to Oklahoma just so you could have a cheeseburger?"

River laughed at her. "No, but I did get a Tinker Burger every time I went through there."

"I'm glad to hear that. Back to the lightning story."

"We were returning to the base, and a big line of thunderstorms was between us and the airport, so I had to fly around them, and it got really turbulent. We were descending through the clouds, and I had just told the copilot to turn on the Fasten Seat Belt sign, when I saw this bright, white flash, felt a big thump, like we'd hit something—then I heard BOOM."

"Shit. What'd you do?"

"I had everyone check in, since I had crew in the back. Then I checked the engines, which were all good, and scanned the rest of the instruments. The plane appeared to be fine, and just as I was about to make a PA announcement—white flash, big thump, and BOOM again!"

"You got struck by lightning twice?"

"Yes, we did. I determined that we needed to get out of that weather and on the ground immediately. I think my exact words at the time were 'I need to get the fuck out of this shit, ASAP!' I threw the gear down, did a screaming-assed descent to the final approach fix, and landed five minutes later.

"After landing, when I went outside to look at the plane, it had only a two-inch hole in the nose cone and a few burn marks on the exterior paint. Maintenance told me the lightning also blew out the weather radar antenna. As I said, it was quite startling at the time."

"That sounds almost as fun as getting shot at. Glad I wasn't on your plane that night."

"Oh, no. What you did in the Middle East was much more dangerous than anything I ever did."

"Didn't you have any defensive weapons on your plane?"

"Nothing but harsh language."

"It sounds like you did some very cool stuff flying the KC-10, River. I bet you loved it."

"I did, very much." She grew quiet and stared into the distance. "Well, let's get back to work."

It was clear River's business face was firmly in place again. No more idle chitchat about the past.

Too bad. I would've liked to hear more.

Chapter Nineteen

River carefully searched her side of Angel Creek while also keeping an eye on Dee on the other side. She was still irritated with herself for not noticing an entire missing section of the aircraft underside. Fortunately, Dee had seen it and told her about it before she wasted more time running down a dead-end lead.

It was nice taking a break with Dee on the banks of the creek, almost like having a normal conversation with a real person, instead of just shop talk about aircraft accidents. It was fun to tell one of her flying stories to someone who was genuinely interested, even though doing that always made her a little melancholy afterward. Not being able to fly anymore was just another loss in her life, added to the pile of losses already there.

"Hey. I think I found something, in the water."

River interrupted her pity party and went over to where Dee pointed at rocks in the middle of the creek bed. "Where? I can't see what you're looking at."

Dee took off her boots and socks and waded into the shallow water. "Over here, at the base of this little waterfall, wedged between two rocks."

"Oh, geez, Dee. Don't walk into the creek with your bare feet. You might step on some sharp metal in there."

"I'll be careful, and thank you for being concerned about my feet."

Dee gingerly maneuvered across the slippery river rocks to the middle of the creek bed, bent down, and put both hands in the cold water. "I know it's here. I saw something shiny between these two rocks."

Dee continued to feel around underwater. "Got you." She stood up holding her prize. "Here. Check this out."

River stood on the bank of the creek and extended her arm toward Dee. Instead of giving her the object, Dee took hold of her hand and held it while she waded through the water to River's side.

"What is this?" Dee asked.

River turned the object over, examining it. "This small section of shiny metal was deformed, either by impact forces, high temperature, or something else. There's a scorch mark on the underside, and this jagged metal on the end looks like it broke off something. Probably no chemical residue, since it's been in the water. I don't know where this goes, and I'm not sure what it is, but it's definitely from our airplane. Good find, Dee."

River photographed it, cataloged it in her notepad, marked the spot with a metal stake flag, and plotted its location on her map. They continued searching for about an hour, found nothing, and then River realized she was hungry. "How about we take a break for lunch. I brought sandwiches from the food cart."

"Great. I'm ready to eat. I've worked up an appetite with all this hiking."

River found a shady spot next to the creek. "I should think this type of hiking would bore you, after your experience as an MP in the army."

Dee sat down next to her. "True, it's not too strenuous compared to marching with a forty-five-pound pack, but I haven't done any hiking in a long time. This is actually kind of nice, walking through the woods with the sound of this creek. I like it here."

River took a moment to be quiet and look around them. "It is really pretty here. Very peaceful, and I like the sound of the water too."

"Do you know why they call it Angel Creek?"

River pointed at the top of the small waterfall. "The lady at the Madras airport said it was because of the rock that resembles an angel. Up there, just above the waterfalls where you found that shiny metal piece, you can make out two rocks that look like wings, and the whole rock formation resembles the Angel of Bethesda, in Central Park."

"That's in New York City, isn't it? I've heard of it but never seen it in person. It does kind of look like an angel," Dee said.

"Have you been to the City?"

"Just once, with my friend, Marci, after I got back from my first deployment to the desert."

"I adore New York City. It's such a cool place."

"It kind of overwhelmed me, to tell you the truth. I'd never seen so many people crowded onto the sidewalks and in the subways. Walking by the skyscrapers made me feel like I was at the bottom of a canyon. But we did have fun."

"My favorite thing to do there is go to Broadway musicals. They're truly amazing."

Dee set down her sandwich and stared at River. "I never would have guessed you were a Broadway musical fan."

"Don't judge a book by its cover."

"I should have guessed you were a fan of musicals by the hiking boots and flannel shirt. They do go together, if you're a gay man."

River couldn't help but laugh. *She's funny and quick. I like that.* "Okay, so I'm not a gay man, at least not the man part, but I can't help that I love musicals, and the museums. I love going to all the different ones, especially The Met."

"The Met?" Dee asked.

"The Metropolitan Museum of Art. They have this sculpture gallery, with giant windows looking out onto Central Park, and a gorgeous, poignant statue of Sappho. It's a beautiful place to relax, have coffee, and watch the world go by."

"That sounds like heaven." Dee became quiet.

"I'll take you there someday, when this is behind us." River grasped Dee's hand. She wanted her to know she wasn't alone.

"Will this ever be behind me? How did you survive this?"

She took a deep breath. "I told you about my friend, Betty, the nurse in the Iowa National Guard, and Captain Al Haynes, my mentor. They helped me find a reason to live, a purpose for my life. Betty would visit me on drill weekends when I was going through physical therapy, and she helped my dad find a counselor for me. After I was better, Al took me up flying in a little Cessna 150."

"That's cool. What'd you think of it?"

"I think Betty probably set this up, but he showed up at my house one Saturday and said, 'Come on, young lady. We're going flying.' He took me out to the local airport, had me follow him as he did the walk-around inspection on the Cessna, then put me in the left seat, cranked the engine, and off we went. He didn't try to instruct. He just wanted to fly around, kind of low and slow, and he pointed out cool stuff on the ground. We did that, nice and easy, and then he had me fly.

"When I had my left hand on the yoke and my right hand on the throttle, I was in control and wasn't scared anymore. Flying made sense to me. I felt like I was home, and this was where I wanted to be. He showed me how to land, and then he let me land the plane myself, and I knew I'd be okay. Al encouraged me to complete my private pilot's license when I was sixteen, and he helped me get accepted to the US Air Force Academy. He pinned on my air force wings and even watched me fly a KC-10 in an air show once. Al and Betty showed me there was life after a plane crash and that I was strong enough to get through it. I survived because I had to, and you'll survive this too."

Dee held onto her hand, and together they watched the waters of Angel Creek flow past them.

It began to rain as they were finishing their sandwiches.

"I think we've found as much as we're going to. Let's head back," River said.

They didn't talk much on the drive to the hangar. Dee had a lot to think about. She appreciated River sharing her story, and it was nice to know someone understood what she was going through, but her situation was different. River didn't betray and abandon her mother like Dee had abandoned Naomi. No mentor or flying lesson could fix that.

The hangar was buzzing with activity when they returned. River took one of the new packets of test results, and they went over to a table to review them.

"This is very odd," River said. "These test results don't show anything."

"What do you mean?"

"There's no chemical residue on anything, other than the usual hydrocarbons from oil, fuel, and hydraulic fluid. This would rule out a bomb, or missile, until we find the rest of the missing pieces from the lower center of the plane. But it doesn't add up. A plane doesn't just blow up for no reason. Let's see if there's anything new on the airplane reconstruction."

After they walked over to the airframe, Dee could see more progress in the tail section and the wings. But the underside of the plane still had that large void area.

"What's supposed to be in this part of the plane that's missing?"

"Hydraulic lines, flight control cables, electrical wires, and the center fuel tank. In the passenger version of a DC-10, there's also a lower galley, beneath the plane's main floor," River said.

"Why is it below the floor?"

"Mainly for space. On long international flights with three hundred passengers, they would need six hundred meals on board, cold-storage in carts, and ovens. A special elevator in the plane let a flight attendant go down to the lower galley, cook the meals, and send them back up to the cabin for the other flight attendants to hand out. It would have water lines and several electrical connections for the chillers and the ovens."

"Could all that electrical stuff have shorted out and caused the explosion?"

"It's hard to tell. Without those modification records, we don't even know if this plane had a lower galley. When it was converted from a cargo plane to a passenger airliner, the Chinese mechanics could have installed a new lower galley here, but we can't be certain. We need to see the rest of the maintenance history."

They walked over to the Maintenance Records table, and River asked the records clerk, "Do you have the maintenance records for the airplane before it was modified?"

Dee noticed that he looked flustered. Something was up with him.

"Ah, sorry, Dr. Dawson, but what you have is everything we have so far. We can't find anything before it was converted. We're still working with Relax Air to get them to release the records, but they claim they don't have them. They said they bought the airplane at an auction in Kenya."

"This is unacceptable." River's brow furrowed, and her eyes looked like they could melt steel.

Dee pulled her away from the table before things escalated. "Let's go find Ronald Moore and have him get those records for us."

Before they could find him, Ronald Moore intercepted them. "Why are you threatening my records technician?"

Dee observed his balled fists, wide stance, and red face. He was trying to physically intimidate River. *He's dangerous.*

River stood up to her full height and squared to face him. Her voice was low, measured, and controlled. "I never threatened anyone. I simply told your technician it was unacceptable to have an incomplete maintenance history. So when do you plan to have the rest of the records here? Or do I need to go over your head. Again?"

Dee saw veins bulging in his neck and stepped into Moore's field of view, just behind River's shoulder, feeling for the secure presence of her weapon next to her breast.

"Don't you dare threaten me, you bit—"

Dee quickly moved between them, put her hands out to block him, then gave him her biggest Texas smile and said, "Hey. No need for raised voices. Everyone's a professional here. Let's just figure out what we have to do to get the documents we all need. Mr. Moore, who would we need to contact to obtain those records?"

He relaxed his posture slightly. "Well, I suppose we could put in a request with the Chinese embassy in DC. I can call my boss."

"Great idea. Would it be faster if we routed the request through the Chinese Consulate office in Portland? I have a contact there who could help."

"That would be very helpful. I'll get that request written up right now. Thanks." He turned and walked away from them.

She turned to River. "Could you please tell me what's going on between you two?"

"Let's get out of here, and I'll tell you the whole story."

They drove back to the hotel, ordered room service, and River went to her room to shower. Dee listened to the water running, closed her eyes, and wondered what River looked like with her wavy, blond hair slicked back and rivulets of soapy water rolling down her back. She felt a tingle deep within. *Hmmm. That's nice. I haven't felt that in a while.*

The water shut off, ending Dee's lovely vision, and she heard a knock at her front door. She retrieved their room service food and set River's tray on the desk. She sat on her bed, leaning against the headboard, her tray on her lap. "Food's here, River."

"Be right there."

River walked into Dee's room wearing baggy gym shorts, a sleeveless USAFA tee shirt with a few holes in it, and her damp, golden hair slicked back.

Oh, my. The deep tingling became more noticeable. *Down, girl. Down.*

River ate her food at the desk, set her tray aside, then came and sat next to Dee on the bed. "Here's the issue with Ronald Moore. I'm a better investigator than he is, and he can't stand it, so he likes to be as difficult as he can with me to try to get even and to show dominance."

"He sounds like a very insecure guy. I've had to work with my share of those guys in the army and the police department."

"He is, and he'll do anything to cover his ass, including throwing team members under the bus. When we both worked for the NTSB, he tried to rush an investigation and came up with the wrong cause factors. I couldn't let my name be attached to an aircraft safety investigation that I knew was wrong, so I went over his head and gave my findings to the US Secretary of Transportation, who directed that the investigation be reopened and the report be revised. I knew I'd burned a bridge with him, but I didn't feel like I had a choice. In this business, your reputation is everything."

"Did you get fired?"

"No, but I knew it was time to go. He'd created a toxic work environment, and I was definitely no longer welcome. The good news is, I saved a big insurance company millions of dollars in damage awards, so they hired me as an independent accident investigator, and I started my own business."

Dee remembered Moore's threatening body language earlier. "Can he still cause trouble for you?"

"No. He can't. He has to send the completed report to all parties, and the insurance company won't pay out any money until I say the report is complete, so he can't touch me."

"All the same, you need to be careful around him, River. He has a violent temper. I recognize it."

River looked at her for a long moment. "You're right. He does have an ugly temper, and thank you for warning me."

River smiled at her, resulting in more tingles.

Dee hopped off the bed and went to the minibar for a Coke. "So, more searching tomorrow?"

River's dark-blue eyes twinkled. "No. I think tomorrow we should go on a field trip instead."

CHAPTER TWENTY

Day 7

River and Dee were on the road at six a.m. heading to the Portland airport. Dee was driving her car through the winding mountains and set her large coffee cup in the holder.

"I've had my morning coffee, so you can speak to me now. Where are we going?"

River tried not to laugh at grumpy Dee, who was clearly not a morning person. "We can't do anything more with the investigation until we get the rest of the maintenance history, and I can't figure out what I'm not seeing, but I'm sure it has to do with that missing underbelly section. So we're going to look at an intact DC-10 to try to see what puzzle piece we're missing."

"And where are we going to see a DC-10?"

"We're flying to Tucson, Arizona, to the Pima Air and Space Museum. They have a DC-10 freighter we can look at. Maybe you'll be able to see something I don't."

River had first-class tickets waiting for them at the main ticket counter at the airport. They were flying from Portland, through San Francisco, to Tucson. River went through regular security while Dee proceeded to the law enforcement checkpoint.

As they were finding their seats on the plane, she asked Dee, "Do you prefer the window or the aisle?"

"Doesn't matter to me. Which one do you like?"

River indulged herself. "I always like the window seat."

"I figured as much, fly girl. You enjoy your window seat, and I'll indulge in a few *zzzs*."

Dee plopped down in her seat and promptly closed her eyes. River hoped she wouldn't snore. It was a smooth takeoff and climb out, with another beautiful summer day in Portland. Sunlight sparkled on the Columbia River, and she watched the puffy white clouds out her window. She looked back inside to tell Dee something, then stopped herself.

She had such a peaceful expression, and River didn't want to disturb her. Her companion, who was also her team member, her new friend, and her fellow survivor, was beautiful when she wasn't stricken with PTSD or immobilized by grief.

As River studied her, she became fully aware she was attracted to Dee. The feeling had been slowly building for the last several days, but now she knew the warmth around her heart was for Dee. If they'd met under different circumstances, and not in the midst of destruction, she would have pursued her, or at least told her how she felt. For now, she'd have to keep her feelings to herself. Dee was in no condition for any romantic entanglements.

She would have to be content with trying to help Dee get through this and stealing glances at her when she could. She was drawn to Dee's full, expressive lips and her beautiful smile, which was especially effective when she was pouring on the Texas charm. River was impressed with how easily she'd disarmed Ronald Moore. She was quick, smart, and could read people well. She could stare at Dee's intense, dark-green eyes, freckled nose, and strong jaw all day. Auburn highlights caught the sun in her tousled brown hair. Her fingertips ached to run through it. Dee was strong and wiry and appealed to the deepest part of her. The warm sensation in her chest drifted lower and spread throughout her belly. *This is going to be difficult.*

❖

Dee woke up at the sound of the landing gear coming down and found River looking at her.

"We'll be landing in a few minutes."

She glanced out the window, sat up, and saw they were over water, with another airplane right next to them. "Why is that plane so close to us?"

"They're doing visual approaches to parallel runways today. That's just another airplane landing on runway 28 Right, and we're landing on 28 Left. As long as the pilots of both aircraft can see each other, it's perfectly safe. I think it's kind of cool, almost like formation flying."

"I'm happy you think it's cool, but after everything I've seen in the last week, I wish we weren't quite so close."

"Are you nervous about flying? I'm sorry. I should have thought about that."

"No. Not really. Flying in any airplane is better than sitting on a nylon jump seat in the back of a C-130 cargo plane, freezing your ass off."

After they landed, River took her to her favorite sourdough bread place on the way to their Tucson flight. "If Texas has the best brisket in the world, then Boudin Bakery in San Francisco has the best sourdough bread. You'll thank me for this later."

It was nice to see River away from the intensity of the investigation. She seemed happy at the simple act of buying bread. Dee hoped she would see this look more often. They boarded the flight to Tucson, and Dee was enjoying her nice first-class seat again. "I could get used to traveling like this."

"I'm glad you enjoy it. We should have a good view of the Grand Canyon today, and maybe Hoover Dam."

Dee chuckled at how nerdy River could be at times. It would be fun to play with her. "So what kind of airplane are we in, and tell me everything you know about it."

River was excited. "This is an Airbus 319, its nickname is The Short Bus, and it's a very popular airliner, built in Toulouse, France. It uses a side stick instead of a yoke to fly it, and see those little things sticking up on the wingtips? That's called a sail, and it reduces drag from the wingtip vortex, which saves six percent fuel burn."

Dee burst out laughing. "You can stop. I was just kidding."

River smiled at her. "Well, I'm glad I can entertain you with airplane minutiae."

"Seriously, River, are you required to memorize all this information about different planes for your job? Or do you have some kind of photographic memory?"

"Yes. I have a freakish memory for all kinds of information, not just airplane-related, but this work also fascinates me. No two days are ever alike."

"Why's it so fascinating? I would think it could very difficult to be around massive casualties."

"That part's certainly hard, but it's rewarding in other ways. This is a very interdisciplinary field, where you have to understand not only how an airplane flies, but also meteorology, human psychology, metallurgy, electronics, structures, aviation regulations, and pilot procedures. I find it extremely challenging."

Dee really wanted to understand why River did what she did. "Is that why you do this, because it's challenging?"

River looked deep in her eyes. "I do this because I love flying and don't want anyone else to go through what you and I have been forced to."

"I get that. It's kind of how I feel about police work. I want to protect people too and, hopefully, get some justice for the bad guys."

Maybe she and River weren't so different from each other after all.

After they landed in Tucson, River got a rental car, and they drove toward Davis-Monthan Air Force Base.

"This is the US Air Force Boneyard, where all military airplanes no longer in service are stored."

She drove past a huge, fenced area of desert with row after

row of B-52 bombers, F-4 fighters, trainers, cargo planes, and reconnaissance jets, spread out for acres in every direction.

"That's a lot of hardware. It kind of looks like an airplane graveyard."

River changed the subject. "Here we are, the Pima Air and Space Museum." She pulled into the parking lot, drove past airplanes on display pedestals, then they walked over to the main museum building. The cool air in the building was a welcome relief from the Arizona summer heat.

Dee wandered around the large building looking at the aircraft on display. "This is so cool. Look at the planes hanging from the ceiling, like they're flying overhead. Oh, I like this one. It's very sleek. What's this?"

"That beauty is a Lear jet, one of the early business jets."

Dee was like a kid at an amusement park, running from plane to plane. They went into another big hangar. "Oh, my gosh. Look at that."

"That's one of my favorites, the B-29 Superfortress, the largest bomber of World War II. It's magnificent, isn't it?"

She led Dee up to the giant gleaming, silver bird that filled the entire hangar. She wished she had time to give her a full tour, but she had a mission to accomplish. "Let's go outside to see the rest of the planes, and one in particular."

It was late afternoon, and most museum guests had left for the day, which was good for what River had in mind. She led Dee past a section of military fighters, then through the attack helicopters, and finally toward the back of the large outdoor area, where the biggest planes were on display.

"Here's my baby. Dee, let me introduce you to the amazing KC-10."

Dee had to lean back to take in the whole airplane. "This thing is the size of a building. How in the world do you get this beast into the air?"

"By magic and mirrors, and a whole lot of power. Look at these massive engines, and this is the air refueling boom under the tail section."

"So gas comes out of this boom, which looks like a giant pipe with wings on it, and goes into another airplane in midair?" Dee asked.

"Yes. After we rendezvous with the receiver airplane, which is a thousand feet below us, the boom operator, who's in the back of the plane, lowers the boom and flies it into the receiver's receptacle. Then we pump fuel into the other aircraft, which can take up to thirty minutes for a big plane."

"Damn. That sounds crazy. Do you do it at night?"

"Yes, and in the weather too. That gets very sporting."

"So, other than reminiscing with your baby, why are we here, River?"

"This airplane is in the freighter configuration of the DC-10, like our plane. I want to see if we can discover any clues as to what's in that missing section of the accident jet, from seeing an intact plane."

They walked to the center of the airplane, looking all around it, hoping to recognize anything.

"I can't see anything missing from the outside. Could we possibly see inside this section?" Dee asked.

"Maybe, but I'll need your help. Come over here to the center landing gear. There's a maintenance hatch we might be able to open. Make sure no one can see us."

In front of the center gear, River found a silver handle recessed into a small square door on the underside of the plane, just big enough for a mechanic to crawl through. She had to reach high over her head to push a button, which made the handle move down. Then she rotated the handle, and the hatch popped open. The door swung downward, toward the ground, held in place by a hinge on one side.

"Give me a boost."

River put one foot on the tires of the center gear, grabbed the edge of the hatch, and, with Dee's hands pushing up on her bottom, pulled herself up into the darkened compartment. She turned around, leaned out through the opening, and extended her arm to Dee.

"Just do what I did, and I'll pull you up."

Dee looked suspicious but complied, and River pulled her into the compact space.

"Where are we?"

River turned on the light in her phone for a flashlight. "This is the center accessory compartment, called the CAC. The aircraft batteries are in here, plus radios, coax cables, and other electrical components." She shone her light throughout the section and took photos. "Nothing too exciting in here."

"What's this big pipe for?"

"That's the air refueling manifold. It's the part of the fuel system where we transfer fuel from our various tanks through the manifold, out the boom, to the receiver aircraft. The KC-10 has five fuel tanks and can pump different types of gas out of any of those tanks through the air refueling boom. Want to see the rest of the airplane?"

"Sure, but aren't we going to get busted for breaking and entering?"

"Hopefully not. Follow me."

River climbed up a metal ladder in the CAC compartment, then opened another hatch in the ceiling above them and went through it. They emerged into a dark, cavernous space with only dim rays of light coming through a few small windows. River took her hand so she wouldn't trip in the unfamiliar place.

"We're in the main cabin, where the cargo pallets are loaded and secured to the floor. We can also take rolling stock, like jeeps and trucks, plus seventy passengers in this section. The boom operator's station is at the back of the plane. Let's check out the flight deck."

It was almost a hundred-foot walk across the metal floor from the CAC to the cockpit, and the interior was hot, like being inside a giant oven. They couldn't stay in here much longer, or the heat would be deadly, but she did want Dee to see the flight deck, her former office. White protective film covered the big cockpit windows, so they could move around freely, unseen from the outside. Dee stood in the middle of the flight deck, looking at all the dials and buttons.

"Would you like to sit in the captain's seat?" River asked.

"Of course I would."

She reached down by the side of the left seat, moved a lever, and pulled the tall seat out and over so Dee could climb in. "Have a seat, Captain."

Dee smiled at her like a little kid as she climbed into the seat. River reached down for the manual seat lever, just under Dee's thigh, then pushed her forward.

"This is very comfy. I like it," Dee said.

"Put your left hand on the yoke and your right hand on the throttles. Now you're ready to fly."

It made River happy to see the big grin on Dee's face, finally. She was having fun turning the yoke and pushing buttons, then making engine noises when she pushed the throttles up. But River saw beads of sweat on Dee's face from the heat. *I need to get her out of here before she gets heat stroke.*

"Well done, Ace, but it's time to go. I think we've seen everything of importance, and this place is closing soon."

"It is getting toasty in here. Very cool, River. I'm impressed. Thank you for showing me your airplane. Can you help me out?"

River leaned down over Dee to reach the seat lever, brushing her thigh on the way. She slowly pulled the seat out and back, her face next to Dee's shoulder. "You look great sitting here," she whispered.

As Dee climbed out, River noticed the tops of her ears were bright red. She took a few more photos of the flight deck, turned to leave, and saw Dee fixed in one spot, staring at the sides of the plane.

"Can you tell me where row sixteen is?"

River knew what she was asking. "So you want to know where seat 16A was located?"

Dee nodded.

River took her hand and led her to the left side of the jet, about thirty feet aft of the main cabin door, then turned her around to face forward.

"There was a window next to Naomi in our airplane. She was sitting just forward of the wing root and would have had a pretty view of the clouds."

Dee crouched into a sitting position and looked around. "It's spacious in here, not claustrophobic, like in little planes. I'm happy she got to see the sky." She looked at River with pleading in her eyes. "You're sure it was instantaneous?"

River pulled her into her arms and held her tightly. "Yes, hon. I'm positive. She didn't suffer, she wasn't filled with fear, she was just gone. I'm so, so sorry."

They held each other, their grief entwined as their tears mixed and became one.

"Hey! Who's in here? Come out of this airplane now!" A stern male voice was yelling at them.

"Damn it," River said. She reluctantly pulled away from Dee, then yelled back, "Hi, Mack. It's just me, River Dawson, leaving now."

"You know this guy?"

"Yes. He's a retired air force chief master sergeant who works as a museum docent. We go way back, so it's not a problem."

They found their way back to the CAC floor hatch and climbed down the ladder into the compartment, where Dee grabbed the edge of the exterior opening and hopped to the ground like a jackrabbit. She held her arms out to help River.

Mack was waiting for them outside the CAC. "Jesus Christ, River. I told you before, you can't go into the airplanes without prior permission. You're going to get me fired."

"Mack, I apologize, but we're in the middle of an accident investigation. I would've asked, but this is time-critical. It won't happen again. Oh, and let me introduce my colleague, Detective Dee Rawlings."

River looked behind her, where Dee had walked over to the left engine tail cone. "River, come look at this."

River joined her, and Dee positioned her to face the right engine. "Stay here."

Dee went to the open CAC hatch door and pushed it up, so it looked almost closed.

"Look at the side of the right engine. What do you see?"

River studied the spot Dee had directed her to, but the CAC

hatch was in the way. Then she saw what Dee did. The side of the CAC hatch was the same shape as the hole in the side of the right engine on the accident plane.

"Dee, lower the hatch a little bit. Yes. Right there. Hold it." She took out her camera and took several pictures, from close-up and different angles. "It's perfect. The profile of the hatch door fits exactly into the hole in the side of the engine on our plane. This proves the CAC hatch blew off first, and then it impacted the engine. The explosion must have originated in the center accessory compartment."

River walked over to Dee, pulled her hands down from the CAC hatch, and held both her shoulders. "You just broke this case wide open."

Chapter Twenty-one

Back in the car with River, after Mack had hustled them out of the museum, Dee tingled with adrenaline. Goose bumps covered her arms, and she didn't care if they were from excitement or from cold air-conditioning blowing across her sweat-soaked skin. She looked over at River. She also had goose bumps on her arms, and it was thrilling to share this moment with her.

As if she could read Dee's mind, River turned to her and put her hand on her cheek. "You're amazing. I can't believe you saw that connection between the hatch door and the hole in the side of the engine. You're an exceptional detective, Dee."

Dee blushed at the compliment, knowing her ears were probably bright red, and she loved the sensation of River's warm palm touching her face. "Thank you. We should celebrate. Do you know a place where we could get a good margarita?"

"Excellent suggestion, and I do. They serve great margaritas and Mexican food."

River removed her hand from Dee's face and backed the car out. As they drove, Dee looked around at the scenery. The desert was mainly brown, with spots of green cactus and rugged mountains in the distance. Its stark beauty appealed to her, but it wasn't as lush and green as Oregon. Now that they were out of the giant airplane oven, she was starting to cool down, still buzzing after her discovery.

River drove to downtown Tucson and parked behind a cool hole-in-the-wall place, BOCA Tacos. When they walked into the crowded, lively place, the smell of Mexican food made her mouth water. They found a small table at the back.

"The food looks great." Dee's stomach growled. "I didn't realize how hungry I was."

"Me either. I built up quite an appetite crawling around that KC-10. I haven't been here in ages, but the food was always good."

"Well, I love Tex-Mex."

River put down her menu and stared at her across the table. "This restaurant does not serve greasy, cheap Tex-Mex. That is not real Mexican food. This place serves food from the state of Sonora, in northern Mexico. I think you'll see it's far superior to Tex-Mex."

Dee was amused at how indignant River was over Tex-Mex. "I guess if I'm a snob about barbecue brisket, you're entitled to be a snob about Mexican food."

"That's exactly right."

Their pitcher of margaritas arrived, and River poured two glasses for them. She raised her glass and smiled. "To Dee. Congratulations on your find today. You did outstanding work."

They clinked glasses, and Dee took her first sip. The taste of chili salt on the rim, fresh lime juice, and very good tequila, all swirled together in a frozen delight, made her feel like she was having a party in her mouth. "This is really good."

"I'm glad you like it."

River was looking at her with a slight smile on her face, almost like she knew something but wouldn't tell Dee what it was. River was beautiful when she smiled, which wasn't very often when they were at the crash site.

She understood the need for a serious expression at work. She'd observed that if women laughed or smiled too much, the men wouldn't take them seriously and dismissed their opinions. River made sure the men respected her at work, but it was nice to see her away from that environment.

Their food arrived, and all talking stopped as they both ate. Dee had to admit, this food was a thousand percent better than any Tex-Mex she'd ever eaten.

"Try this. It's a green-chili chimichanga. I think it's fabulous." River reached across the table and fed Dee the tasty bite from her own fork. The flavors exploded on her tongue, but the intimacy of River's gesture made her stomach do flip-flops. River kept looking into her eyes, expectantly waiting for a response.

"This is delicious. Thank you for bringing me."

"You're welcome. I'm glad you like it. It's nice to be able to have dinner with someone."

Dee sensed River wanted to say something more but had stopped herself. After stuffing themselves, they paid the bill, and River drove them to a Westin hotel in the foothills of the Tucson mountains. The sun was setting behind the mountain ridge, extending long shadows across the grounds and bringing the welcome relief of shade.

Dee wandered around the spacious lobby, then walked out to the courtyard to a large, sparkling swimming pool surrounded by palm trees and cabanas. It called to her. River came up behind her, and she felt River's warm breath on her neck.

"Would you like to go for a swim?"

Tingles ran down her spine. "I'd love to, but I don't have a swimsuit with me."

"They usually have bathing suits in the hotel gift shop. Let's check."

Dee found a bathing suit with cute boy shorts and a royal-blue top. They went to the suite to change, where Dee noticed two bedrooms. She was feeling very relaxed after her two margaritas and couldn't wait to jump into the pool.

River came out into the living room of their suite wearing a one-piece, red Speedo and had a white towel around her neck. It was snug and showed off her curves, her toned legs, and the creamy skin of her broad shoulders. With River's wavy blond hair, she looked like she could be on the old TV show *Baywatch*.

"Ready?" River asked.

"I sure am."

❖

The pool area was mostly deserted by the time they got there. It was evening, and the air was warm, but not hot, since the intensity of the Arizona sun was behind the mountains. It was a beautiful setting, with soft lights illuminating the palm trees, steeply rising mountains behind the resort, and a view of the city lights of Tucson to the east. It was peaceful and quiet, until River heard a splash. Dee dove in and swam underwater to the opposite side of the large pool.

When she surfaced for air, she called back to River. "Jump in. This feels great."

Dee swam the length of the pool back to where River was watching her. She emerged with water running off her smiling face, then reached out to River. "Come in the water with me. You'll like it."

Her voice was soft, so only River could hear her, and as seductive as a siren's song. River couldn't resist her any longer. She took Dee's hand and jumped in. The water was warm from the sun but still felt refreshing.

She came up from the water, pushed her wet hair off her face, spread her arms, leaned back, and floated on the surface. The warm air across her wet skin gave her goose bumps. She opened her eyes to see Dee watching her as she floated. Dee gave her a small smile as she openly admired her body, moving her gaze up and down. Arousal flowed through every part of her. They were crossing into dangerous territory, but River didn't care.

She'd been fighting her attraction to Dee for some time, but her resistance was quickly fading; especially now that she knew Dee wanted her. The desire on Dee's face was clear and unmistakable.

"This is so pretty. I could stay here for a while. Here. I'll float you to the deep end." Dee got behind her, put her hands under her shoulders, and gently pulled her through the water. River looked at the stars twinkling overhead and wondered if this was Heaven. Even if it wasn't, this was a piece of it. It was a perfect moment, a beautiful place, at exactly the right time, and with a woman she would never forget. River drank up every second of Dee's strong hands guiding her through the warm pool, as she floated both on top of the water and in the air. She closed her eyes, trusting her body to Dee's hands. She felt Dee's lips by her ear.

"Do you like this?"

More goose bumps, this time from her ear, down her neck, across her breasts, and into her center. "Yes, I do. Very much."

Dee kept her lips against her ear, and she could feel Dee's smile on her cheek. "Good. So do I."

She continued to float River around the pool, her hands shifting lower to her shoulder blades, then her ribs, and finally Dee grazed the sides of her breasts with her thumbs. *Oh, God.* Her nipples were standing at attention, painfully erect, with the warm breeze blowing across her wet swimsuit. She knew Dee was watching her breasts when she moved her thumbs in small circles. *What the hell. This feels too good to stop.*

As if reading her mind, Dee stopped pulling her, turned her around, and set her on a small bench in the pool wall. The pool area was dark and empty. They were alone, except for the stars. She faced River, put her hands on River's hips, and pulled herself in. They looked at each other for a long moment, breathing the same air, feeling the same electricity, and she opened her knees for Dee. *I have to touch her.*

She placed her palm on Dee's cheek, with her fingertips slowly pulling Dee to her, as natural as if they'd done this a thousand times. There was no rush, no surprise, only desire. Dee had the sweetest smile as she parted her lips, the tip of her pink tongue showing. River closed the remaining inches between them and pulled Dee's lips to her own. They were the softest lips she'd ever known—luscious, sensuous, warm velvet. Her kiss was slow, her lips caressing, and River opened her mouth fully. She wanted Dee's hot kisses on her lips, the taste of Dee's slick tongue in her mouth, and Dee's beautiful body pressed against her own.

Dee wrapped her arms around her back, while River drew Dee closer to her with her knees. She was lost in Dee's kisses, hungry for more, as moans emerged from deep within her throat. Then Dee moved her hand around to River's front and caressed her neck and collarbone as she explored her mouth with her tongue. Electricity flowed from Dee's hand to River's pounding heart.

"Don't stop," she said, but then she heard a noise.

Dee withdrew her hand from River's chest and backed away slightly. "Maybe we should take this upstairs."

❖

Dee couldn't wait to get her hands on River back in their room. She was throbbing and wanted River naked in bed with her. They had a long walk to their suite on the other side of the resort. River had surprised her so much today, not just by breaking into a museum airplane, but by her tenderness when she showed her Naomi's seat. Dee also remembered all the times River had held her hand, or touched her thigh, or when she stole glances of her.

When River let her pull her around the pool, that was the confirmation she needed to know the attraction was mutual. River was so beautiful floating on the water with her eyes closed, like an alluring water nymph. Dee enjoyed every second of her unabashed gazing at River's toned body. She studied every inch of her, from her shapely leg muscles to her round hips, her firm arms, and those gorgeous full breasts, with prominent peaks begging to be sucked.

"Finally," River said as they rounded the corner to their suite.

River put the key in the lock and they rushed into the room. She closed and locked the door, and when she turned around, Dee pushed River up against the door and pressed her hips into her. She kneaded River's breasts and took the kisses she had to have. River returned her passion with her darting tongue and hungry lips. She pulled Dee to her and moved her hands lower to squeeze Dee's cheeks. Dee yanked River's bathing suit straps off, kissed her, and pressed her thigh into River's center all at the same time. River broke their kisses, putting her hands on top of Dee's.

"Wait. Please, wait."

Dee was confused. "Am I pushing you?"

"Yes, well, no. I don't know. You're making my head swim."

Dee smiled. "What's wrong with that? You make my head swim too."

River held Dee's face and kissed her again. With desire blazing in her eyes, she pressed her breasts into Dee. When Dee reached around and squeezed River's tantalizing round bottom, River broke their kiss again, moved her hands up to Dee's shoulders, and pushed her away.

"No. I can't. You have no idea how much I want you, but I just can't, Dee."

"I don't get it, River. I feel our connection, and I know you do too."

River moved past Dee and sat on the couch. "Please sit with me."

Dee joined her on the couch and took her hand.

River looked deep into her eyes. "Yes. I feel a connection with you too, a very powerful one. I would like nothing better than to follow our attraction, but we can't do this, at least not now while the investigation is ongoing."

"We've already figured out where the explosion started. We just have to determine why it exploded. The investigation's practically done. Why wait?"

"Because you're not ready for this right now. Dee, your sister just died six days ago."

Dee put up her hand. "You don't have to remind me of that. You and I both know we have some kind of chemistry. I want you, River, and I thought you wanted me too. Sorry I misread the situation. I'm going to bed."

Dee stood up from the couch and walked over to her room. She turned to face River.

"Who are you to decide what I'm ready for? I make my own decisions, and you don't know me at all."

Chapter Twenty-two

River was a mess. She finally shows Dee what she feels for her, Dee returns her desires, and then she slams on the brakes. *I'm an idiot.*

She wanted to run after Dee, retract what she'd said, throw her on the bed, and make love to her all night. Instead, she'd ruined a perfect day that could have been the best one of her life. Gone now, like a wisp of smoke, never to be recaptured.

River went through her usual tasks of checking the room's security, turning off lights, and setting her alarm. She took one last look at the bottom of Dee's bedroom door but saw no light. Upset with herself, she didn't think she could sleep. Plus, she was still thrumming all over from Dee's hot kisses and roaming hands.

She should have kept her attraction to Dee a secret, at least until the investigation was complete. And she should never have kissed Dee, but, to be truthful, she was just too irresistible. Her strong hands on River's shoulders as she glided her through the pool made her feel like she could finally let go, that she could trust her. She was powerfully drawn to Dee, and it wasn't just her big Texas smile or the cute freckles across her nose, but the intensity of her deep-green eyes and those very expressive, dark eyebrows. When they were alone together, Dee's eyes showed every emotion as it crossed her face. River was privileged to have this rare, intimate connection.

She climbed into bed, turned off the light, and tried to sleep, but Dee wouldn't let her. As soon as she closed her eyes, she felt Dee's sensuous kisses on her lips, her hands squeezing her bottom, and Dee's fingertips teasing her breasts. She briefly contemplated touching herself but stopped. With Dee in the next room, such an act somehow seemed disrespectful to her. She tried to ignore her throbbing center and punched the pillow. *I deserve to suffer.*

❖

Day 8

After a fitful night of hoping Dee would climb into bed with her, River woke up tired and disappointed, mainly in herself. The sound of running water meant Dee was already up and in the shower. She went to the living room to make herself coffee and noticed something blue in the wastepaper basket. It was Dee's bathing-suit top from their swim last night, discarded in the trash. Apparently, Dee didn't care to keep any memento of their first kiss. Could things get any more awkward?

The water shut off, and Dee came out of the bathroom wearing a towel. "Oh, hi. The bathroom's all yours." She quickly retreated into her room and closed the door.

River answered her own question, and no, it could not possibly get more awkward between them. She took a quick shower, dressed, and returned to the living room to see Dee on the phone.

"How is this my fault? I simply asked for a favor. I need to get this straightened out. I'll call you back. Thanks, Marcus."

She turned to River. "Have you heard anything about a problem with the maintenance records from China? It sounds like there may be an issue with them."

"I haven't heard anything, but I was just about to call in for a status check."

She dialed the accident investigation headquarters. "This is Dr. Dawson. Can you transfer me to maintenance records? Thanks."

While she waited, she looked at Dee, who appeared closed off, like her shield was firmly in place.

"Have you guys gotten the rest of the records? What do you mean, they're not cooperating? Did you tell them we can get a federal subpoena for them? Let me speak to Ronald Moore. Yes. I'll stand by."

She looked at Dee, whose expression was all business, the moment of happiness from last night gone. "Do you know what's going on, Dee?"

"When you're done, I'll tell you what my partner said."

River returned to her call. "Really? That's very strange. Yes. I can get there in about three hours. I'll let you know what we find out."

"So what did Ronald Moore say?" Dee asked.

"This is one of the more bizarre things I've ever heard of. The Chinese government is upset that we're demanding the records from their aircraft-overhaul facility. They claim they supplied all known records, plus all their modification records, to the company in Kenya that paid to have the plane converted from a freighter to a passenger jet. The company in Kenya has certified letters stating that all records were included in the sale of the aircraft to Relax Air two years ago. And now, Relax Air claims they don't have them. The FBI in Las Vegas is serving them a subpoena for the records today. Ronald wants us to go to their company headquarters in Las Vegas to make sure we get them back. What does your partner know about this?"

"Essentially the same about the Chinese government. Marcus told me they're upset because the request came through my friend in the consulate's office, and not through their normal protocol. He also told me the hotshot CEO of Relax Air, Lorenzo Franklin, has some very questionable business associates. Marcus thinks money is funneling to them from international crime bosses, namely Russians."

"Russians can't own a US airline," River said.

"Exactly. That's why even though Relax Air is a US company, it's controlled by an international holding company in Turkey, which is a subsidiary of another company in Africa. It's a big shell game designed to be difficult to track, in order to hide the money."

"Well, this should be an interesting trip to Las Vegas."

❖

River had decided to drive the ninety miles from Tucson to Phoenix because they could find more flights to Las Vegas from there. It was difficult for Dee to sit next to her in the car, knowing she couldn't reach over and hold River's hand. In fact, after everything that had happened between them last night, it was closer to torture. She still felt hurt and rejected.

Ordinarily, if a woman rebuffed her, she was able to shrug it off, not that she hit on women that frequently. But she couldn't dismiss River so easily. She'd showed Dee a side of herself that was a surprise, a vulnerable, tender, and very passionate side. During the time they were making out in the pool, she'd sensed that something broke, a dam of restraint and control that she rarely let go of.

When River had trusted her in the pool, she'd felt honored. She'd also been overwhelmed with desire when she realized River wanted her too. Thinking about the electricity that flowed between them when she'd kissed River aroused her all over again, and when River had pulled her close with her knees, she was done for. Dee couldn't go there, especially after River was so firm with her that no romantic entanglements were possible.

She couldn't be mad at River. Dee understood she was attempting to keep their relationship professional, but she still didn't have to like it. Maybe River was right, and they shouldn't explore the possibility of anything romantic. As the survivor of a plane crash, she knew what she was talking about, but Dee certainly didn't like anyone telling her they knew what was best for her. That brought back bad memories of her father doing the same thing.

"You're very quiet this morning," River commented.

Dee formulated her response carefully. "Look. I'm sorry about last night. I misunderstood and pushed you to take things further, but I don't want there to be any awkwardness between us. I can assure you, it will not happen again. You're probably right. Getting involved in the middle of an investigation is a bad idea. I suppose

I should be glad at least one of us kept her head. Let's just forget it happened and move on."

"Okay, and thanks for understanding. You're right about one thing. I don't know anything about you, except that you're an army vet and a cop, but I would like to know more. Did you always want to go into the army?"

Dee laughed out loud. "Hell, no. It never even crossed my mind until my high school principal suggested I enlist."

"Will you tell me about that?"

"It's a long, boring story, but I will, if you insist. When I was eighteen, my father kicked out of my home for being a lesbian."

The fear and shame crept up on her like an old ghost as she retold her story. She hated remembering anything about him, or about that awful night.

"Why did he kick you out for being gay?"

"It was my eighteenth birthday, the youth group at church had a cake for me, and my friend, Mary Ellen, wanted to give me a birthday kiss. We went behind the church building, and it was definitely a mind-blowing kiss, which turned into several, and my father walked up on us. Because he was a fundamentalist Baptist preacher, he told me, 'You are a disobedient sinner and an abomination. You're a bad influence on Naomi, and you're no longer a part of this family. You have to leave, and don't come back.'"

Dee almost choked on his words as she spat them out.

"Oh, my gosh. What did you do?"

"I had one friend during that terrible time, my high school principal and tennis coach, Dr. Catherine Wilkinson. She and her partner, Gretchen, had a small cattle ranch outside Killeen, Texas, where I grew up, and they let me stay for free in their garage apartment. Otherwise, I'd have had to sleep in my car, my trusty Ford Pinto." *I wonder how she and Gretchen are doing? I need to call them and tell them about Naomi.*

"That sounds like quite a risk for a school principal to take. Why'd they let you stay at their house?"

"Because no one else would help me. Everyone in town was

afraid of my father. He would stand on an actual soapbox in front of the county courthouse and publicly call out people in town, naming their sins, such as adultery, sloth, or greed, and telling them to repent. I was allowed to have friends only at church, and he made sure everyone shunned me. My principal, Dr. Wilkinson, wasn't afraid of him because she'd already had battles with him over textbooks and other stuff. So Doc and Gretchen took me in, or I would have been just another homeless gay teenager living on the streets."

"That's awful, Dee."

Remembering Doc and Gretchen, and their happy home, made her smile. "When I showed up on their front porch sixteen years ago, I was a hot mess. Doc and Gretchen took care of me and told me I wasn't a worthless piece of shit. They gave me a safe haven when I really needed it. One day, out of the blue, Doc asked me, "Have you ever thought about the army?" I remember I laughed so hard, Coke came out of my nose, and I made quite a mess."

River laughed at her description.

"I think at the time I said, 'No, that was one of the many subjects Daddy didn't let us talk about.' But then the lightbulb went off when Doc said these magic words, 'You've got enough credits to graduate with your high school diploma, and you just turned eighteen, so you don't need your parents' permission to enlist.'

"Doc knew I wanted to go to college to study medicine, but that was impossible after I got kicked out. She told me the army would pay for college classes I could take in my off-duty time, and I could work toward my bachelor's degree. She signed me up for the next entrance test and took me to talk to an army recruiter. The recruiter really liked my test scores and told me I was qualified for any military specialty. The idea of protecting my fellow soldiers appealed to me, so I chose military police, and that's how I ended up in the army. That's when my life went from lost to found."

"So if you'd never considered military service, how'd you like the army?"

"The training was difficult, but I took to it like a duck to water. I adapted well to the discipline of army life. They kept me busy, and things were very simple. Every minute of our day was scheduled, and I just had to follow orders, be where I was supposed to be, help out my squad, and wear my uniform correctly. The structure of my life in the army was predictable, it gave me something to hold on to, and it was such a relief from the chaos back home."

"What'd you think of your training?"

"I liked learning about law enforcement and force protection, but I really loved weapons training. I scored well on my marksmanship tests and I especially liked defensive tactics. I got real good with close hand-to-hand combat and mixed martial arts. They sent me on my first deployment to the desert six months after I completed my MP certification."

"What'd you think about being deployed to the Sandbox?"

"It was dangerous, difficult, dirty, but also exciting. We worked our asses off. I learned a lot, and that's when I met my first real girlfriend, Marci, an air force air traffic controller."

"Well, at least you had the good taste to get involved with an air force woman. So what happened to Marci?"

"Turns out, I was just a wartime romance, and she already had a partner waiting for her back at her home base. It was a 'TDY-rules-apply' situation for her."

"I remember that from our overseas KC-10 trips. I'd never heard the term 'temporary duty rules' before, but then the guys in my squadron would take off their wedding rings as soon as we'd land in some foreign country, and some of them would screw anything. This one guy, a real hound dog, was married to a woman pilot in our squadron. He would screw around behind her back, and all the guys kept quiet about it. I thought it was gross."

"Yeah. There were plenty of guys in the army like that too."

"It sounds like you really liked the army. Why'd you get out?"

"Because I couldn't do what they ordered me to do."

"What do you mean?"

Dee grew quiet remembering the bitter decision she'd been forced to make ten years ago, a decision that had changed her life. River seemed genuinely interested, so she continued.

"I loved the service and was doing really well. I took college classes, got my bachelor's degree in criminal justice, graduated from

US Army Officer Candidate School, and was number one in my class at Advanced Investigation School. I was a second lieutenant, I was doing important, interesting work, I had money to spare, and my life was great, until my boss assigned me to investigate a soldier accused of homosexuality. I knew this guy and we were friends, but I couldn't rat him out to the army just so they could take away his career and ruin his life. He was a good soldier, and they tried to give him a dishonorable discharge."

"I'm sorry you had to do that. The air force had witch hunts too when I was in. I came very close to getting outed. So what'd you tell your boss?"

"First of all, I informed Michael, my friend, that he was under investigation. Then I told him what not to do and what to say when he got interrogated. I filed my report, with no evidence of any misconduct, and they left Michael alone. After that, I knew I couldn't hide who I was while at the same time prosecuting my fellow soldiers for being gay. So I stayed on the down-low until my time was up, got out, became a civilian cop, and moved to Portland."

"Do you ever miss it?"

"Only a little. I loved the army, and it probably saved me, but I couldn't lie about who I was anymore. I'm happy I'm free now."

Chapter Twenty-three

River could identify with much of what Dee said about the army because of her own time in the air force. She'd learned the necessity of hiding her true self from her first days at the US Air Force Academy. That was the price you paid to serve your country and fly military jets, if you were a lesbian. River had reached the same conclusion as Dee about one thing: lying about yourself damages your soul. Even though River had been medically discharged from the air force, she would've faced the same difficult decision as Dee did if she'd been able to stay.

"Thank you for telling me about your time in the army. It's too bad you weren't able to continue your career on active duty. It sounds like you were doing very well. And I'm really sorry to hear about your father. I can't comprehend why any parent would do that to their own child."

River wanted to reach over and take Dee's hand, but she stopped herself. She didn't want to give Dee any mixed messages.

"You're lucky you weren't raised by fundamentalists. My father could take any verse from the Bible and twist it to justify his actions. Everything was very black and white in that world, and unquestioning obedience was required. I'd planned to escape from my parents by going far away to college, but that didn't happen. Even worse than getting kicked out of my home was that my father wouldn't let me see, or speak to, Naomi anymore."

Dee's voice had a catch when she mentioned Naomi.

"So you didn't talk to her for sixteen years because of your father?"

Dee hesitated before answering. Clearly it was hard for her to talk about the subject. "Yes. Our father kept us apart because he hated me for being a lesbian. Only after he died, four weeks ago, was Naomi able to get in touch with me."

"You mean you couldn't call her or write her at all? That's just cruel, to both of you."

"Yeah. He was. I wrote to her several times but never heard back. I saw her only one time after I left home—after I'd finished basic training and went back to Killeen to see her. By then she'd started high school, so I wore my uniform and showed up at our old school. I remember I found Doc coaching the tennis team and saw Naomi from behind, hitting tennis balls against the backboard. Doc intercepted me before I could talk to her and told me I had to leave the school grounds immediately."

"Why did she say that if she was your friend?"

"I'll never forget what she told me that day. When I asked why, she said, "Because your father is a vengeful man. He said he'd have you arrested if you ever showed up here looking for Naomi." She also told me my father had threatened to cause trouble for Doc and Gretchen if they helped me. So I had no choice. I turned around and left before Naomi saw me."

River's heart broke for both Naomi and Dee. She also felt grateful to her own father. He hadn't been around much, but at least he'd never tried to hurt her. She didn't care if their situation was awkward; she reached for Dee's hand. "I'm sorry you had to go through that."

"Stupidly, I thought if my father could see that I was doing well in the army as a soldier, he might not think I was an abomination anymore. I was wrong. After that visit, I realized he was so rigid in his thinking that he would never change his mind about me. After I left Killeen for the last time, Doc called me and warned me to not try to see my sister again, and she promised to look out for Naomi." Dee removed her hand from River's and reached into her pocket for a tissue. She turned her face away and looked out the side window.

River was miserable driving knowing she couldn't say anything, or do anything, to help her. She didn't have a right to. Hearing about Dee losing her family at eighteen brought back her own loss of her mother when she was thirteen. She and Dee had an intimate knowledge of each other that neither of them wanted. They both knew what it was like to walk through Hell, they knew what the pit of despair looked like, and they both knew their loss would never go away.

River wanted to curse Dee's father, and, if he wasn't already dead, she would've liked to punch him in the face for what he did to his precious daughter. *She is precious to me.*

River wasn't doing very well at containing her emotions. Her eyes teared up, and she couldn't see clearly, so she turned off the highway into a rest area. When she came to a stop and shut off the engine, she reached for Dee, and they held each other tightly until the tears passed.

"I'm sorry. I didn't mean to make you cry," Dee said.

"It happens, and when it does, I just have to ride it out. Are you okay?"

"Yeah. I'm just tired of it. I want this investigation to end so I can figure out how to go on with my life."

River separated herself from Dee's arms, and they drove the rest of the way to the Phoenix airport in silence.

❖

After taking their seats on the flight to Las Vegas, River said, "Pull your lap belt tight. This is always a very bumpy flight."

"Why is it always bumpy?"

"Thermal updrafts from the sun's uneven heating of the desert floor."

"In other words, because it's hot?"

"That's what I said."

River was truly a nerd about flying. It was kind of cute when she used technobabble like that and assumed Dee knew what she was taking about. Just as River predicted, as soon as they were airborne, the airplane bounced around like they were driving over logs. It reminded Dee of riding in the back of a helo in Afghanistan. Unlike many of her male buddies, she was proud that she'd never hurled in the back, although this plane ride was pushing her right to the edge.

After a firm landing and a walk through the noisy airport with its slot machines, they emerged into the hot desert air. A black limousine with a Relax Air logo on it stood waiting for them.

"This is nice. Think they'd mind if I had a bottle of water?"

"I'm sure they won't," River answered.

"So exactly what are we doing here?"

"We're supposed to meet the FBI guys at the company headquarters, where they'll serve a warrant for all maintenance documents. We'll check that the records are complete, take them with us, and fly back to Portland."

"Sounds easy enough."

When they arrived at the garish, ultra-modern, glass-walled headquarters building, an attractive young woman in a very snug dress and stiletto heels met them.

"Good afternoon, Dr. Dawson. I'm Giselle, Mr. Franklin's secretary. If you and your assistant will follow me, I'll take you to Mr. Franklin's office."

River started to correct her, but Dee stopped her. It was better they not know she was a cop right now. Something here didn't feel right. She would play River's assistant for now and keep her eyes open.

Giselle took them to the top floor of the high-rise building and into an opulent office decorated with original art, a huge desk, and a panoramic view of Las Vegas. "Please take a seat. Mr. Franklin will be with you very soon."

Dee glanced around the room. No family pictures, very expensive furniture, and a wet bar with crystal decanters. This guy was a player who liked to show off his money. As she was about to tell River, Lorenzo Franklin came into the room like he was entering a stage. He wasn't tall, maybe five-foot-six, wore an expensive silk suit with chunky gold rings, and had a manufactured smile of white porcelain veneers that could light up The Strip. A cloud of expensive cologne following him, he looked like he'd come out of central casting for *The Godfather*.

"Ladies, ladies, welcome. It's a pleasure to have you visit. Dr. Dawson, what an honor. Would either of you care for a drink?"

"No, thank you. We're just here to pick up the maintenance records."

He moved to sit behind his big desk, leaned back, and put his feet on the corner of the desk in an obvious show of his power. Dee tried not to laugh at him.

"Well, you see, Dr. Dawson, that's where I'm confused. We've already released all the aircraft records to the NTSB. I'm afraid you made a trip here for nothing." He smiled at them with his big fake grin.

He's lying.

River walked over to the edge of his desk, put her hands wide on it, and loomed over him.

"All records of any mishap aircraft will be immediately surrendered to the National Transportation Safety Board, where they will be impounded for examination. You will produce all records and deliver them to me now."

"Dr. Dawson, you don't need to get upset. Please calm down. I can't give you what I don't have. It's as simple as that."

His smarmy grin appeared again. River locked eyes with him, took out her phone, and dialed a number. She spoke loud and clear. "Agent Farris, are you and your men in the lobby? Very good. I'll have Detective Rawlings bring you up to the CEO's office. He would like for you to personally hand him your federal warrant. Then you can begin searching this entire building, starting with his office, until we find the records we need. See you in a minute. Thanks."

She ended the call and put her phone in her pocket, while still staring at him. "Mr. Franklin, this is your last opportunity to cooperate fully with this investigation, or things are going to happen that you will greatly regret. What's it going to be?"

"You don't need to make threats, little lady. Just relax, and I'll see what I can do for you."

"Your choice." River turned to her, "Detective Rawlings, please bring Agent Farris and his men up here to start their evidence search."

"Yes, Dr. Dawson. I'll be right back with them."

Dee ran down to the elevator and punched the button for the lobby. This guy was an ass, but he was hiding something. What possible reason could he have for withholding those records?

River remained standing in front of Franklin's desk, waiting for Dee to return.

Franklin spoke quickly, "This really isn't necessary. Why don't you call off your dogs, come back tomorrow, and I'll have everything you want all ready for you."

"So you do have the records. I don't think you understand what's about to happen. If you don't produce them immediately, I call the FAA Administrator, tell them you're refusing to cooperate, and they will revoke your FAA Operating Certificate. That means all your planes are grounded, all your flights are canceled, and no more money is coming in. How well do you think that will go over with your investors?"

Fear flashed across his face. "Look. You don't want to do that, and you don't know what you're talking about. We had to cut a few corners when we started up, but everything is good now."

His delusional thinking stunned River. "One of your aircraft blew up in midair, over three hundred people died, their families are devastated, and you think everything is good now? If you, or anyone in your company, caused this accident to happen, I will find out who's responsible. I will report your refusal to cooperate to the insurance company, and they will not make any liability payouts until I tell them the report is complete. You'll be on your own to cover all the damage awards and lawsuits from this accident, which will be in the multi-millions. You'll probably bankrupt your airline."

His eyes darted from side to side, and he looked very nervous. He picked up his phone. "Tommy, the accident people are here for the records from flight 402. I'm going to send someone down to you to pick them up. Please give her everything." He hung up.

"Fine. You win. We have nothing to hide. Just go down one floor, and Tommy, our records manager, will give you want you want. I'll stay here to talk to the FBI men. Sorry for the misunderstanding."

"Thank you. You know, it doesn't have to be like this. We're only trying to figure out what happened to the plane so we can save lives."

River left his office and walked to the elevator to go down one floor. When she stepped out of it, Tommy was waiting for her and led her to a big room with large file cabinets.

"Flight 402 records are in this cabinet. I'll get you a box for them."

He unlocked the file cabinet, pulled the heavy drawer open for her, and left to get a box. River scanned the folder titles, looking for the ones she needed. As she was reaching for a folder, a hot, meaty hand covered her mouth and pinched off her nose. A powerful hairy arm wrapped around her neck, choking her. River fought back as hard as she could, struggling for air, and then everything went dark.

❖

Dee, Agent Farris, and his three men got off the elevator and walked into the CEO's office, where Franklin was feverishly shredding papers. River was gone.

"Stop what you're doing. Where is she?" Dee demanded.

"I don't know. She's probably in the ladies' room."

Dee ran behind his desk, grabbed his silk tie in her fist, slammed him up against a glass wall, and yelled in his face. "Tell me where she is right fucking now."

"One floor down," he choked out.

She ran down the hall, threw open the stairwell door, and flew down the stairs three at a time. Listening for sounds, she heard a muffled noise around the corner, ran to the sound, and saw the back of a big man, his arm around River's neck and her feet dangling from the floor. Dee drew her weapon and aimed at the center of his torso *Take the shot. No. She's too close to him.*

Dee charged him at him full speed, plowed into him like she was sliding into second base, and directed her feet to hit the back of his knees. He crumpled backward to the floor and let go of River as he fell. Dee jumped up, grabbed River, moved her to safety, turned, and pointed her weapon at his heart. She was focused, calm, with her finger on the trigger. *Just a tiny pull, and he'll never hurt River again.*

River coughed and croaked out, "Don't do it, Dee. He's not worth it."

This ugly, gross pig had tried to kill River. Just a little pressure on the trigger and she could watch his chest explode in a cloud of red.

The FBI agents ran into the room. "We've got him, Detective. You can stand down. Cuff him, Rogers," Agent Farris said.

Dee moved her finger off the trigger but kept her weapon trained on him. After Agent Rogers flipped him over and handcuffed him, she returned her gun to her shoulder holster and went to River's side.

River couldn't speak. She could only rub her red throat and cough.

Dee gathered her into her arms. "Oh, my God."

She turned and shouted to Agent Farris, "We need an ambulance now!"

River's voice was raspy and weak. "Get records." She pointed to the open file cabinet drawer.

Dee went to the cabinet and pulled out the thick folder of maintenance records. Just then, she heard the sound of sirens and looked out the glass wall to see an ambulance pulling into the driveway. "Can you walk, River?"

She nodded and Dee helped her stand up. River turned to look into her eyes, reached for her, and pulled her into an embrace. She held her tightly, her lips next to Dee's ear. "Thank you for saving me."

Chapter Twenty-four

After the doctor took X-rays and examined River, she and Dee sat together in the waiting area. Dee was holding her hand and wouldn't let go. Her neck was sore, it hurt to swallow, and she was getting some wicked bruises on her throat.

The doctor came out to talk to her. "Good news. The X-ray doesn't show any damaged vertebrae in your neck, and the swelling in your throat will gradually go away. Keep ice on it, take the pain meds, minimize talking, and come back if you have any trouble breathing. I don't want you to leave town for at least twenty-four hours. I'd really like to admit you, just to keep an eye on you tonight."

River shook her head. "No, thanks," she said, her voice barely above a whisper.

The doctor turned to Dee. "And you're staying with her tonight? Keep checking on her every hour."

"Yes. I'll be with her, and I'll check on her. Thank you so much."

He looked at River. "You're going to be all right, but you had a very close call. The nurse will come back with your discharge papers. Please take care."

As they left the hospital, Dee turned to her. "Can I get you anything?"

River nodded. "Ice cream."

Dee chuckled. "You almost get your head torn off, and now you want ice cream. What flavor?"

"DQ."

"Dairy Queen soft-serve ice cream?"

River nodded.

"Excellent choice. We'll stop at a DQ on the way to the hotel. I got us a room at one off the Strip, where it's not so noisy."

After they got into the car, River reclined her seat and closed her eyes, exhausted.

"We're here, River. Are you okay to walk?"

She nodded, got out of the car, and followed Dee into the hotel. Still shaky, she found a chair to sit in while Dee got the room key. Her eyes drifted closed, and she shuddered, feeling the hairy arm choking her again. She jumped when Dee touched her shoulder and saw a concerned look on Dee's face.

"Come on. Our room's ready."

After Dee opened the hotel room door, they went inside, she put the ice cream in the minifridge and then came over to River and pulled her into a gentle hug. She didn't say anything, just held on to River, then she held her tighter. "I can't believe I almost lost you."

River returned her embrace. Feeling the solidness of Dee's body pressed into her own confirmed what she already knew. She was in love with Dee and wanted to be with her from now on. Everything thing else in the world seemed meaningless. Her work, her reputation, airplanes, other people—it all meant nothing if she didn't have Dee.

They slowly separated, then sat down to eat, the cold Dairy Queen ice cream a great relief to her sore throat.

"Does it hurt bad?" Dee asked.

"Not too much. The pain pills help. Could I have some of your fries? I guess I am hungry."

"Here. I got you your own order. We have to keep ice on your neck, or you're going to have some very nasty bruises."

River was overcome with fatigue, plus she felt just the edge of a migraine starting. When she got up to get her medicine, she felt light-headed. "Crap." She had to sit down again.

"What's the matter? Do you need something?"

"I just need to sleep, and I need my migraine medicine. Could you please get it for me?"

"Sure. Let me help you."

Dee brought her the meds, put her arm around her waist to steady her, and guided her to the bed. She turned down the covers, sat her down on the bed, then knelt to take off her shoes.

"Will you lie down with me?"

"Of course. Just give me a minute."

River heard Dee check the hotel room door locked, brush her teeth, and change into a tee shirt and gym shorts. After she closed the drapes, she finally climbed into bed with River, where she moved over and curled up next to her back. Dee put her arm around her waist and scooted next to her like a spoon.

"Is this all right? I'd like to hold you."

"Yes. You feel perfect. I'm fading fast. Good night."

She took Dee's hand and held it between her breasts. Dee's body felt like Heaven next to hers. As she drifted off to sleep, she knew she was safe in Dee's arms.

❖

Dee stayed awake most of the night guarding River. She tossed and turned, and cried out in her sleep twice, but Dee was able to get her back to sleep by gently rubbing her back. When Dee closed her eyes, the image of River being choked brought her to the edge of panic. Having her hand next to River's heart, where she could feel her steady heartbeat and her deep breathing, helped her calm down.

Even though she was watching over River, the smoldering desire was still there. She wouldn't do anything about it, though. She simply relished the feel of River's body next to hers, but she needed to figure this out.

Maybe River was right that she had to go through the grief process before they had any chance at being together. But she was certain about one thing. She wanted to explore the possibilities with River. She had no idea how to make it work, but she was determined to find a way. Maybe when the investigation was over, which should be soon, they could talk.

River would figure out what caused the accident, and then Dee would go see Naomi's family, and she'd attend counseling with Dr. Lopez. She needed her work back, her life back, and maybe even a future with River. She would walk through Hell to get it.

After Dee finally fell asleep, she sensed movement against her back. It was warm and sensuous, with light pressure on the back of her legs. She moved her own hips in reply. A soft hand moved across her waist, pulling her closer, then inching lower. Hot breath blew on her neck, and firm breasts pressed into her shoulder blades. Her consciousness slowly came to the surface, and she was fully aware of River touching her, wanting her. Ignoring what River had told her earlier, she put her hand on top of River's and guided it to where she needed it most, her throbbing center.

Dee was already soaking wet and swollen with desire. River would soon discover the depths of her arousal when she slipped her fingers under the waistband of Dee's shorts. She continued lower, lightly tugging at Dee's hair, then tracing her fingertips achingly slow across her hard ridge. Dee ground her bottom into River's lap. When River caressed her slick flesh, Dee rolled onto her back, pulled off her shorts, and opened for her.

River drew circles on her skin, then moved lower, teasing her entrance. Dee raised her hips. "Kiss me."

River kissed her deeply as she slid her fingers into her. She was deliberate, slow, and fully in control. Dee's desire made her grind her own pelvis into River. Her hungry kisses matched the rhythm of River's pummeling fingers. She was taking Dee to the moon. She wanted River everywhere, all over her, in her, and gripped her torso as River's pace increased. She trusted her and clung to her as River took her over the edge of a cliff. River was relentless and wouldn't stop, even after wave after wave of pleasure made her shudder like a rag doll.

"Stop, please. I have to catch my breath."

River stopped her strokes but kept her fingers deep inside her. "You're so beautiful."

She placed tender kisses all over her face, then rested her damp head on Dee's heaving chest. She slowly withdrew and put her thigh between Dee's legs, pressing against her still-throbbing center. As her pounding heart slowed back to normal, a nagging question interfered with her bliss. "I'm not complaining, but I thought you said we couldn't do this."

River propped herself up on one elbow, the streams of soft morning light through the drapes making her blond hair look like a halo.

"I know what I said, but I was wrong. Today was almost my last day on earth, and I'm not going to lose one more day with you. I don't care what anybody else says. I love you, Dee, and I can't live without you."

Dee was stunned and overjoyed. "I love you too."

She wrapped her arms around River and breathed in her scent. The roller coaster of emotions she'd been on the last several days made her hold tight to River. She had gone from seeing her almost killed before her eyes to making love with her. It was almost too much. She kissed River's forehead. "So how are you feeling? You were pretty restless last night."

"I'm good. Sore around my neck, but not too bad. How's it look?"

"Yikes. It's bad. I hope you have a hoodie to cover your bruises. Are you hungry? Can I get you anything?"

"Are you in a hurry to go somewhere? Because I'd like to stay in bed with you for a while." River moved her hand up under Dee's tee shirt and started massaging her breast.

"No. I don't want to go anywhere. I just wanted to make sure you're okay. Oh, that feels amazing."

River kissed Dee while she tugged at her nipple and pressed her leg into her.

"I want to make love to you, River, if you're up for that?"

"Only one way to find out. Take me."

That was all she had to say. Dee ripped off her remaining clothes, removed River's, and threw the covers back. She rolled River onto her back and admired her luscious curves, especially her perfect round breasts. Dee settled between River's legs and lowered her mouth to feast on River's prominent nipples. River ran her fingers through Dee's hair as she sucked and kneaded. Then she felt slight pressure on the top of her head as River urged her lower.

Dee felt heat radiating off the apex of River's thighs. She took her time kissing the length of River's stomach. Her mouth watered to taste her. She dragged her own breasts across River's folds, opening her like the petals of a delicate rose. When she tasted River's flesh for the first time, she felt such a rush of electricity, she thought she might explode. With her tongue, she tasted every part of River, and with her hands, she pressed River's knees open. They moved as one, with their own unique ebb and flow. River's body told Dee what she wanted, and Dee followed her undulating hips, accelerating her tongue and entering her. River gasped and grabbed Dee's hair, pulling her face in.

Dee was unstoppable as she stroked River, taking her higher and higher with both her tongue and fingers. River relinquished her last bit of control and let Dee have her. She writhed, and moaned, and sang for Dee, until River gripped her fingers with her flesh and climaxed, shuddering with each wave. Dee held her firmly but didn't stop.

"Please. I can't take any more."

"You surrender?"

"Yes. Completely. Come here."

River pulled Dee's face to her and kissed her deeply, longingly. Dee raised herself up to look at her. River's face was so beautiful, so content, and she radiated happiness. Dee traced her fingertip over River's swollen lower lip, across her jaw line, down her slender neck, and then she kissed along her collarbone. River answered by moving against her again. Dee never wanted it to end.

CHAPTER TWENTY-FIVE

Day 9

After a luxurious morning of lovemaking with Dee, River was floating on air. Dee was so much more than she'd ever expected. Her passion came through every time she kissed or touched her. Dee made love to her with such abandon and intensity, River thought she might never return to earth.

When she felt Dee's arms around her and put her head on Dee's shoulder, she was encircled with love and tenderness. It was different, but it was the most love and security she'd felt since her mother died. River was aware, for the first time in a long while, that she was hopeful for the future, as long as it included Dee.

After a lovely shower together, they packed up their things, including the precious maintenance records River had almost lost her life over, and left for the airport to catch a flight back to Portland. It was so great to be open and honest with Dee about how she felt, and so amazing to know Dee loved her too. Only one thing remained between them. She had to give Dee the suitcase with Naomi's letters.

Now that they'd determined the explosion had originated in the center accessory compartment, the small suitcase filled with letters was no longer relevant to the investigation. She would return them to her, Dee could go through them as she was able to, maybe even with a therapist, and then they could talk about building a life together.

The plane flight to Portland was uneventful, and River was

still tired from her near-death experience, so she closed her eyes, held Dee's hand, and slept for most of the flight. After landing in Portland, they drove to Redmond to deliver the records and check the progress of the airframe reconstruction.

On the drive through the mountains, River tried to figure out the best way to tell Dee about the letters, but instead, Dee wanted to ask her questions.

"So, why are you single?"

"Well, I used to be, until last night. Why are you?"

"It's not like I'm opposed to being in a relationship. Quite the opposite, in fact. I just haven't found a woman I could really trust. My first girlfriend, Marci, the air traffic controller, led me to believe she was single, but she wasn't. I dated a few women in the army, but we were all so afraid of 'Don't ask, don't tell,' it never worked out."

"What about after you became a civilian and moved to Portland?"

"That was better, because I didn't have to fear losing my job if they found out I was a lesbian, but it certainly wasn't easy. I met a woman I really cared for on a softball team, but she wasn't good with fidelity, so that didn't last. I also was gone too much with work. That lady required a great deal of attention, and I just couldn't give it to her. That's something I really like about you."

"What is?"

"That you're very independent and self-sufficient. So, you still haven't answered my first question. Why are you single?"

River was quiet as she thought about her long and checkered past, with many attempts at love and many failures.

"I think I've had the same problem as you, with being away too much for work. In my case, the phone would ring in the middle of the night, and I'd be gone for a month. Not too many women are willing to put up with a partner who's out of town half the time. When I was in the air force, we were always leaving for a new assignment to a new base, so we could never be stationed together. I was with one woman for five years. We met in graduate school at USC after I was medically discharged."

"What happened with her?"

"I'm not really sure why it didn't work out. She wanted a white picket fence and kids, but I wasn't ready for that. We tried, but I couldn't give her the commitment she needed. We're still friends, but I don't see her too often anymore."

They both were quiet for a while, and then Dee squeezed her hand. "I don't care about our pasts. I'm only interested in being with you now, and in making a future with you."

"Me too, Dee."

River was filled with a happiness she hadn't felt in a very long time.

❖

When they arrived at the hangar, everyone was buzzing with activity. Major progress had been made on the airframe reconstruction, and they'd found the digital flight data recorder. As Dee and River walked into the big hangar, all noise stopped, and everyone turned to look at them. Then the applause started. Everyone was clapping for them, even Ronald Moore. He approached them with his hand extended, shaking hands with both of them.

"Well done, both of you. The FBI filled me in on what happened at Relax Air headquarters. We're so glad you're all right, River, and I'm very happy you were with her, Detective Rawlings. Both the man who attacked you and the CEO, Lorenzo Franklin, are in FBI custody. The FBI intercepted Franklin at the airport as he was trying to skip the country in a private jet. Let's get these maintenance records scanned into the computer."

Dee noticed River was uncomfortable with the applause, so she raised her arm and gave the men a thumbs-up to acknowledge them.

"Let's see if they found any more pieces," River said.

They walked around the airframe within the scaffolding, then went to the CAC area on the underside of the plane. The missing section was more defined, with the perimeter filled in by more found parts.

"This confirms the CAC was definitely the origin point of the explosion, but we still need to figure out why it exploded," River said.

"Someone could've planted a device in here. You had no trouble opening the hatch from the outside."

"That's certainly a possibility. There's no lock on this hatch when it's closed because only maintenance uses it, so it's not hard to open if a person has access to the ramp."

"Where's the stuff from inside the CAC? Like all the batteries and radios we saw on the plane in Tucson?"

"Excellent question. We have some shelves against the wall where we put the unidentified parts. They might be over there."

Considering the size of the aircraft, there weren't that many unidentified parts on the shelf racks. The unknown pieces were grouped according to where they were found on the site map.

"Here's the part I accidentally stepped on at Angel Creek, when we were out there the first day."

River added, "And this is some wall insulation I found, also from Angel Creek."

Dee spotted something. "Look at this. I think this is the CAC hatch door."

River helped her as they lifted down the heavy mangled metal from a high shelf, and then River examined it.

"The inside surface is burned, and there's a deformed area in the center, like it was pushed outward from pressure. Let's see if it fits."

They carried the two-foot by two-foot hatch over to the side of the right engine, and two engine techs came over.

"Could you guys get a ladder and help us lift this?" River asked them.

A crowd of investigators gathered around them to watch what they were doing. The techs brought over two ten-foot ladders and carefully raised the hatch to the side of the engine cowling.

"A little higher. That's good. Now rotate the hatch ninety degrees to the right."

They did as River directed, and the edge of the hatch fit into the gash in the side of the engine like a key into a lock. The crowd gasped.

"Hey, River. Come over here."

Dee was staring at a curved piece of metal, black on one side and lime green on the other.

"I recognize this shape from when we were inside the CAC. It looks like it's part of that big pipe that went through the compartment." Dee reached for it from the top shelf. It was in a plastic evidence bag, with a numbered tag on it.

"Let's see where they found this," River said.

They located the item number on the site map. It was discovered just before Angel Creek in the debris path. River opened the plastic evidence bag, and the smell of jet fuel and scorched paint assaulted them.

River looked at it in disbelief. "Oh, no. This can't be."

❖

"What is it, River?"

"I have to see the first maintenance records on this airplane, before it was modified. I hope to God I'm wrong."

They ran over to the Maintenance Records desk.

"Let me see the records you just scanned into the computer system."

The technician handed them to River, and they went to a table to examine them.

River was irritated with herself. "I should have gone through these as soon as I got them."

"And when would you have done that? When you were in the hospital after that guy tried to kill you, or when we were in bed together in the hotel room?"

"I see your point."

"What are you looking for in these records? They're from several years ago."

River turned the maintenance book over, so she could read it in reverse order. She flipped open a page and her face fell.

"It's right here. The original tail number. It was changed when this plane was converted into a passenger airplane, like it was rebuilt into a completely new aircraft. Dee, this airplane wasn't just a cargo freighter. It used to be a KC-10."

"Why's that important? It's kind of the same plane, isn't it?"

"No. It's not. The piece of pipe you found is only in a KC-10 because it's part of the air refueling system. This is the shroud that goes around the air refueling manifold in the CAC. It's a pipe within a pipe, to prevent fuel from leaking. They had to put this in because the fuel leaked into the electrical CAC compartment from this very beginning of this airplane's life."

"Are you saying this pipe caused the explosion?" Dee asked.

"This pipe leaked fuel into the CAC. Then just the right combination of fuel vapor, oxygen, and a spark from an ignition source blew up the plane. These people never even had a chance. The worst part is, this was a known problem in the KC-10 fleet. It was a design defect by the manufacturer."

"Explain, River."

Ronald Moore had walked up behind River and heard her comment. A crowd of investigators stood around her to listen.

"When McDonnell Douglas made the DC-10 into an air refueling tanker for the US Air Force, the forward and aft baggage compartments were converted into fuel tanks, and the manifold pipe was installed to carry fuel from the different tanks out to the air refueling boom. The problem was, it cost more money to route the pipes around the CAC compartment to keep the fuel lines out of an electrical area. They knew the fuel pipes could leak because we carried different types of gas, which made the seals leak. So instead of moving the pipes properly, they put a pipe shroud around the manifold, but it leaked anyway. Fuel would soak the insulation whenever maintenance opened that compartment door. There was an accident at Barksdale Air Force Base when fuel vapors in the CAC were ignited by a spark, and it caused a KC-10 to blow up on the ramp. This is the reason our plane exploded, but there were contributing factors."

"What contributing factors?" Ronald asked.

"The tail number of this aircraft was 79-0433 when it was a KC-10. I know this plane because I was the US Air Force chief accident investigator when it was damaged in a ground mishap many years ago. It was repaired, so it was safe to fly, but the crews said it flew like it was crooked. It was in the maintenance hangar so much, the air force returned the plane to the manufacturer to be used for spare parts. It sat for several years, then was transferred to a third-party aircraft-leasing company. They sent it to the Chinese facility to be converted into a passenger plane. The Chinese mechanics should have removed the air refueling manifold and these pipes from the CAC, but they didn't."

"Why wouldn't they remove the fuel manifold if it was no longer needed?" Dee asked.

"Because it cost more money, just like always. The fact that the Relax Air management wanted to maximize their profits was the proximate cause."

"What's that term mean?"

"It is the last thing in the mishap chain of events that led to this explosion. After the air force KC-10 blew up on the ground, the FAA issued an airworthiness directive requiring the CAC to be inspected for fuel leaks before every flight, and that the insulation be removed from the compartment. Lorenzo Franklin had his mechanics ignore that directive to save time and money. If the Relax Air management had complied with this directive before flight 402 left Chicago and they'd found and repaired the fuel leak, this aircraft would not have blown up."

"So not removing the manifold allowed fuel to leak into the CAC, and failure to inspect it allowed fuel to accumulated there, but what's the ignition source?" Ronald asked.

River went over to the unknown-parts shelves and picked up the small silver piece of metal Dee had found in the creek bed.

"I believe it was this—a battery cable from one of the batteries in the CAC, which shorted out, caused the spark, and then ignited the fuel vapor."

River could see confusion on Dee's face as she tried to put this together.

"Ultimately, the Relax Air management is responsible for this accident. It wasn't a bomb, or a missile, or a lightning strike, or even pilot error. It was a chain of events that could have been prevented."

All sound in the hangar stopped. Everyone was very quiet as the real reason for the accident sunk in.

River reached for Dee and held her. "I'm so sorry."

Chapter Twenty-six

Dee didn't say anything on the drive back to the hotel. Ordinarily, she would be celebrating with her team when they solved a case, but she didn't feel like celebrating. This was personal. Part of her wished she could beat the life out of the greedy, smarmy CEO with her bare fists, but that wouldn't accomplish anything. He'd just be replaced by another CEO, who'd probably do the same thing.

Is this the futility that crime victims feel when the system that's supposed to bring justice fails them?

River reached for her hand and held it. The warmth of her touch grounded Dee in the present. She was proud of the investigative work they'd done together, but now she had to face the aftermath.

"I have to go see Naomi's family in Chicago and explain what happened."

"Would you like me to go with you?" River asked.

"That's very sweet, but I need to do this myself. There's so much I don't know about Naomi's life, but I desperately want to. I hope her husband, Bill, can fill in the gaps for me. Mostly, I want her daughters to know they have an aunt who cares about them."

River squeezed her hand.

Back at the hotel, the guys were going out to dinner, but Dee wasn't in the mood to be around them. She only wanted River.

"What will you do while I'm in Chicago?"

"I need to stay here for a few days to write my final report and make sure Ronald Moore has the correct cause factors in his NTSB report."

"Will there be any consequences for that Relax Air CEO? Will anyone go to jail over this?"

River sat down next to Dee on the bed. "He probably won't see any jail time, but his life is ruined. I recorded every word he said to me with my phone, right before he had his goon try to kill me. I also have a journalist friend who writes for the AP news service, and she'll be very interested in what he said. He'll never work in the airline business again. As for the company, Relax Air will probably go bankrupt after the lawsuits, all their employees will lose their jobs, and their planes will be resold. It's amazing how much damage one bad man can cause to so many people."

Even though Dee now understood how Naomi had died, the knowledge didn't give her any solace, and it certainly didn't give her any closure. Maybe she and Naomi's family could help each other get through this. She had to walk through her grief before she could go on with her life and before she could ever consider a future with River. The sooner she dealt with her loss, the sooner she could come back to River. She called Bill.

"Hi. Is this Bill? I'm Dee, Naomi's sister. I was hoping to come and see you in Chicago, if that's all right. Tomorrow? Yes. I can get a flight tomorrow and probably get to Chicago by late afternoon. You will? Thanks. I guess I'll see you then. Bye."

"What'd he say?"

Dee had a lump in her throat. "He's really nice. I thought he'd be upset with me for not calling sooner. He's picking me up at the airport and asked me to stay at their house with them. He said his girls, Brin and Taylor, want to meet me. This is going to be so hard, River."

"It will be, but you'll get through it, and maybe you can help Naomi's kids too. You've learned how to be resilient, Dee, and you can be there for them."

"How can I possibly help Brin and Taylor when I don't even know them, and I can barely keep it together myself?"

"Because you all love the same woman. When I was thirteen, my friend Betty told me something that really helped me. She said, 'Love never dies. Your mother will always be with you because she lives in every cell of your body, in your very DNA.' This thought gave me a great deal of comfort when I missed her, and it still does. I feel my mom's presence fairly often, like out at Angel Creek, because she loved the water. That's why she named me River. You and Naomi share the same blood, and she still lives in you, and in her daughters. That's how you can help them, and yourself, get through this."

She put her face in her hands, and River put her arms around her. They would hold each other through the dark night.

❖

Day 10

Watching Dee suffer broke River's heart and brought back memories of her mother's death. Even learning the cause of the DC-10 crash she and her mother were in hadn't eased the pain of her loss. She was glad Dee had family to go to. It was also imperative that she give the pink suitcase with Naomi's letters to Dee before she left. She was worried about not giving them to her earlier and had to find a way to make her understand.

"I'd like to take you somewhere before you go to Portland."

"Sure. That'd be nice," Dee said.

River had Dee follow in her own car, since she'd be leaving for the airport after their excursion. She led her to the Madras airport.

"This place has fabulous pancakes."

Sharing breakfast, they looked through the cafe windows and watched the small planes take off and land. River was concerned about Dee leaving, especially since she didn't know when she'd see her again. The pending separation was weighing on her.

"Love the pancakes," Dee said.

"Glad you like it. We might as well enjoy life while we can."

"What do you mean?" Dee seemed confused.

"I mean life is fickle, and it can change in an instant. So we should enjoy it now, because we can't count on it in the future."

Dee looked stunned. "You don't believe in the future?"

"I have a hard time believing things will work out, because, in my experience, they rarely do."

"Is that because you lost your mom?"

River was quiet. "Yes. But I also lost my flying, and other people I've loved, so I don't plan for the future. Maybe it's because of what I've seen and the work I do."

"Does this mean you don't believe in a future for us?"

"No. Not at all. That's what's changed for me, Dee. I do believe in us. It's the first time I've felt hopeful in a really long time."

"I'm glad to hear that, because I'm planning to come back to you after I deal with my family."

"I'm so happy to hear that. But now I have a surprise for you. Come on."

They left the restaurant, and Dee followed her out to Angel Creek. After they parked, she took Dee by the hand and led her to the place on the creek with the rock angel.

"This is such a beautiful, special spot. I love it here. Thanks for bringing me here before I have to leave," Dee said.

"Sit on this rock and close your eyes, and I'll be right back."

"Have I ever told you cops hate surprises?"

River ran back to her car and got the pink suitcase from the trunk. She carried it over to Dee and placed it at her feet. "Open your eyes."

Dee looked at the suitcase, and a puzzled look crossed her face. "What is this? It kind of looks like a funny old bag my mother…" Her expression changed when she recognized it.

"I found it, Dee, over there by the cargo container. Open it."

She flipped open the old latches, raised the lid, and stared at the letters. Then she untied the twine and picked up the first letter. Speechless at first, she turned to River. "I gave these Minnie Mouse stickers to Naomi. She was crazy about anything with Minnie on it." Dee pulled out the yellowed paper and read Naomi's first letter to her. She held the letter to her heart, bent over, and rocked back and forth.

With tears in her eyes, she stood up and pulled River into her arms. "I can't believe you found these. You have no idea what this means to me. You just answered the first prayer I've said in sixteen years. I love you so much."

River was so relieved. Her cheek was wet from Dee's happy tears. "I'm so sorry I couldn't give it to you before today."

"Did the evidence guys just release it?"

"Well, no, not exactly. Because they didn't have it. I did."

Dee looked surprised. "So you didn't turn it in, and you saved it for me? When did you find this, River?"

This was the question she'd been dreading. "A few days ago."

Dee was confused. "A few days ago? How many?"

"It was when I came across the cargo container here, five days ago."

Dee's brow furrowed. "Five days? You found this five days ago and didn't say anything to me about it. Please explain."

She took a deep breath. "At first, I didn't know what it was until I opened it."

Dee put her hand up to stop River. "Wait. Did you open Naomi's letter to me and read it? I assumed the evidence guys opened it. You knew those were letters from Naomi to me. Why would you not tell me about these for five days? I don't get it, River." Her last words were clipped.

"Well, I couldn't let you see the letters right away because the investigation wasn't complete, and you were involved with it. Also I didn't know you like I do now. I thought seeing these would be too much for you. I was afraid it would cause you to have another PTSD attack. I didn't want you to be in anymore pain."

Dee was quiet, and then she took a step back from River, still holding the precious letters. "You've made quite a few assumptions about me. You didn't think I could handle letters from my sister? Is that the only reason you kept these from me?" Dee didn't blink, waiting for her answer .

The words stuck in River's throat. "Of course I still needed your help with the investigation, and I was trying to maintain my professional integrity. I wanted to tell you, but I was worried how you'd take it. I'm sorry I didn't give these to you sooner. I apologize, and I hope you can forgive me."

Dee looked like she was made of stone, her muscles trembling, barely containing herself.

"I trusted you, River. After everything I confided to you about my past, you know what Naomi means to me. You knew how important they were to me, and yet you chose to withhold them from me for five days. Who are you to decide what I can and cannot handle? You made a decision you didn't have the right to make. The most important thing in the world to me is honesty, and you just stabbed me in the heart."

"Dee, you don't understand. I was trying to protect you."

"I don't need you to protect me. I can take care of myself. You're not the woman I thought you were. I hope your professional integrity keeps you warm tonight, because I certainly won't. Don't contact me."

She picked up the small pink suitcase, turned her back, and left. River's heart was breaking. Her philosophy of never believing in the future was confirmed once again as she watched her hope vanish into a cloud of dust.

Chapter Twenty-seven

Dee drove as fast as she could, on the verge of losing control. She screamed in the car from rage and from hurt, but worst of all was knowing that River had betrayed her. She'd been a fool to let herself fall for a woman after knowing her only ten days, and also in the midst of an aircraft crash. The shock of losing Naomi had obviously impaired her judgment when it came to River, and she should've never crossed the line with her. It didn't matter how beautiful she was, or how passionate. It was a mistake to get involved with a woman she couldn't trust. She wanted to get far away from her.

At the Portland airport, Dee checked her roller-board suitcase so she could carry on her mother's old pink Samsonite. After they were airborne, Dee opened the case and picked up the stack of letters. She looked at the first envelope again, the one River had opened. Her eyes filled when she saw her baby sister's handwriting.

Dee carefully put the letters back in the case. She couldn't read them now, or she'd be a blubbering mess. She'd read them later, maybe in a quiet place outside, away from other people. She noticed her own letters to Naomi in the blue US Army envelopes in the stack. It would be excruciating to see these letters because she'd written them during the first five years she'd been away. After that, since she'd never gotten any replies, she'd figured Naomi didn't want to hear from her, so she gave up.

She tried to sleep on the four-hour flight, but every time she closed her eyes, a vision of River naked came into her mind. She let her visions continue for a while, until she was feeling bothered, but then she had to shut them down. She opted instead for a few drinks on the plane to numb her brain.

After landing in Chicago, she looked out the window at the airplanes taxiing back and forth, like an organized ant colony. Planes were everywhere, crisscrossing so close, she was sure they'd hit each other. She imagined River taxiing her big plane through this traffic with ease. Then she saw a Relax Air DC-10 slowly taxi past them, a majestic beast dwarfing almost all the other airplanes. She looked for the CAC hatch to see if any fluid was leaking. She closed her eyes and envisioned the giant airplane covered in golden light, safe and protected from harm.

After walking through an underground tunnel with rainbow neon lights flashing overhead like a retro disco, Dee was slightly less apprehensive at the prospect of meeting Naomi's family. Her new family, maybe.

When she came out of baggage claim, Dee recognized Naomi's girls immediately. They looked just like her and Naomi when they were kids.

A handsome man with a warm smile came up to her. "Dee? I'm Bill."

They looked at each other, and Dee recognized her own sadness in his eyes. They awkwardly hugged.

"I'm so glad you're here. This is Brin, our youngest, and this is Taylor. Let me put your bags in the back."

He opened the back of their well-used family van.

"Daddy, look. It's Mama's suitcase."

They all stopped and looked at the pink suitcase.

"How'd you get that? They told me everything was destroyed," Bill said.

"My friend, who's an accident investigator, found this in the debris field and gave it to me today."

"This is a miracle, Dee. I can't believe this survived. We have so much to talk about."

❖

After Dee left her at Angel Creek, River stayed for a while, but the beautiful, serene place only made her more heartbroken. At first, Dee had been so happy to see the letters, but the look of betrayal on her face when she realized River had kept them from her was devastating. She couldn't do anything but wait for Dee to contact her and, possibly, give her another chance.

She drove back to Redmond to collect the last data for her final report. Ronald Moore came up to her and got in her face as soon as she walked in the door.

"Why didn't you tell me Dee Rawlings was a surviving family member? I never would've let her work on this investigation if I'd known that."

"That's why I didn't tell you."

"This is very unprofessional. I'm going to have to report this. You may not be allowed on any future investigation teams if you can't keep your personal life separate from your work."

"You go right ahead and do that, Ron. But I'll make sure Detective Rawlings gets the credit she deserves in my report for her major contributions to this investigation."

River gathered her documents for the last time and left the hangar. Her work here was done. She couldn't bear to stay by herself in the hotel room she'd shared with Dee for the last nine days, so she stopped there, packed her clothes, checked out, and drove to Portland to go home. She could finish her work from Denver and remove herself from Oregon. It was too painful to stay in this place where she'd fallen in love with Dee, then ruined it all because she'd underestimated her.

River would complete her official report, but then she needed to do some serious thinking about where to go from here. Being forced to work with petty jerks like Ronald Moore was wearing her down. Seeing the tragedy of an aircraft accident affect the life of a survivor like Dee brought up so many difficult memories of her own trauma. Maybe she needed to take an extended break from airplane crashes.

She would reevaluate her options and patiently wait for Dee to call.

❖

Dee was impressed with Bill and Naomi's tidy home. It was a modest size with an immaculately trimmed yard. Walking into the house, she could feel Naomi. She also sensed love and deep longing. She looked around and noticed several Lone Star decorations, plus a Dallas Cowboys clock in her kitchen. *She was always so proud of being a Texan.*

Brin, the nine-year-old, came over to Dee. "Aunt Dee. Will you open Mama's suitcase and read us her letters?"

"You know about these?"

"I found them in Grandpa's box when I was helping Mama clean out his stuff."

Dee was stunned. She had no idea her father had saved these letters.

Bill came over and sat with them on the couch. Taylor was hiding out in the kitchen.

"Your dad came to live with us two years ago, when his dementia got bad. I put his things in the attic, and Naomi was his caregiver. After he passed away a month ago, Naomi and Brin came across these letters he'd been hiding since you left home."

"Since I was *told* to leave home," Dee said.

"Yes, so she and Brin opened the first letter, and then she wanted to wait and read the rest of them with you. Naomi thought these letters could help you two reconnect."

Dee wasn't quite sure what to do, but Brin could be as persistent as her mother when she wanted something. Since they were all here, she decided to read them together.

She opened the small pink case, took out the stack of letters, and opened the first one, with the Minnie Mouse sticker on it, and read it out loud.

Dear Sissy,
   Where are you? I need you to come home! Mother

and Daddy are yelling all the time. I miss you SO MUCH.
Please come home.
  I love you, Squirt

Dee could picture Naomi's thirteen-year-old, tearstained face as she read her anguished words. She was drowning in guilt for leaving Naomi unprotected from their father. Dee loved Naomi so much and never wanted to hurt her, but obviously she broke Naomi's heart when she abandoned her.

Brin snuggled up next to Dee on the couch and put her little warm hand on top of hers. "Don't be sad, Aunt Dee. Mama told us all about why Grandpa made you go away because you were gay. He was a bad man when he did that."

"She told you that?"

Taylor stood at the doorway watching them from a safe distance. "Yeah. She did. She also said you taught her how to stand up to Grandpa. Will you read the next one?"

Taylor reminded Dee so much of herself. She looked like a little clone, with the same dark-green eyes and some of her bad-ass dyke attitude. She certainly might be a future lesbian in training. Dee pulled out the next letter from the stack, in one of her blue army envelopes.

Dear Squirt,
  I miss you so much! So far, I really like the army. We get up real early and it's hard work, but I'm learning a lot, and I've made some friends. I hope I can come home and see you after I graduate from basic training in a few weeks. Please write to me!
  I love you, Sissy

"So she never saw any of your letters because your father took all of them. I'm surprised he kept them, especially since we weren't allowed to say your name in his presence," Bill said.

"Wow. I knew he was a control freak, but I never thought he

wouldn't let Naomi see my letters. She must have thought I didn't care about her anymore. That fucking old bastard. Sorry. I didn't mean to swear in front of you girls."

"That's nothing compared to what Mama used to say." Brin seemed almost proud of her mother.

"I wish I could have heard her cuss just once. She was such a goody two-shoes growing up."

"Well, we have a really funny video of Mama cussing up a storm. Want to see it?" Taylor asked.

"Sure I do."

Taylor sat on the other side of Dee, punched buttons on the TV remote, and brought up the video clip of Naomi on the screen. It was Christmas, with a decorated tree in the background and holiday music playing. Naomi was teaching Taylor how to make cookies, and when she opened the oven door, thick smoke poured off burned cookies. Naomi was so mad, she let loose with a string of curse words, stomped over to the back door, flung it open, and hurled the smoking cookie sheets outside into the snow. She stomped back into the kitchen, still cursing. The video ended with Naomi looking directly at the camera and saying, "Merry fucking Christmas!"

They all howled with laughter, which then turned into tears, with Brin and Taylor holding on to Dee. Clasping Naomi's daughters in her arms, Dee felt her sister in each one of them. River was right. Naomi still lived in both her girls, and in Dee. Overwhelmed with love for Brin and Taylor, she silently promised to protect them for the rest of her life.

"Read another one," Brin asked.

Dee opened the next white envelope, also with a Minnie Mouse sticker on it.

> *Dear Sissy,*
>
> *I miss you so much. It's really lonely without you. I'm not allowed to talk about you, or Daddy gets mad. Why did you leave? A big sister is supposed to look out for you, not go away. Please come home soon.*
>
> *I love you, Squirt*

She could hear Naomi's young voice in her pleading words. The guilt was crushing her. She held the letter to her heart and rocked back and forth. "I'm so sorry. I'm so sorry, Naomi. I never meant to hurt you."

Brin and Taylor both hugged her, and Bill gave her a tissue.

"You don't have to read any more letters, Aunt Dee. We don't want you to cry."

She wiped her eyes. "I'm okay. I'm glad I get to look at these with you girls. Then it's not too hard."

She read more letters to them and told them about her life in the army as an MP when she wrote her letters. Then she noticed a change in the tone in Naomi's writing. She still missed Dee and wanted her to come home, but her words conveyed a new strength, especially with regard to their father. Naomi was angry with him, and she wasn't afraid of him anymore. She wrote about making her own decisions for her life and no longer doing what he told her to. It became clear that Dee's absence had made Naomi learn to defend herself and stand up to him. *I'm proud of you, Squirt.*

The girls would have stayed up all night listening to the letters and watching their mother's videos, but Bill made them go to bed. Both Brin and Taylor hugged her before they went upstairs, and Taylor said, "Thank you for coming, Aunt Dee."

Bill came over to Dee after he put his daughters to bed. "I can't thank you enough for being here. I've been so worried about them, especially Taylor. I don't know how you did it, but Taylor said more to you this evening than she's said since the plane crash. Maybe it's because you're so much like Naomi."

"I am?"

"Oh, yeah. Your voice is the same, your gestures are the same, your eyes, even the way you laugh. It's uncanny. You've been able to connect to them, and I'm so grateful."

"They're great kids. You and Naomi have done a wonderful job raising them."

Dee was surprised she felt so comfortable talking to him. She'd been filled with apprehension about meeting him and had expected him to blame her, but he'd showed her only kindness. He was a good man, and a great dad, and so different from her own father. She wanted to get to know him better. "So how did you and Naomi meet?"

"We were high school sweethearts. My dad was a tank commander in the army and got stationed at Fort Hood. So we moved to Killeen, and I transferred to Naomi's high school when we were both seniors."

He smiled as he gazed into the distance, clearly remembering Naomi.

"I never believed in love at first sight, until I met her. The first time I saw Naomi, she was speaking at a school assembly, asking for everyone to elect her to our student council. She was so smart, and funny, and she really cared about our classmates. I couldn't take my eyes off her. She had the most captivating dark-green eyes, so expressive, like she was looking directly into my soul. I knew right then I was in love with her, we were meant to be together, and I would marry her. Amazingly, she felt the same about me."

"That's incredible. So what'd you think about my father and mother?"

"I liked your mother, but she was so quiet and submissive. And she didn't smile very much. I thought it was because she missed you. Your dad, well, he was a piece of work. He was a bully, and he warned me to stay away from Naomi, which didn't work. I think he was really a frightened, small man. He was so desperate to control all of you, he only succeeded in driving you all away."

This was all news to Dee. She was surprised, and pleased, that Naomi had followed her heart, against their father's wishes, to be with this kind man who was so clearly in love with her.

"So when did you and Naomi get married?"

"Well, she got pregnant in December of our senior year, and we got married in the chapel at Fort Hood on Valentine's Day. Your father refused to attend, since we were 'sinners,' but your mom came, and so did everyone in my family. They all loved Naomi. She was going to drop out of high school, but Dr. Wilkinson wouldn't let her. She arranged for Naomi to complete her classes online, and she and Gretchen let us move into their garage apartment for free."

"They let me live there too, after my father kicked me out. We were lucky to have them."

"Naomi and I sure were. Doc helped us get scholarships and student loans for college, and I got a full-time job at a tire shop. Doc insisted we both walk across the stage to receive our diplomas when we graduated, even though Naomi was six months pregnant. Then three months later, Taylor showed up, and we both started junior college. Two years later, we transferred to the University of Texas, I finished my degree in mechanical engineering, and Naomi got her degree in social work. Taylor was three, Naomi was pregnant most of our senior year, and then Miss Brin joined us the week before we graduated. Naomi graduated with honors."

Dee was blown away. Instead of falling apart by her absence, Naomi had grown a spine of steel and a will of iron to accomplish everything she did, especially with no help from their parents.

"That's an incredible story, Bill. I'm so happy you and Naomi found each other."

"We were very lucky. Naomi and I had fourteen happy years together and two beautiful girls, but I really miss her." He wiped his eyes. "Well, you must be tired after they talked your ear off. I'll show you to your room."

Dee got settled in the comfortable guest bedroom and stood at the window looking at downtown Chicago. She'd been so afraid to meet Naomi's family, thinking they'd blame her for their mother's death. But they were sweet to her and surrounded her with love, though they didn't even know her. She checked her phone to see if River might have sent her a text. She ached to call her and tell her all about Naomi's family, but the knife of betrayal was still deep in her heart.

Chapter Twenty-eight

Day 11

River was relieved to wake up in her quiet, peaceful house. The stress of the investigation and the way she'd left things with Dee had drained her. She could manage basic tasks such as laundry, but that was all. She was worried about how Dee was doing with Naomi's family. Hearing her cell phone ring in the kitchen, she ran to answer it, disappointed it wasn't Dee.

It was her assistant. "Oh, hi, Maggie."

"Nice to hear your voice too. The insurance company wants to know when they'll be getting your report."

"Tell them three days. I need a little more time to finish it."

"Okay. They have another job for you. They want you to the review the report from a cargo plane accident in Indonesia."

"Tell them I'm not available."

"Did you pick up something else? You don't have to travel for this one."

"No. I just need a long break, maybe a permanent one. I'll call you later."

River needed to make a change in her life, and she needed to begin today. Cleaning out her attic was the first step, and then she'd work her way through the rest of the house. She'd get rid of everything non-essential, then put the house on the market.

It was too difficult to face any more accident investigations, so she would make inquiries at USC. Maybe she could find a purpose in the world of academia and train the next generation of investigators. Nothing was keeping her in Denver anymore, not even her grandparents' old house.

❖

After a restless night, Dee woke up to the smell of coffee and made her way downstairs to find everyone dressed and ready to go.

"Good morning. We have a big favor to ask Aunt Dee. Don't we, girls?"

"Sure. Anything."

"We have an appointment in one hour with a family therapist, and Taylor just agreed to come with us, but only if you will too."

Outplayed by a thirteen-year-old. "Let me get ready. I'll be happy to."

Everyone was quiet in the van during the drive. Maybe they were all as apprehensive as Dee. The woman therapist was very gentle with Brin and Taylor. Bill expressed his worry for his kids, and Dee mainly listened.

Then the therapist turned to her. "And what are you feeling, Dee?"

I hate this. She took a deep breath. "If I hadn't been so stubborn when I was eighteen and could've keep my mouth shut with my father, I could've stayed at home, stayed connected to Naomi, and she never would've been on that airplane. I never thought he'd kick me out. Daddy expected me to come crawling back, to repent at church in front of everyone, and act right after that. But I just couldn't do it, so I had to abandon Naomi to save myself, and I'll regret that to the end of my life."

The woman looked at her with great sympathy.

"Dee, you did nothing wrong. You simply survived, when a lot of gay teens weren't able to. Your father, not you, was responsible for all the pain he caused your family. He tried so desperately to control you, your sister, and your mother that he suffocated all of you."

When Dee took in her words, a cloud lifted. Leaving the session, she felt lighter. Everyone was quiet on the way home, and the tension level in the van had lessened.

Bill pulled Dee aside after they went inside. "Thank you for your honesty in therapy today. I think it really helped Brin and Taylor. I talked to the girls, and we need your help. Can you stay with us for the next few weeks? I have so much to do with the funeral, the paperwork, the house, and the therapy that I'm overwhelmed. If you could stay until Taylor's comfortable with the family therapy, I'd be very grateful."

"Of course, Bill. I'll do anything you want."

Over the next many days, Dee, Brin, and Taylor went through the difficult task of sorting through Naomi's things. They saved beloved mementos, attended therapy, watched family videos, told stories of Naomi, and Dee read them the rest of the letters. One letter really touched her.

Hi Sissy,

I have the best news. I met a boy at school and he's super nice, plus he's gorgeous. I really like him, but Daddy said I can't see him. We'll see about that! I know now why you had to leave. Daddy tried to force you to be something you weren't. I'm not mad at you because you left home. You had to save yourself. And Daddy can't stop me from seeing Bill. That's his name, by the way. I miss you and I hope you'll write back to me.

I love you, Squirt

Naomi understood why she'd had to get away, and she'd grown into a strong woman, who could stand up to their father and seize her future. Reading about her falling in love with Bill was an amazing gift.

❖

Day 16

In the last few letters Dee read to them, Naomi wrote about their mother.

Hey Sissy,

Mother's not doing well today. She's very tired. The doctor says it won't be long now because her cancer has spread. I'm so glad she was well enough to come to my wedding and got to see our baby, Taylor. She told me to never give up on you, no matter what Daddy says, and I never will. I know you didn't have a choice when you left home, and I understand now. I will find you again, I promise.

Love always, Squirt

Dee carefully folded the letter and put it back in the envelope. There was only one more letter left in the pink suitcase, at the bottom of the stack. It was in a new envelope. Dee would save this one until later. She wanted to spend as much time as she could with Brin and Taylor learning about their life with her sister. Naomi had not only survived her absence, but she'd thrived and created an amazing family.

Then she heard a familiar voice in the background. It was coming from the den, where the TV had been left on. When she pushed the door open, she gasped and put her hand over her mouth.

"Do you know her, Aunt Dee?" Brin had followed her.

Dee put her hand down. "Yes, I do. We worked together on the crash investigation. Where's the remote? I need to turn this up."

River's image was on the TV screen, and Dee's heart pounded. River was sitting at a table with Ronald Moore and three other NTSB investigators in a press briefing answering questions about flight 402. Enlarged pictures of the reassembled DC-10 were displayed in the background. A reporter asked her a question.

"Dr. Dawson, what was the key evidence that led you to find the cause of this terrible crash?"

"We had exceptional teamwork and support from many federal and state agencies on this case. In particular, I'd like to thank the Portland Police Bureau for sending us Detective Dee Rawlings. Her work was essential in discovering the critical evidence of this accident."

Taylor turned to her. "Wow, Aunt Dee. Who is that lady?"

"A very special friend."

❖

Day 22

River kept herself busy, but she constantly thought about Dee. She was eager to know how things were with Dee's family. She longed to hear her voice, with her little hints of Texas twang, and to gaze into her green eyes. The last time she'd looked into Dee's eyes, she'd seen only hurt and betrayal.

Her time alone, when she didn't have a thousand demands on her, had brought her life into sharp focus, and she didn't like what she saw. She'd worked so hard for prestige and professional success, but she came home to an empty house. Her whole life was empty without Dee.

River had grown a tough shell to survive in a career field where women make up less than seven percent of all pilots. She hadn't even noticed, but over time, she'd become a person she couldn't stand. In a world where men treat knowledge as power, she was now someone who had to be right about everything. The depth of her own arrogance stunned her.

She'd been so sure she knew what was best for Dee. And she'd made so many wrong assumptions about her, she didn't blame Dee for not speaking to her. Keeping the letters from her because she didn't think Dee could handle them was a huge mistake, based on her own feelings about her mother's death. At age thirteen, her fear, anger, guilt, and hopelessness had overwhelmed her, and she'd seen Dee through those same thirteen-year-old eyes.

Dee Rawlings was the opposite of fearful and hopeless. She

was courageous when she'd joined the army at eighteen and learned to fend for herself. Then she demonstrated fearlessness when she worked on the investigation, and she showed such grace when she talked about how much she loved her sister. River kept replaying their conversations and kept seeing images of her, especially at bedtime.

When she closed her eyes at night, she longed to curl up next to Dee. She wanted to touch her skin, inhale her scent, and kiss Dee's lips. Even though it was torture, she remembered every detail about their lovemaking and the way Dee had touched her body and her soul. When she experienced the full force of Dee's desire for her, she trusted her and finally was free enough to lose control, to give herself to Dee.

I can see your face, I can hear your voice, I can almost touch you.

River relished every moment with Dee, when neither of them held back, when their passion combined into a swirl of fire. Nothing in the universe mattered as much as joining with her and becoming one. She'd given herself to Dee with complete abandon and with the hope of forever.

Chapter Twenty-nine

Day 23

Dee lingered over the shoe box of treasures from Naomi's closet. Baby-ultrasound pictures, her girls' footprints, their graduation and wedding pictures, and Dee's wooden Camp Fire Girl beads.

Bill watched her sort through the box. "I asked her why she kept those beads, and she said, 'Because they're important to Dee, and she'll want them.' Ready to go?"

"I guess so."

They climbed into the van and drove to the Elk Grove cemetery. Today was the day they would put Naomi to rest. They had an urn with her name on it and remembrances of Naomi from each of them inside it. When they found the wall, a group of teenagers was waiting for them. They were all in bright clothing and holding rainbow-colored balloons.

"What's this?" Dee asked.

"These are the kids from the group home Mama founded," Taylor answered.

Bill added, "It's for homeless LGBTQ kids."

Her baby sister surprised her again. Naomi had turned their family dysfunction into a chance for hope for these kids. Dee's heart was filled with pride and longing as she watched their rainbow balloons ascend into a perfect blue sky. She felt Naomi's spirit ride them into Heaven.

When they returned home, the house seemed brighter. Dee was thankful her grief had lessened and relieved both girls were okay. "There's one more letter from your mom that I was saving. Want me to read it to you?"

"Yes," they all answered.

Dee opened the last letter in Naomi's pink suitcase, the one in the new envelope.

> *Dear Sissy,*
>
> *I don't know why I still write to you after all this time. I guess it's because I feel like I'm talking to you. Daddy's getting real bad. He doesn't know who I am, and he shouts like he used to on the courthouse steps in Killeen. He won't let me turn off the light at night. The hospice ladies have been so sweet to him, even when he yells at them. He's a pain in the ass to the bitter end!*
>
> *I wish you were here to go through this with me, but I know I can't look for you until he's gone. He would freak out if he saw you, and I don't want you to remember him like this. Don't hate him, Dee. In the end, he was a scared little man, afraid to stand before God and account for his life.*
>
> *I miss you and I love you forever, Squirt*

Dee held Naomi's last letter to her heart. "And I love you too, Squirt."

❖

Day 25

River was pleased her housecleaning was going well. Without the burden of work, she sorted through every room, threw out half of the contents, donated what was left, and kept only a few clothes, plus her pictures.

She'd come across some boxes in the attic that belonged to her grandfather. Now that the house was cleaned out, she had time to sit down and open them. In the first box, right on top, carefully wrapped in old newspaper, was her mom's favorite bowling trophy. She smiled holding it in her hands and remembering the night her mom won it.

They were in their smoky neighborhood bowling alley, and her team had just won the league championship. Mom was the high scorer, and she jumped up and down with joy in her red-and-gray bowling shirt. What a great night. River held the trophy to her heart, then wiped off the dust and set it in her "Keep" box.

Her mom's competitive spirit was one of their strongest connections. Even though she was a flower child from the Sixties, a free spirit, and a brilliant woman, she always had to be the best. River inherited this trait in abundance, and it had served her well at the US Air Force Academy, in pilot training, and during her doctoral program. Most of the other items in the box brought back happy memories with her mother until she came across her parents' divorce papers. When her family broke up was the first time love was taken from her.

After that, River and her mother moved to Denver to live with her grandparents. Their house had been her safe place to land after the divorce, then after the plane crash, and after the air force took away her flying. This was where she'd come to patch herself up, deal with another loss, and grow strong enough to stand up and put one foot in front of the other.

Something was different now. She was no longer willing to accept the role of brave survivor who suffered with quiet stoicism, while learning more resilience as she went on with her life. This time River would not let Dee end up in her pile of losses, not while she could still fight for her. She'd respected Dee's orders not to contact her, but now she needed to take action. Her mother's voice rang in her ears. "Go for it!" She picked up a pad of paper.

❖

Day 30

"This came for you today." Bill handed her an envelope.

Dee took it and recognized River's neat handwriting. *I can't face this right now.*

"Who's it from, Aunt Dee?" Taylor was watching her.

"Just a friend."

She put the letter away in her room. She wanted to rip it open and consume River's words, but she had to steel herself before she could read it. She was starting to see light at the end of the tunnel. Grief no longer overwhelmed her every day. She'd learned so much about the amazing life Naomi had, and she was grateful for her memories.

Dee didn't want to risk derailing her progress by thinking about River right now. She needed to wait a while longer before she dealt with that whole situation.

❖

Day 44

After River listed the house, it sold in three days, and now she was doing her final inspection before she turned it over to the new owners. She'd thought it would be hard to say good-bye to the old place, but it no longer felt like home. She was ready to let go and move on to something else. Though she wasn't exactly sure what that was, she was optimistic. The only thing missing was Dee.

She'd almost called Dee a thousand times in the last two weeks and was eager to know if she'd gotten her letter. She also wanted to know how everything was with Naomi's family. She really missed hearing Dee's voice. She missed everything about Dee, but not talking to her was excruciating.

She was flying to Los Angeles to interview for a professorship at USC but wasn't sure it was the right fit. She couldn't commit to anything until she heard from Dee, and so far, only silence. River could stay in a holding pattern for a long time, but at some point she had to accept the reality that Dee was done with her. For the moment, she would continue to wait for Dee as long as she could.

❖

Day 45

Dee knew it was time to go home and get on with her own life. She'd loved her time with Bill, Brin, and Taylor, and they'd become a real family. They'd had a beautiful funeral for Naomi, the girls had a good therapist, and Dee knew she could call them whenever she needed to. She had only one more thing to do—open the letter from River.

Dee opened the envelope carefully, took out the letter, and smoothed the folds. Seeing River's handwriting made her heart race.

Dear Dee,

I hope reading Naomi's letters has brought you closer to her. You've survived so much already, and I know you have the strength and the grace to get through this. I was wrong when I underestimated you, and I hope you can forgive me. You and I both know we have something very special, and I don't want to lose you. I want my life to be with yours. If you're willing to take a chance with me, meet me at the dedication of the Flight 402 Memorial at Madras airport.

I love you,
River

She sat on the side of the bed, rocking back and forth. "Oh, River."

Then she heard a soft knock at her door. Taylor was standing before her.

"Are you all right, Aunt Dee?"

"I wish I could talk to your mama. She always had great common sense."

"Maybe you could talk to me. Mama said I was a good listener. Are you upset because of the lady on TV?"

"What lady on TV?"

"Your special friend, Dr. Dawson. She's the one who sent you a letter, isn't she? I saw her name on the envelope."

"You're a very good detective, Taylor."

"Thank you. So why are you upset about your friend?"

Dee hesitated. She didn't really want to go into her romantic life with a thirteen-year-old.

"Well, Dr. Dawson, I mean, River—that's her name—is more than a special friend to me."

"Is she your girlfriend?"

"My girlfriend? How do you know about that?"

"Mama told me everything. I know what all the letters mean in LGBTQ, she told me about safe sex, and I even know about birth control. So is she your girlfriend or not?"

"Yes. Maybe. I don't know." Dee's head was swimming.

"If Mama was here, I think she would ask you, 'Are you in love with her?'"

Dee knew without question, after everything they'd been through together, that she was.

"Yes, I am."

"Then I'm pretty sure Mama would say that you need to tell her. She always told us, 'Life is too short to miss out on the miracle.'"

She pulled Taylor into a hug. "You are a very smart girl, and I'm so proud to be your aunt."

Dee had learned so much about love and forgiveness from Naomi and her family. She now understood what it was like to be part of a loving, accepting family. She didn't know if it was possible, but she wanted this kind of family for herself, and she could no longer deny she wanted this family with River. She pulled out her phone and sent River a text.

I'm coming home. I'll meet you at the dedication in two days.

❖

River felt her phone buzz before she boarded her flight to Los Angeles. When she took it out of her pocket, she saw the text from Dee and stopped.

"Dr. Dawson, are you boarding?" The gate agent was calling her.

She smiled. "Not this plane. When's the next flight to Portland?"

"It leaves in fifteen minutes, gate B17, on the other side of the concourse. I'll switch your ticket."

"Thanks so much."

River ran over to B17, giddy with excitement, and boarded the plane just before they closed the door. She had no idea what to expect when she saw Dee again. She didn't know if Dee would say "Good-bye and get out of my life" or "I love you." This could be the best day of her life, or the worst.

❖

Day 47

Dee was nervous driving out to Madras Municipal airport. She'd never expected to step foot in this place again. She still didn't know what she'd say to River when she saw her, but she had to face her. Walking toward the small terminal, she saw a large crowd assembled on the tarmac, many in uniform; Oregon State Police, Portland Air National Guard, Civil Air Patrol, Relax Air employees, and then she saw River. She was more striking than she'd ever seen her, with sunlight on her golden hair. Instead of her familiar flannel shirt, she was wearing a tailored black suit and looked gorgeous.

River spotted her and made a beeline to her. "Thanks for coming. I'm so happy to see you. The team is over here, or they have chairs up front for family members."

"I'll stand with you guys."

The team members waved at her as the ceremony started. There were a few short speeches, with Ronald Moore giving one, and then they pulled a cord to reveal the Flight 402 Memorial.

The crowd was silent as they took it in. It was simple and

elegant, with wings carved into a large granite stone and the names of all the passengers and crew engraved underneath, as if they were sheltered by the wings.

She reached for River's hand. "Let's find her name."

The mood was somber but also reverent. As they got closer, Dee saw a brass ring at the base of the monument. "What is that, River?"

"It's a compass rose with the monument on a three-one-zero-degree heading to Portland, their destination."

"It's like they're flying into the sunset. It's magnificent."

Looking up at the wings against the blue sky, Dee felt lifted up with Naomi. They would never be separated again because her sister's love lived on inside her.

She turned to River, "We need to talk. I wasn't going to come here, but I couldn't ignore you anymore."

"Would it be okay if we drove out to Angel Creek to talk?" River asked.

"Sure."

When they arrived, they got out of the car, and River turned to her. "So why are you here? I'm almost afraid to ask."

"I'm here because you and I understand loss and because we're both survivors. I know you didn't intentionally try to hurt me, and I've learned a lot about forgiveness, for my family, and for myself. I want you to know I forgive you, and you cannot judge me based on your own experience."

River let out a little laugh. "Yes, ma'am."

"What's so funny?"

"You're pretty hot when you get stern."

Dee couldn't help but smile. "I've had a lot of time to think, and I believe we were meant to find each other. The question is, are we willing to take the risk to make this work? Facing Naomi's death taught me to value my own life and to be willing to take a chance. I think you're worth the risk."

River looked into her eyes. "I've wasted years running away from love, and I'm done with that. Dee, I need you, and I love you."

Dee's future lay before her, and she reached for River. "I love you too, and I want to make my life with you."

A full smile spread across River's face. "I know you hate surprises, but I hope you'll like this one."

She handed Dee a cardboard box. She opened it and found a flat square wrapped in gold paper. "What is this?"

"This is from my favorite poem, 'Last Night the Rain Spoke to Me,' by Mary Oliver. Open it."

Dee tore the paper off to reveal a stainless-steel plaque with engraved letters.

"It's beautiful, River."

"It represents my hope for a long and wondrous journey with you. Look underneath it."

She reached into the box and pulled out a folder. Dee opened it and saw a land deed to Angel Creek with both their names on it, and blueprints for a house.

Dee was shocked. "How did you... Never mind."

She pulled River into a long, deep kiss. Then she stepped back, looked into her sky-blue eyes, and held River's face. "You are my family now, and I am yours. Let's build our log-cabin home here."

About the Author

Julie Tizard (www.JulieTizard.com) is the multi-award-winning author of *The Road to Wings*, Gold Crown Literary Society 2017 Debut Novel of the Year; and *Flight to the Horizon*, winner of two Lesfic Bard awards and a finalist for two INDIES awards.

A professional pilot for over forty years, Col. Tizard was one of the earliest women US Air Force pilots. She flew as a T-37 instructor pilot, an aircraft commander on the KC-10 air refueling tanker, an aircraft accident investigator, chief of flight safety, and a Squadron Commander. She served for over twenty-five years.

Captain Julie Tizard was a commercial airline pilot for thirty years and flew the Boeing 737, 757, 767, the Airbus 320, and the DC-10. She was also an instructor pilot and line check airman on the 737 fleet. She also flies a T-67 Firefly, a two-seat military trainer. When not writing about flying or attending air shows, she can be found playing a baritone horn in the local LGBTQ band and traveling like a normal person. *Free Fall at Angel Creek* is her third novel.

Books Available From Bold Strokes Books

Can't Leave Love by Kimberly Cooper Griffin. Sophia and Pru have no intention of falling in love, but sometimes love happens when and where you least expect it. (978-1-636790041-1)

Free Fall at Angel Creek by Julie Tizard. Detective Dee Rawlings and aircraft accident investigator Dr. River Dawson use conflicting methods to find answers when a plane goes missing, while overcoming surprising threats and discovering an unlikely chance at love. (978-1-63555-884-5)

Love's Compromise by Cass Sellars. For Piper Holthaus and Brook Myers, will professional dreams and past baggage stop two hearts from realizing they are meant for each other? (978-1-63555-942-2)

Not All a Dream by Sophia Kell Hagin. Hester has lost the woman she loved, and the world has descended into relentless dark and cold. But giving up will have to wait when she stumbles upon people who help her survive. (978-1-63679-067-1)

Protecting the Lady by Amanda Radley. If Eve Webb had known she'd be protecting royalty, she'd never have taken the job as bodyguard, but as the threat to Lady Katherine's life draws closer, she'll do whatever it takes to save her, and may just lose her heart in the process. (978-1-63679-003-9)

The Secrets of Willowra by Kadyan. A family saga of three women, their homestead called Willowra in the Australian outback, and the secrets that link them all. (978-1-63679-064-0)

Trial by Fire by Carsen Taite. When prosecutor Lennox Roy and public defender Wren Bishop become fierce adversaries in a headline-grabbing arson case, their attraction ignites a passion that leads them both to question their assumptions about the law, the truth, and each other. (978-1-63555-860-9)

Turbulent Waves by Ali Vali. Kai Merlin and Vivien Palmer plan their future together as hostile forces make their own plans to destroy what they have, as well as all those they love. (978-1-63679-011-4)

Unbreakable by Cari Hunter. When Dr. Grace Kendal is forced at gunpoint to help an injured woman, she is dragged into a nightmare where nothing is quite as it seems, and their lives aren't the only ones on the line. (978-1-63555-961-3)

Veterinary Surgeon by Nancy Wheelton. When dangerous drugs are stolen from the veterinary clinic, Mitch investigates and Kay becomes a suspect. As pride and professions clash, love seems impossible. (978-1-63679-043-5)

All That Remains by Sheri Lewis Wohl. Johnnie and Shantel might have to risk their lives—and their love—to stop a werewolf intent on killing. (978-1-63555-949-1)

Beginner's Bet by Fiona Riley. Phenom luxury Realtor Ellison Gamble has everything, except a family to share it with, so when a mix-up brings youthful Katie Crawford into her life, she bets the house on love. (978-1-63555-733-6)

Dangerous Without You by Lexus Grey. Throughout their senior year in high school, Aspen, Remington, Denna, and Raleigh face challenges in life and romance that they never expect. (978-1-63555-947-7)

Desiring More by Raven Sky. In this collection of steamy stories, a rich variety of lovers find themselves desiring more: more from a lover, more from themselves, and more from life. (978-1-63679-037-4)

Jordan's Kiss by Nanisi Barrett D'Arnuck. After losing everything in a fire, Jordan Phelps joins a small lounge band and meets pianist Morgan Sparks, who lights another blaze—this time in Jordan's heart. (978-1-63555-980-4)

Late City Summer by Jeanette Bears. Forced together for her wedding, Emily Stanton and Kate Alessi navigate their lingering passion for one another against the backdrop of New York City and World War II, and a summer romance they left behind. (978-1-63555-968-2)

Love and Lotus Blossoms by Anne Shade. On her path to self-acceptance and true passion, Janesse will risk everything—and possibly everyone—she loves. (978-1-63555-985-9)